RAFT

A Novel

STU KRIEGER

ISBN: 978-1-960146-31-1 (hard cover)
      978-1-960146-32-8 (soft cover)

Edited by: Amy Ashby

PipeVine

Published by PipeVine Press, an imprint of Warren Publishing
Charlotte, NC
www.warrenpublishing.net
Printed in the United States

*This book is dedicated to Hillary,
Gus, and Rosie for allowing me to steal a little
bit of their souls to bring these characters to life.*

*To Drina and Bobby for rounding out
our family in the most beautiful way.*

*And to Gwendolyn for leading the charge
of the next generation of fearsome warriors
crusading for kindness and positivity.*

Praise for RAFT

"*Starting with an unlikely comic premise, Stu Krieger has created a memorable, funny, and surprisingly touching family tale.*"
–MERYL GORDON (MRS. ASTOR REGRETS AND BUNNY MELLON)

"*RAFT is an absolutely hilarious and heartwarming family story with a very clever off-the-wall twist. Stu Krieger's second novel nailed the speech of both parents and two teenagers. Something, as a writer, I know first-hand, is extremely difficult. The graduation and aquarium antics had me in hysterics. I actually fell in love with a penguin! I know you don't know me, but trust me on this ... you're going to love it!!!*"
–LAURA NUMEROFF (IF YOU GIVE A MOUSE A COOKIE)

"*Stu Krieger's L.A. is a riotous landscape of family—human and animal—and the myriad ways all these beings try to discern who they are, who they love, and what they're willing to do for happiness.*"
–SUSAN STRAIGHT (NATIONAL BOOK AWARD FINALIST, MECCA AND IN THE COUNTRY OF WOMEN)

"*Stu Krieger, a uniquely talented and successful screenwriter, has gifted us all with a magical and surprising, laugh-out-loud novel. It should not be missed. Read it!*"
–PARKER STEVENSON

"*I enjoyed RAFT immensely; it's very entertaining and illuminates a modern dilemma: man's eternal search for elusive happiness.*"
–HAYLEY MILLS

raft – (raft, rahft)

noun
1. a more or less rigid, floating platform made of buoyant materials, often used to transport one to safety
2. a pod of penguins floating on water

CLARK

There are certain experiences you go through in life that can't be properly shared until you've gained some distance from them—and taken some time to digest exactly what happened. That's definitely true of the story I'm about to tell you. To set the scene of what was going on with me at the time, I feel like it may be best to begin by sharing an entry I wrote in my journal exactly one year ago today ....

Jesus Christ—I hate my life.

Yeah, I know, the Christmas-card version looks perfect: smart, great-looking wife; two happy, healthy kids; a big house tucked into a safe, well-manicured canyon. (Okay, my brother-in-law calls it a "mansion," but let's not get carried away.) In any case, I clearly have no reason to complain, right?

But ya know what? Every once in a while ... not every minute of every day, not necessarily even once a day ... but occasionally, just occasionally ... it would be nice to feel like I'm more than an ATM with a dick.

You'd think that wouldn't be so hard for Julia to understand.

But this morning, before I even had the chance to throw down my first cup of coffee, we had a nuclear-scale fight. Nasty shit, name-calling, tears—not my favorite way to start the day.

What can I tell ya, Julia? I write and *illustrate* kids' books. It's what I do. It's how I pay the bills. And guess what? Sometimes my subconscious speaks through my pen.

Yesterday afternoon I was on the phone with my editor's secretary. We were trying to schedule a meeting to go over a few preliminary sketches for the latest book in my crazy-successful *Cow on the Lam* series. Apparently I was doing some absent-minded doodling. Like I said, it's what I do. It's what I've done since I was a kid. It's such a part of who I am that I usually don't even notice I'm doing it.

But Julia did.

And this is what set off the Battle Royale.

I mean, it's not like our kids are babies. Even if they had happened to see it, they would have thought it was funny. Especially Charlie. He's a senior in high school, and I don't think that kid has had a single thought that wasn't dictated by his cock in the last three years. I'm pretty sure he's still a virgin, but trust me, it certainly isn't from lack of trying.

At fifteen, Katie is barreling through ninth grade, aching to finish school so she can attack the world. Her biggest reaction to my sketch would have been a fleeting "Ewww," followed by a whip-smart commentary on the patriarchy's determination to wave their penises like scepters while issuing dumb ass proclamations designed to keep women subjugated. Then she would have added a cogent critique of the doodle because, despite her outrage, she is and has always been my best critic.

Anyway, before my eyelids were even above half mast yesterday morning, I drifted into the kitchen and was instantly attacked by the snarling pit bull that had once been my sweet wife. She was furiously brandishing the ATM sketch.

"Clark Alexander Whitaker!"

(If she was pulling out the middle name, I knew I was in deep shit.)

"Is this your passive-aggressive way of telling me you think I'm spending too much? You're the one who encourages me to buy the strawberries at Whole Foods, even when they're nine dollars a box. I would never do that on my own. Oh, and I suppose it's my fault I had to call the plumber when the toilet in the kids' bathroom overflowed because Katie tried to flush down a condom filled with whipped cream? And to be clear, pal, if you have something to say to me, come right out and say it because I am not someone who will sit by and silently tolerate your covertly hostile assault-by-doodle."

I tried to defuse her with a calm and quiet, "Well good morning to you, too, my love," but Julia wasn't having it. I followed up with the standard, "It's just a stupid scribble" defense, but that wasn't flying either. She said that, lately, I'd been perpetually angry and withdrawn, filled with a barely concealed hostility toward her, the kids, and the entire world.

And ya know what? Not that I could ever admit it, but she wasn't wrong.

I told you: at this moment, I hate my life.

Setting aside the previous success of my *Cow on the Lam* series, the new book isn't happening, despite a looming deadline. Every idea I've come up with so far has been rejected by my editors. They have no problem telling me what they hate, but they never offer even a scant suggestion of what they might like. I don't get paid until I deliver, and I can't deliver because they've paralyzed me. I conjure a million different ways to approach the story but then reject each one out of hand as a preemptive strike before the idiots-in-charge have the opportunity to demolish another dream.

Not getting paid, trying to navigate my freelance life, having bills sailing in through the mail slot like a coven of ghosts ... I feel like there's an invisible sumo wrestler sitting on my chest, making it impossible for me to catch my breath.

And trust me, this has nothing to do with the fact that I'm about to turn fifty.

Some days lately, I wake up with a screaming voice in my head, asking me, "What's the point of any of it?" Who cares if I bang out another book? Do parents even read to their kids anymore, or do they just stick a screen in front of their toddlers' faces and then snatch up their own phones to see if their TikTok followers approved of their latest post about the most amazing pizza they had the night before? We've become a society of idiots, and I fear reading will soon become as extinct as the Tasmanian tiger.

Have I mentioned that my mother-in-law recently moved in with us? I love Honey. I do. But even though she does her sincere best to not be a burden, she's very high maintenance. (Which, admittedly, is not as much of a problem for me as it is for Julia.)

For the past two years, Julia's full-time job has been taking care of her parents. Her dad died three months ago after a protracted battle with cancer that hollowed him out before it carried him away. During that time, Honey had a heart attack, then open-heart surgery; she was diagnosed with type-2 diabetes, followed by a period of having scary-as-hell hallucinations (like the two-headed ebony horse hiding in her bedroom closet) brought on by one of her new meds. Julia bore the brunt of it all.

You see, Julia has a brother we call Tits-on-a-Bull because he couldn't possibly be more useless. Once Julia's dad was gone, and Honey wasn't ready to move into an assisted-living facility, the only thing that made sense was to move her in with us. We have the room—this is not a goddamn mansion, but we do have a few spare bedrooms—and it was the best way to cut down on Julia's stress. How many times could she race back and forth across town in snarled L.A. traffic every time her mother had another— pretty much daily—crisis?

So while my wife takes care of her mother, I'm often charged with looking out for the kids ... while being the breadwinner ... and maintaining the house and yard ... and trying to pay the endless stack of bills.

Ya know what I wanna know?

Who's left to take care of me?

I swear to you, as long as I left my credit cards behind, I could completely disappear, and my family would hardly notice.

Here's what I crave more than anything: one long weekend away with my nuclear crew. Just me, Julia, Charlie, and Katie. Alone together. (Which, by the way, is not an oxymoron, so don't start with me.)

It doesn't have to be anything fancy. When the kids were little, we'd go camping quite a bit. Up to the mountains, down to the beach; sometimes we'd go to a state or national park. It was great. We also did a bunch of road trips: Hearst Castle, Coronado Island, a cabin in Idyllwild, hanging out in San Francisco. So many of the major developmental leaps my kids made early on came during vacations where they had that concentrated "just us" time. That's something I truly miss.

Look, I know the kids are practically adults, into their own lives. I get that. Charlie's graduating next month and heading off to college back East. Katie has a huge circle of friends, plus she's a crackerjack student and a voracious reader. But we're still a family.

Aren't we?

I want some time to enjoy each other, to be relaxed together, to laugh. That's what I miss most. The way we used to laugh.

Hey, fuck you.

This has nothing to do with the fact that I'm turning fifty.

Damn, Katie's calling me. Or, more accurately, she's *bellowing* for me. Would it kill her to come find me? She's gotta know I'm in my office. It's where I always am this time of day. When I'm not writing or drawing, I'm in here, hiding. Hoping to stay out of the line of fire.

Shit. The kid will not stop yelling, "Dad!"

★★★

Okay, I'm back.

I tracked her down in the bathroom off the family room. She was halfway through plucking her eyebrows—God knows why that's a thing—but anyway, she was doing what she felt needed to be done when one of the overhead light bulbs blew.

"You need to change it, Dad," she snapped.

An added "please" would have been nice. It also would have been fine if her tone wasn't laced with disgust over the fact that I didn't know the light bulb was going to die in the middle of her beauty regimen. Apparently in her world, I should've been able to anticipate the blowout and get it changed before she ever had to suffer such an inconvenient interruption.

I could have expressed my displeasure with her attitude, but I didn't. Desperately needing her approval, I scurried off to the utility closet, fetched another bulb, and dutifully changed it ASAP.

Oh shit. Yeah: it's trash day tomorrow. I need to empty the indoor recycling bin into the big blue can, then empty the kitchen trash into the black can, and then drag them both down to the curb while making sure they're sufficiently out of the way so Julia doesn't crash into them backing out of her side of the garage; the last thing I need is the expense of one more knocked-off side-view mirror.

"Thanks, [my love/Dad/Clark]. It's so wonderful the way you automatically take care of everything around here to maintain our perfect lives."

Yeah, good luck waiting to hear that, my friend.

Anyway, where was I? Right. See, the thing about Charlie leaving for college is that it truly feels like the end of an era. Like it'll never be Us Four again. How the hell did we get here so quickly? I mean, wasn't he just out in the garden, running naked while he made potions in his little blue bucket, mixing grass and mud and those red-orange berries that fall over the fence from Mrs. Inckel's mountain-ash tree? And, yes, I know he's ready to spread his proverbial wings, but does he need to fly three thousand miles away to do it?

We used to talk all the time when he was younger. He seemed to sincerely enjoy hanging out with me, asking a million questions, wanting to explore things together. When he was a real little guy, after he'd get tired of me reading the same old picture books to him over and over, he'd press his tiny hand to my lips and say, "Tell me a story from your mouth."

That shit kills ya, right?

And now he's getting ready to go to college.

Another thing I thought would be easier is the whole idea of them growing up and convincing themselves they're ready to have sex. Knowing it's inevitable, Julia and I have always tried to be open and honest with them; we've made it clear that they can ask us any questions they want, but now Charlie finally has a serious girlfriend, and while I don't think they've done it yet, when they finally do? Oh man ... how do we allow nature to do its thing while still maintaining a few appropriate boundaries?

We'd rather have them here than off in some parked car in a dark alley where serial killers roam, but how do we know what Amy's parents want or what their house rules are? We try to ask Charlie about this, but he'd rather die from fire ants devouring his scrotum than discuss anything even remotely sexual with his parents. No matter how cool we think we are.

I also pride myself on making a concerted effort to raise my son and daughter with the same rules, but who am I kidding? I'll be incredibly happy for Charlie when he finally sheds his virginity, but it's just fine with me if Katie wants to wait until she's thirty. Sorry. I realize that's so not evolved. But it's the way I feel, so deal with it.

Charlie's girlfriend Amy is a formidable partner for him. She's got the energy and passion to match his, but she also has no hesitation in challenging him when he goes into full "the world revolves around me" mode. Right now they're both in a school production of Romeo and Juliet. He's Romeo, and she's Juliet's mother, Lady Capulet, and therein lies the rub. She doesn't understand why he gets to be the dashing leading man while she's in a frumpy, padded dress and a gray-streaked wig. Somehow this has become Charlie's fault. Welcome to the wonderful minefield of romance, son. Nobody ever promised you a ho's garden.

Which brings us to another dilemma that's shoveling additional stress onto the slag heap of tension that is my current life.

It's Julia's birthday a week from Saturday. I would love to do something nice for her, but I have zero disposable income right now. She's well aware of this and has told me repeatedly that we can just have a simple family dinner at home with no presents necessary, but it's a trap. I haven't survived twenty-one years of marriage without being able to recognize this. She says she doesn't care, but she obviously does. She *claims* she'd be fine with no presents, but she doesn't mean it. Oh, I think she *thinks* she does. Sincerely. But that one year I got her Mother's Day cards and a present from the kids but then forgot to get her my own "to the wonderful mother of my children" card? Let me tell you, it wasn't pretty.

So here's what I'm going to do: I'll take Katie down to that little boutique jewelry store on Montana Avenue and have her help me pick out a bracelet or a pair of fancy earrings, then put our gift of choice on the credit card and not think about it one minute longer.

Eventually I'll get paid again.

Right?

And when I do, I'll pay off the credit card bill and be done with it. A few months of 18 percent interest is far better than trying to pretend that showing up without a birthday present is an actual repercussion-free option.

★★★

It's a brand-new day.

When I couldn't fall asleep last night, instead of trying to count sheep or some other fruitless bullshit, I decided to silently recite all the good things in my life. Of course, fighting to tamp down the negative stuff made that sumo wrestler on my chest feel like he'd gained another eighty pounds, but I did try. I thought about the fact that the four of us are healthy. We don't live in some bleak "… stan" country. We don't have a pharaoh with a whip, forcing us to schlep enormous boulders up steep inclines to build the pyramids. (Okay, I probably should pump the brakes here; even *I* think I'm starting to sound like an asshole.) But, on the bright side, my Prius is averaging fifty miles to the gallon.

Then today when I woke up, Julia was preparing to take her mother to a vital appointment at Kaiser to get Honey's blood-pressure medicine adjusted. The hitch was Julia's car refused to start. It might be the battery or the alternator or the starter. Who the hell knows? I'm a writer, not a mechanic. I could have just sent them off in *my* car, but I had an equally important meeting with our mortgage broker. I wanted to see if it made sense to refinance the house so we could take out a little cash to cover things until the current crisis ebbs.

We all know Kaiser appointments are never brief or efficient, so it seemed logical for me to drive Julia and Honey there, go off and do my thing, and then return to pick them up. Simple, right?

Have I mentioned that my wife's a compulsive backseat driver? And she most often does it from the front seat. She'll be the first one to tell you she's a terrible passenger. No matter how many times we've discussed this, sometimes in a fit of mutual rage, she simply cannot help herself. One of these days, she's going to put her foot right through the car floor, trying to stomp her imaginary brake when she thinks I'm getting too close to the car in front of me. (I'm not.)

So this morning, I followed her instructions into the Kaiser parking garage that got them closest to the wing they needed to report to (to spare Honey from having to walk farther than necessary). I was coming up to a second level clearly marked One Way, Do Not Enter when Julia started yelling at me to make a right-hand turn. "Here! Right here!"

And I did ... only to find a big black Escalade coming directly at me, destined for a head-on collision. Because, just like the sign said, it was a one-way passage. I couldn't back up due to a steady line of cars (going the correct way), moving up to the next level. The Escalade had nowhere to go because there were several cars behind it. The square-headed driver of said Huge Vehicle decided his best response was to lean on his horn, issuing a bleating, unrelenting blast that ricocheted off every wall in the claustrophobia-inducing parking structure.

In response, I only did what any reasonable man in my position would have done.

I threw the car into park, turned to my wife, and yelled, "You got us into this, you deal with it!" Then I got out, slammed the door, and walked away. How she extricated herself, I have no idea because she's still not speaking to me.

I walked down to the ground level, called an Uber, and went off to meet with the mortgage broker.

In trying to deal with my sad state of unremitting stress, I've been reading a book on "Conscious Living." It might be total bullshit, but the underlying concept teaches you how to assess and deal with things in the moment so you can release anxiety before it builds up. It also comes with a series of exercises and techniques for trying to let go of that angst before it escalates.

Returning from my appointment, I stormed into my office, yanked the book off my desk, and flipped to the "How to Deal With Your Stress" page of activities. Following the instructions, I bolted up to the spare bedroom, grabbed a wedge pillow from the guest bed, then charged into the backyard to track down the bucket of sports equipment stored on the side of the house. Finding the plastic baseball bat I was seeking, I raced to the hall outside my office, slammed the wedge pillow onto the floor, raised the bat, and began to beat the crap out of said pillow. As I did, I screamed out all my frustrations, taxing my soon-to-be hoarse-with-rage throat:

"DON'T TELL ME HOW TO DRIVE! I AM A GROWN-ASS MAN! I COULD HAVE GOTTEN US ALL KILLED! LEAVE ME ALONE SO I CAN WRITE MY BOOK! I WANT TO GET PAID! I WANT TO GET LAID! I WANT TO BE TREATED WITH RESPECT! I WANT TO BE LEFT ALONE! WHY DO I FEEL SO ALONE?

I WANT MONEY! I WANT LOVE! I WANT A FUCKING BEAN-AND-CHEESE
BURRITO FROM TACO BELL!"

I kept on beating, panting, raging. Stuffing began to fly out of both sides
of the pillow, sending white cotton clouds up into the air. I didn't care. I
needed to keep going, no matter how much my chest was heaving and my
voice was giving out.

"I NEED TO RUN AWAY! I WANT US *ALL* TO RUN AWAY! IF MY LIFE IS
SO GOOD, WHY DOES IT SUCK SO BAD? HELP ME. DON'T HELP ME. LEAVE
ME ALONE. AM I ALONE? I FEEL SO ALONE. HOW AM I ABOUT TO TURN
FUCKING FIFTY?"

More tufts of stuffing. More screaming. Then tears. But I could not stop
slamming that stupid plastic bat into the nearly flattened pillow.

That's when I was snapped back by a tremulous voice behind
me: "Dadda?"

KATIE

Okay, even though this all happened a year ago, I can still totally remember how freaked out I was to find my dad there, beating the daylights out of that pillow. I mean, I love my dad. But in that moment, I was absolutely convinced he was going next-level cray.

See, for the final month of the school year, on Wednesdays, we had a minimum day because the teachers had mandatory afternoon meetings. So that day, I had come straight home to get started on research for this huge AP History paper that was due soon. When I walked in, Dad was in the hallway, screaming and totally beating up the purple wedge pillow I'd use when I watched *Real Housewives*. I couldn't compute most of what he was screaming about because in my head, I was all, like, *What's he doing? What's happening here?* But I know he sounded *really* upset.

As soon as he saw me, he sprang straight up and tried to make some lame dad joke about needing to teach that pillow a lesson. It was totally weird. The stuffing was all over the place. There was even one big tuft stuck to the side of his sweaty temple. So gross.

And it kinda looked like he'd been crying.

So I go, "Dad, is everything okay?" And he's, like, "Yeah. It's fine, never better." Then he quickly gathered up all the stuffing and the pillow corpse and muttered that he needed to take a quick shower so he could start dinner.

It turned out Mom and my Nonnie Honey were stuck at Kaiser because Nonnie's blood pressure was way up when the doctors were trying to get it down; that meant Dad was on duty to make dinner for Charlie and me.

I would never tell Mom 'cause it would totally hurt her feelings, but I'm always glad when Dad's the cook. Honestly, he's way better at it. Mom has major trust issues, so she thinks you have to cook everything to death, otherwise, we'll all get salmonella and die a swift and painful death.

Anyway, Mom and Dad were obvi having some major issues, but nobody wanted to talk about it. I tried. I asked my brother what he thought was up, but that guy lives in his own private world on Planet Charlie. As long as his needs are being met, a bomb could go off next to him, and he'd just step around it and go back to talking about himself.

Oh, and please don't even get me started on how I felt about his relationship with Amy. They thought it was love, but I knew it was more about the fact that they were a pair of theatre-nerd weirdos who were the boy-and-girl version of the exact same person. My best friend Lauren told me that one day between third and fourth period, they were running down the hall, holding hands, singing that "For Forever" song from *Dear Evan Hansen*. Really, really loud. Oh my God, who does that? It's so embarrassing.

But, anyway, about Mom and Dad …

Mom says I've always been the perceptive one. She says even when I was little, like, preschool age, I'd listen to everything and ask a million questions that always caught her by surprise. She said one time, I told her I'd heard her on the phone with Aunt Lily and asked why a lady would want to be married to a dirty dog. (I thought, *Wouldn't she at least want to give it a bath if they were going to be together?*) Two weeks later, Aunt Lily filed for divorce.

I know my parents seriously do love each other, and most of the time, they get along much better than any of my friends' parents; I guess that's why it was so easy for me to tell when something wasn't right. Nobody was yelling, nobody was being barky or nasty, but there was hardly any eye contact. Plus, there was a lot more silence than usual.

Well, it's never totally silent if Nonnie's around. She just chatters all the time. She's so cute. Nobody needs to be listening, nobody needs to respond, but Nonnie likes to talk. She tells stories—usually the same ones we've heard, like, a billion times—and she loves to reminisce. Did you know she once waited on Jack and Bobby Kennedy when they were teenagers? She was working at a drugstore soda fountain in Boston. "Soda fountain"—doesn't that sound so cute and retro?

Anyway, I tried talking to my brother about all this. I go, "C'mon, Charlie. You've got to feel it. There's just … can't you tell how much more tense it is around here these days?" He gave me this fully blank stare, shrugged, and then asked who ate the last ice-cream sandwich he'd been dreaming about since breakfast.

When Mom finally got back from Kaiser, she was wiped out, stressed out, and very worried. They were keeping Nonnie in the hospital to try to determine why none of her meds were working properly; plus, Nonnie had started having these little mini strokes that were making her talk gibberish, which is *so* scary.

Dad was up in their room with the door closed. Charlie was out back in the pool, furiously swimming like a maniac even though it was early May and not at all warm out. Ya know, when we get the "May Gray" that comes before the "June Gloom"? Gross.

Anyway, Mom came looking for me to see what was going on.

I didn't do this to start some big thing—I swear! But she wanted to know what the deal was with Charlie, and I knew what an awful day she'd had—have you ever had to spend an entire day in a hospital? It's disgusting. And guaranteed to be full-on stanky.

Anyway … it didn't seem fair to lie to her, so I told her Amy and Charlie had had a big fight, and he was out there trying to swim it off. It's not my fault he'd left his door open so I heard the whole battle from his end. After he hung up, I called my other best friend, Ori. (People think you can't have two best friends, but you *so* can and anyway, I'm getting off track.) *SO* … I called Ori to get filled in on the deets because I knew she'd be down to spill the tea on whatever happened at rehearsal for *Romeo and Juliet*. Ori's the assistant stage manager, which meant she had to have been there to witness the whole sitch.

Charlie was playing Romeo, and Amy was Juliet's mother. That meant if everybody didn't die, Amy would have been her own boyfriend's mother-in-law. Like, that's not weird, right? Well, on top of that, when Charlie and Melissa (who was playing Juliet) had to do their big kiss, Charlie got a boner that everybody could see. And, obvi, *everybody* included Amy.

Okay, see, this is one of the zillion reasons why I'm so glad I'm not a boy.

Their junk is like an Instagram account you have no control over, posting messages that were meant to stay private. No thanks.

Amy acted all hurt and humiliated for the rest of the rehearsal, but Charlie didn't pick up on it because, remember, he lives in his own "it's all about me" bubble. It was only that night on the phone that Amy went ballistic, accusing Charlie of loving Melissa more than he loved her, even though any woman who thinks a guy has even a teeny bit of sway over his penis has to be seriously impaired.

I told Mom not to say anything unless Charlie brought it up first, but the second he came in from the pool, she couldn't keep from launching into Mother Mode. She tried to comfort him and said something about his penis having a mind of its own. Charlie instantly turned his wrath on me. He said the only way Mom could know any of this was because of my stupid, big mouth and why did I have to be such a "goddamn, fucking, endless pain in his ass"?

Next thing you know, Mom was yelling at him about his filthy mouth, and he was yelling at me about how I'd ruined his life by being born, and Dad never once, not even for a second, poked his head out of their bedroom.

That was how I knew for sure that something was going on between the two of them.

Well, after a few days, Nonnie didn't seem to be getting better. Mom spent another entire day at Kaiser, and even though it was almost ten o'clock at night, she still wasn't home. She called to say goodnight to Charlie and me and then asked me to put Dad on. At least that meant they were talking again. I really hated them thinking they had to protect us from whatever was going on because, seriously, it only led me to make up stuff in my head that was probably ten times worse than the truth. Bottom line? Like I said before, I knew they loved each other; no doubts there. Whatever the deal was, it would all be fine. Soon.

I hoped.

Charlie had an evening rehearsal for his lame-ass play, so Dad and I had gone out to dinner together. Whenever it's just the two of us, I can always get him to take me to sushi because I'm the reasonable and respectful one, unlike Charlie who orders practically everything on the menu and costs Dad a fortune. When we got to the restaurant—OMG, they have this *in-sane* salmon-skin hand roll—I asked Dad to take off his wedding ring so we could pretend he was a divorced dad on his night out with his daughter. He wasn't going for it. I just thought it would be fun to have the ladies in the restaurant be all, like, *Oh, look at that nice dad spending time with the poor daughter he probably only sees every other weekend.*

Okay, over that weekend, things rocketed to Insanity and Beyond.

It started on Saturday. Mom was still running back and forth from the hospital every second; Nonnie seemed to be getting a little better (at least the ministrokes had stopped, and her blood pressure was under control), but they still didn't know when they were going to send her home. Dad, the Parent-in-Charge, was freaking out because he couldn't focus on his next book and had a major deadline coming up; I thought I was doing him a favor by trying to get out of the house for the day.

My friend Benny Seelig from AP History wanted me to come over so we could work on our congressional-procedure project together, but Dad got all, "Who is this boy and how can I believe all he wants to do is study on a Saturday afternoon?" I said, "Since when are you some suspicious fifties dad who thinks every boy is, like, some out of-control, horny maniac?" And he goes, "I *was* one. They all are."

I told him he was being gross and finally got him to agree to drive me to Benny's house in the Palisades. The whole way there, Dad was giving me these rules, like, "You don't go anywhere else but his house, you call me if other boys show up, and I'll be back at four o'clock sharp to pick you up." Fine. Then he goes, "And keep your phone on and near you so if I need to call or text you, I can—and if I do, I expect an immediate response."

He didn't appreciate it when I told him he needed to chill. *God! Seriously, Dad, when did you turn into such a nervous wreck? I thought that was Mom's job.*

At three, Benny and I were at his kitchen table, making a chart on how bills get introduced in Congress, and there was, like, this crazy pounding on the door while the doorbell was ringing nonstop. It was like some drug bust going down except there weren't any drugs. Benny opened the door, and it was Dad looking like a wild-eyed lunatic.

I was all, "Dadda? What's wrong?" And he goes, "I texted you six times, called you four times, and you never picked up. I thought you were raped and dead, and I was sure your mother would shoot me through the heart for letting you come here in the first place."

Okay. My bad.

I had left my phone in my purse, and my purse was by the front door near the sweatshirt Dad had made me bring even though it was eighty degrees out; I just forgot I was supposed to check it. Benny and I were working. I swear to you, I was innocent. I wasn't even attracted to him; he's way too tall, and I'd have to practically break my neck off looking up at him all the time. But he does have a really sweet smile.

Too bad Dad didn't care about any of that.

He grabbed me by the arm, snatched up all my things, and yanked me out Benny's front door. I never even got to say goodbye. Dad screamed at me all the way home. He was practically gasping for breath as he described all the terrible, scary things he was sure had happened to me because *I* was his responsible kid; if I wasn't answering my phone, it could only be because the most awful thing in the world had happened.

I would've tried to defend myself, but he never stopped yelling long enough to give me the chance.

This is one more reason why I *knew* something was seriously not right.

Normally, my dad is straight up the sweetest, chillest guy I know. Our favorite thing to do together is to people watch and then laugh at all the stupid things strangers do and say. Or we love to go buy school supplies. It's, like, our thing. Finding the perfect binders and file folders and colored pens. We both get way too excited. But what can I say? It's our messed up "perfect student" obsession. So not healthy, I admit.

Anyhow, by the time we got home, I was crying and apologizing and crying some more, and then he got all upset, saying he probably overreacted but he was so fully terrified that something beyond ugly had happened to me.

He was also petrified that Mom never would have allowed me to go to Benny's in the first place, and she would've hated him forever for putting her precious baby in harm's way. I was all, like, "I don't even know what's happening right now." And then we both finally calmed down and agreed we didn't really need to say anything about any of this to Mom. We'd just tell her I was in my room all day, studying.

The next morning, as soon as Mom went back to Kaiser, Dad asked me to go with him to that cute little jewelry store on Montana. He wanted my help with picking out a birthday gift for Mom. He was being super nice and sweet, and I know it was because he felt bad about the whole Benny flip-out, so I was kind and forgiving too. We found these special spiral, gold earrings for Mom, then Dad insisted on getting something for me. I told him he really didn't have to, but there was this sweet little peace sign on a silver chain and, well, it seemed like he really *wanted* to buy it for me, so how could I say no?

For a hot minute, it was almost like things were back to normal until later that afternoon when, seriously, I still have no idea what I walked into.

I came out of my room to get a snack after studying most of the afternoon—Mom was at the hospital, Charlie was off somewhere with Amy—and there was Dad in his office. He'd strung a clothesline across his big front window, and when I came in, he was taking sopping-wet twenty-dollar bills out of a washtub at his feet and hanging them on the line with clothespins.

I asked what the heck he was doing. Ya know what he said?

"It's a favor for your mother. Don't ask."

JULIA

Please don't act so smug. Are you going to tell me *you* would have paid your housekeeper with bills that smelled like pot? Of course not. And I wasn't about to either.

Spending practically every waking moment at Kaiser, I didn't have the time or the strength to make an ATM stop, and I certainly wasn't going to ask Clark to do one more errand for me. I was quite aware he was still incredibly pissed off about that whole stupid debacle in the Kaiser parking garage.

Okay. It was all my fault. I know that.

But if he didn't drive like such a maniac, I wouldn't have to be on him all the time. I don't get it. He never anticipates anything. There'll be a yellow light in front of us, and he's still barreling along like he has no idea it's about to turn red and he'll have to stop. If I dare to make one gentle, innocent comment, like, "Honey, you might want to consider slowing down," he turns and roars at me like I just asked him to cut off his own dick with a rusty razor blade.

But back to the reason why he was washing that cash.

I'm a casual, recreational pot smoker. I'm not an addict like my friend Laurie who wakes and bakes every single morning, but I do like to unwind two or three nights a week with a few hits to help me relax.

So sue me.

But here's the deal: until they went off to college, I was committed to doing absolutely everything I could to hide it from my kids. How could I tell them I didn't want them doing drugs if they caught me out in the backyard, acting like I was a special guest at Willie Nelson's Fourth of July barbeque?

Look, I do my best to be as open and honest with my children as I can be. I despise those parents who are in virulent denial with their "no kid of mine" fantasies. C'mon, people, they're kids. Breaking the rules is a requirement for being a teenager. But I also think you have to provide modeling they can emulate. So, when it came to smoking pot, I hid. And I kept my stash locked up in our bedroom safe. Which also happens to be where I keep a stack of emergency cash because we live in the land of earthquakes, fires, and your occasional tsunami warning. You must be prepared for the possibility of not having access to an ATM. They say that in a major disaster, we might have to go up to two weeks with no power. How unbearable would that be? I'm telling you, if I hadn't been born a girl, I would have made the absolute best Boy Scout. I am always prepared.

That morning, after I got back to the hospital to check on Mom, I realized the next day was Monday, which meant Esmerelda would be coming to clean the house bright and early, so I needed cash on hand to pay her.

Ever since I quit working to be home with the kids, then went back to work after they were in middle school but quit again to take care of my parents, Clark had given me a monthly allowance. I was supposed to use it for personal expenses and also to pay the housekeeper. He covered all the other bills—food, the kids' needs, household stuff, repairs, our entertainment, and whatever else came up. This arrangement was fine with me. I do better on a budget. I mean, the way some of my girlfriends can piss away money? Seriously. I don't even understand it. My neighbor Natalie's annual fresh flower expenditure alone must be more than the entire GNP of Zimbabwe.

Stuck at the hospital, I asked Clark to pull some money out of the emergency fund to pay Esmeralda and told him I'd refresh the cash stash the next time I had the chance. He did as I asked but then called to report that the money had apparently been too close to my pot supply and, as he said, "It was making the bills smell like they'd spent the weekend with Cheech & Chong." Without me even asking, he gave the money a bath in lemon-scented dish soap and hung it on a line in his office to dry. I had to admit, it was very sweet of him. I saw no need to risk having Esmerelda sell me out to the DEA in exchange for a green card. (Yeah, I know weed's legal in California, but can you ever totally trust the Feds?)

The clearest indication that Clark wasn't yet ready to forgive me over the parking-lot incident was when after I got home, I said, "Well, I guess this gives a whole new meaning to money laundering," and he didn't even crack a smile. I wished he could have gotten a little perspective; I was not the only one who'd been out of line.

Look, I wasn't insensitive. I knew Clark had been under tremendous pressure. I knew he was having trouble with the new book, and his editors were being horrible to him. If I could've stormed in and kicked their collective asses, I would have. I hated it when they tormented my sweet husband. I'm on his side. I always have been.

But he was not entitled to treat me like shit.

It's this thing he does when he's unhappy. He gets curt and condescending and acts like everything I say is the stupidest, most ridiculous thing he's ever heard. I don't know if he's even aware he's doing it, but I can only suck it up for so long.

When I lie in bed, trying to talk myself off the ceiling, it becomes an endless loop: *he's stressed, he's worried about money, he doesn't want to let us down or say no to the kids when they need something* ... I get it.

But that still didn't excuse him for treating me like shit.

And then there's this part of him that lives in la-la land. Yes, his incredible optimism is one of the things that first attracted me to him— especially with my dark heart being positive the world is engaged in a perpetual plot to kill me in the most painful and protracted way possible—but sometimes I don't understand what's wrong with him.

Maybe you need to join us in the real world, pal.

Like the way he was fixated on this cockamamie scheme about wanting the four of us to go off camping or exploring or staying in a quaint little bed-and-breakfast in Cambria for a long weekend. What did he think we'd do with my mother? It's not like we could drop her off at some Old People Kennel. Yes, I know, I could have asked my brother, but then Tits-on-a-Bull would've had a million reasons why he and his useless wife weren't equipped to take Mom in. He'd claim Mom doesn't really like him. He'd say she's much more comfortable with me. He'd even declare she was bound to become so stressed out with me gone that she'd have a heart attack and die, and then I'd never forgive him, which he'd convince himself she'd do just to spite him.

So it was easier to not ask in the first place.

Then there was the whole matter of the kids and their schedules. Charlie was rehearsing for *Romeo and Juliet* nonstop, followed by its two-weekend run. Shortly after that, it would be his graduation. If Clark thought Charlie was going to want to spend a single weekend away from Amy, who still had another year of high school after Charlie went to the East Coast for college ... c'mon, Daddio, wake up. Your boy wasn't going anywhere solo, and we were *not* taking Amy out of town with us. I couldn't even begin to imagine what Katie would have to say about *that*! Oh, and as a side note, hubby, I would dare you to try to separate Katie from her schoolwork for three or four days. It would be like trying to cleave grilled cheese from its bread. Not pretty.

Despite all that, when my dear husband gets a plan in his head, I wish you luck trying to convince him to let it go.

And in case you're naive enough to assume the tension in the house couldn't possibly have gotten ramped up any higher, think again.

Mom was spending at least one more night in the hospital because they couldn't release her until she peed—which she hadn't done in two days. She claimed she'd *never* be able to go with so many people waiting for her to do it, so there was a chance she'd be stuck at Kaiser until Veteran's Day.

After the kids were in bed that night, Clark and I took a walk around the neighborhood. We smoked a little pot and attempted to make peace. We really aren't good at fighting; we've never been able to do the silent-treatment thing for more than an hour or two. It felt nice to be nice, and then we kissed and made up.

Just as things always go when we come out of a tense period like that, it wasn't as if everything was instantly back on track. As usual, the next phase was a tentative, careful way of being with each other because we were both so self-conscious, afraid of saying or doing the wrong thing. It was still way better than being in Chilly Standoff Mode.

We got into bed and started messing around: you know, kissing, a little "you touch me, I touch you" foreplay. It all felt regular and comfortable and like such a relief after the previous few days. Then Clark climbed on top of me ... and instantly lost his hard-on.

I'll spare you all the gory details because it was so sad and painful, but we tried a bunch of different approaches and possibilities; no matter what we did, I could feel Clark's body heading toward rigor mortis—every single bit of him was stiff except the part we needed to be.

Then his anger and the sarcasm came back. Gently touching his shoulder, I whispered, "Sweetie, what can I do to help?" He turned to glare at me and barked, "Get a hot, young, functional husband and leave me the fuck alone."

Ouch.

★★★

In the days that followed, Clark was more withdrawn than ever. He was a million miles away, but I was afraid to try to reach him. I didn't have the strength to take any more of his barking or insults or outright rejection.

Mom was finally back home. That was the good news *and* the bad news. I was consumed with her care, convinced every decision I made was the wrong one. She was unsteady, often confused, and had no appetite. She seemed to be sleeping an awful lot. I wondered if that was okay. Was it to be expected after the trauma she'd been through? I couldn't ... I wasn't ... I was not ready to have her die.

Charlie was in his final week of rehearsal on *R. and J.*, so he was hardly ever home. I assumed he and Amy had made up, but I wasn't entirely sure. That was one powder keg I was perfectly fine avoiding for the time being.

Katie was my savior. She did her thing and helped with Mom; she was aware of the stress in the house and would do whatever she could to not pile anything else on. She stayed with Mom for the evening so Clark and I could go out to dinner with our best friends. I don't think either of us really wanted to go, but we were hoping the distraction would be good for us. We've known Sara and Brent since we first became a couple; Clark and Brent worked together, selling hot dogs at Dodger Stadium one summer after college. The Randalls have three kids, so they know the stresses of this modern life. Clark and I figured it would be nice to be with people who would understand what we were grappling with.

We got that one wrong.

The evening started out fine. We met at our favorite Indian restaurant, ordered our usual array of curries and chicken tikka masala and naan, and asked about each of the Randalls' kids in turn. Sara told a cute story about a recent pediatrician visit with her four-year-old, Zoey. Doctor Mary needed to draw blood, and when she asked Zoey which finger she wanted pricked, Zoey instantly responded, "My mother's."

I know most of you are too young to even get this reference, but Art Linkletter was right: kids really *do* say the darndest things.

We laughed and gossiped about mutual friends while the guys downed giant bottles of Taj Mahal. Then Sara made the mistake of asking how we were. I hesitated, hoping Clark would jump in so I'd be spared the danger of saying the wrong thing. He paused for a second, then sweetly laced his fingers through mine and put our entwined hands up on the table. He released a tortured, twisted sigh.

"To be honest, we're struggling. Honey's just out of the hospital, Julia's exhausted from taking care of her. I'm hitting a wall with the new book, nobody's paying me shit, despite the fact that I'm owed a bunch of back royalties … if we're being candid with you guys, right now, everything pretty much sucks."

"Oh c'mon," Brent cajoled. "The kids are doing great—"

"Sure," Clark snapped, "if you wanna forget that Charlie's on the verge of leaving us and probably won't ever be living at home again."

"That's what we want, isn't it?" Sara innocently asked. "Thriving, independent kids who can make their way in the world?"

Clark practically shouted, "It's not what *I* fucking want. I want my family at home. Happy. Together. There'll be plenty of time for them to move on, but who the hell says it has to happen so soon?"

Brent chuckled and tried to diffuse the tension. "Easy, champ. Things will level out—you'll get through this. You always do. But for tonight, how about we lighten up and enjoy our night out?"

In a flash, Clark jumped up, slapped his napkin onto the table, and snarled, "Ya know what? If you only wanna hang out with people who make you laugh, maybe you should find a Volkswagen full of fucking clowns."

With that, he stormed out of the restaurant.

A few minutes later, I retrieved the car from the valet and found him pacing up and down Ventura Boulevard. I calmly told him to get in the car. He made a gesture to shoo me from the driver's seat, but I silently shook my head. He got the message and went around to the other side. The last thing I needed was for him to drive home like a maniac, nearly rear-ending everybody we encountered. I wouldn't have been able to take it. And I really couldn't handle another fight.

After we got back to the house, Clark remained silent, but this time, it felt different. He didn't have anger radiating off him like an intense sunburn; instead, he was wrapped in a cocoon of sadness.

He got undressed and slid into bed.

When I joined him there a few minutes later, I willed him to make eye contact. I kept my voice soft, low. "You know," I said, "if all this has gotten to be too much, we can make changes. We have options."

He stayed silent, staring at me with a dampness beginning to flood the corners of his eyes. I felt compelled to go on. "You know I love this house, but I love you so much more. Let's sell, downsize, find a house we can pay cash for, and not worry about a mortgage. One day last week when I had a few hours to kill, I went to a couple of open houses in the Valley. There are some perfectly fine three-bedroom places in Sherman Oaks—"

I never got to finish the thought. You know why? My husband, the man I've known for twenty-three years, did something I'd never seen him do before.

He started to wail.

I'm not talking about merely crying. He does that at movies and weddings and when both kids were born, but this was a whole new level. I'm telling you, it was Greek Widow at her Husband's Funeral wailing.

It wasn't long before his shoulders were shaking, and his entire body was trembling. I had no idea what to do. Honestly, it was terrifying. There was so much palpable pain, and I was powerless. There in our bed, under our tie-dyed quilt, I reached my arms out to him, and he willingly slithered into my embrace.

Still wailing.

I held on to him as tightly as I could. His sobs took on a heaving, hiccuping rhythm that seemed to last for ages. (Or maybe it was only six or seven minutes.) When he finally managed to calm down, he spoke in a barely audible croak.

"I ... am so scared."

It broke my heart.

I stayed awake for a terribly long time, staring up at the ceiling, hours after he had passed out from pure exhaustion.

The next morning, I woke up to find Clark on his side, totally buried under the covers the way Charlie used to sleep when he was a little kid. I didn't want to wake him, so I silently slipped out of bed, snatched up my slippers and robe, and escaped the bedroom.

Charlie had already left for school—something about a final costume fitting. Katie was in the shower. Mom was blessedly asleep. I didn't need to get within two hundred yards of her room to know that; ever since I was a little kid, my mother has snored like a grizzly bear sleeping off a bender.

When I glanced at the clock a short time later, it suddenly hit me: it was seven thirty and I remembered Clark had scheduled an eight o'clock phone call with his editor in New York. I needed to get him up so he could poop and have a cup of coffee to fortify himself before what would inevitably be a challenging conversation.

I went back into our bedroom. He was still entombed in the blanket, apparently sleeping quite soundly. I reached out and gently shook him. Even through the quilt, his shoulder felt weird. Cold. Too round. And fleshy.

My heart started to race. My eyes felt like they were drifting out of focus.

I had this unsettling lightness in my head. Then, ever so slowly, I peeled back the covers ....

Okay, you're probably going to have a hard time believing this, but do you know what I found?

There was a penguin in our bed.

Yes, you heard me correctly: a fucking seventy-five-pound, black-and-white penguin. I think it rolled over and blinked at me, but I was too angry and freaked out to absorb the details.

Was this Clark's idea of a joke? Was it supposed to send me some kind of sick message? I mean, it wasn't exactly a severed horse's head, but what the hell? Who would do that? *Why* would he do that?

I raced out of the room and pointedly slammed the door behind me to trap it inside. The last thing I needed was for my mother to wake up and have a close encounter with an arctic bird.

I ran into Katie's room where she was getting dressed for school. I know I must have looked like a madwoman judging by how she was looking back at me, but wouldn't you have been freaked out? When I could finally make my brain form words, I told her her dad was MIA, but he had left a goddamn penguin in our bed.

Katie gaped at me for a long moment, then blinked a few times as she digested my declaration before racing down the hall to our bedroom.

The next thing I heard was my daughter's horror-movie scream. It didn't stop. It rose in pitch and became impossibly louder. Trailing her, I galloped into my room.

My girl's eyes and mouth were both wide open. She was on the cusp of hyperventilating. The screams had faded into panting squeaks.

The penguin was up on its webbed feet in our bed, standing more than four feet tall. Its eyes were locked on Katie as it emitted honking, squeaking sounds in response.

"What's with all the screaming?" I asked my daughter. "I told you there was a penguin in here."

She looked at me as if I were the stupidest human on Planet Earth.

"Mom. That's no rando penguin. That's Dad."

CLARK

All right. I realize I'm going to have a little trouble putting this into words that make sense to you, so you'll have to bear with me.

You know how when you first wake up in the morning, you're kind of in that *Twilight Zone* state? Not really asleep but not fully back to consciousness?

Well, that's where I was when I saw Katie standing beside my bed, staring at me, screaming. Like a lunatic. I tried to ask her what the heck was going on, but I couldn't make the words in my brain come out of my mouth. I'd lost my voice. Laryngitis? Why? From what?

I had a sudden memory of my emotional breakdown the night before—sobbing in Julia's arms until I passed out—but why would that cause me to lose my voice?

As I was still trying to puzzle that out, Julia came charging in, responding to Katie's screeching. They were having some disjointed, crazy conversation about a penguin, and then this is what I heard my daughter say:

"Mom, I know this from school. Baby penguins have gray eyes that get darker as they get older, and some species have brown eyes, plus there's one weird type with yellow eyes. None of them have *blue* eyes—except in *Happy Feet*, but that's animated and stupid, and this is real life." Then she pointed directly at me and said, "That penguin has blue eyes.

Dad's blue eyes—with the little fleck of gold in the upper right corner of his left eye—and that's why I know for sure this is Dadda."

Well, of course I was me. Who else would I be? But what the heck was all that chatter about a penguin?

I hopped off the bed.

Wait … since when do I hop?

My wife and daughter jumped back, getting out of my way like I was radioactive. What the hell? All I was trying to do was get to the mirror on the back of Julia's closet door. Except there was something weird about my gait.

It felt like I was waddling.

Julia and Katie stood together, frozen, gawking at me; they both seemed to be holding their breath. When I reached out to open the closet door, it wasn't my arm that came into view. It was a flipper. A sleek black flipper.

Okay. I was slowly getting it. I obviously *wasn't* awake. I was having one of those dreams where you wake up in the dream, so you think you're awake, but you're actually not. I just had to calm down and let it play out.

I used my flipper to flick open the slightly ajar closet door. I gazed into the mirror. A penguin was staring back at me. A nice-looking penguin with peach-colored patches on his neck and a similarly colored streak down his beak, but a penguin nonetheless.

Seriously … what the fuck?

Wake up. Wake up. I needed to wake the fuck up.

I slapped my face with my flipper and then did it again. Harder. Katie came rushing at me.

"Dad, stop. You're gonna hurt yourself." She gently pinned my flipper to my side. "What happened to you?" she asked. "Why are you a penguin?"

Julia raced into view beside Katie. She was agitated, upset, confused. "Katie, you need to stop this now. This is not your father. It's a messed-up, misconceived … I don't even know what, but I do know there is no way in hell your father could suddenly turn into a penguin."

And then Julia started to cry.

Katie put an arm around her mother's shoulder. "It's all right, Mama," she said, sounding heartbreakingly calm and mature. "I'm sure we'll figure this out."

Julia said there was nothing *to* figure out. She had to get her mother to a doctor's appointment, and she needed to call my publishers to tell them I was too ill to get on a call. Katie needed to get to school. The only logical thing to do was call Animal Control and get that nasty, filthy penguin out of the house.

Then my loving wife told our daughter that as soon as I had the courage to show my face again, she was going to throttle me into pudding for thinking, even for one deranged minute, that bringing a wild animal into her bedroom was a cute or intelligent way to prove my point—whatever my point might be.

"Mom! Please! You can't call Animal Control," my daughter pleaded. "I know I'm right, and we can't send poor, helpless Dad off to some rejected-pet gas chamber. And while we're at it, somebody needs to tell me *this*: how "humane" is a Humane Society that puts innocent creatures to death just because nobody wants them? Look, we need time to figure out what's happened. I'll go to school, and you can take Nonnie to the doctor but only if we can leave Dad right here 'till later. Okay? You have to promise me, or I'm not going anywhere."

With that, she folded her arms resolutely across her chest.

Bless you, Katie.

Julia considered this a moment, glanced at her watch, and then went off on a whole new line of rising anxiety.

"Where will it pee? Where will it poop? I can't just lock a penguin in my bedroom and expect it to not destroy the place!"

"What are you talking about?" Katie asked. "Dadda's potty-trained. I mean, God, he has been for, what, like, forty-seven years?"

And then she turned to stare directly at me and added, "Right?" So what else was I supposed to do? I nodded.

Katie squealed, clapped her hands, and jumped up and down like an excited four-year-old. "Oh my God! Did you see that? He nodded! The penguin nodded. That proves it! He really is Dad."

There was more negotiation, a discussion about them running out of time, and then Julia heard Honey calling out for her from down the hall. That instantly kicked everything into a higher gear. The very last thing Julia wanted was for her mother to see a penguin in the house, so she and Katie dashed out of the bedroom, tightly closed the door behind them, and left me to my own devices.

From somewhere down the hallway, I heard my wife's muffled voice: "How are we supposed to know what to feed that thing?"

★★★

Fun fact: a penguin flipper slapping the remote does not turn on the TV.

Out of sheer boredom, I scanned the front page of the previous day's *Los Angeles Times* on the floor beside the bed, but I couldn't get my eyes to focus. Is it possible for a penguin to need glasses?

I was beginning to feel overheated, yet I couldn't take a shower because, once again, fingerless flippers are not ideal for working the knobs.

By the way, have I mentioned I'm claustrophobic in the best of times?

Feeling trapped in my room, no matter how big it is, (yet far from a mansion's master suite, believe me) was only exacerbating this sensation. Plus, I was getting hungry. See, the problem with having had my little fit that sent me storming away from the table with Brent and Sara the previous night was that I'd never finished my chicken tikka masala or my Taj Mahal.

(*Note to self:* next time you feel a need to flip out on friends, you might want to finish eating first.)

Okay, back to the issue at hand—or issue at flipper, I suppose. I needed to eat. I needed to cool down. I needed to get out of that room.

I knew Julia and Honey would be gone for quite a while, so what harm could there be in me going downstairs to take care of my basic needs?

Unfortunately, the bedroom door was closed tight. Julia really had not wanted the penguin (that she refused to believe was me) to escape.

Goddamnit. Whoever realized hands were so essential to every little thing we do? Like my problem with the shower: How was I going to be able to turn that doorknob?

First, I tried gripping it with my mouth. Or beak. Or bill—or whatever you call a penguin's maw. I could get my jaw open surprisingly wide, but I didn't seem to have any teeth to clamp down on the knob. I waddled back to the mirror and opened my beak to see these little, fleshy protrusions that sort of looked like teeth but had no grip. No bite.

On second attempt, thinking maybe just clamping my bill down over the knob and turning my head would do the trick, I got absolutely nowhere. No matter if I whipped my head to the left or the right, I just couldn't seem to apply enough force to get the knob to disengage from the catch.

Shit.

I stepped back from the door to consider other options. I plopped my weary penguin butt down on the carpet to contemplate. Then, a few moments later, I was sure I was onto something.

I toddled into Julia's closet (luckily, *that* door was still ajar) and hopped up onto the step stool she kept there to reach her upper shelves. What I was after was right where I thought it would be: a gripper! You know, one of those poles where you squeeze the handle at one end and the claw on the other end to grab things you otherwise can't reach.

With the gripper clamped in my bill, I returned to the bedroom door. Great theory, dismal results. With no fingers or tongue to cock the trigger, how was I going to get that claw to open wide enough to latch on to the knob? After fifteen minutes of futile attempts, I'll give you the answer: it wasn't going to happen no matter how many times I tried.

Fuck!

Here's the thing about claustrophobia: the more you think you're trapped, the more you begin to feel like you are. So your heart starts to race. And you start to sweat. And you feel like someone's reaching down your throat to squeeze your lungs until there is no way you can take in any air. My phantom chest-sitting sumo wrestler had returned to torment my penguin self.

I waddled away from the door and paced across the bedroom. I went to the open window and inhaled. I had to calm down. I had to think. I had to get out of that room.

I had to pee.

Oh great! Julia's worst fear that I'd go on the carpet like some excited puppy could not become a reality. I waddled into the bathroom and used my head to push up the toilet lid. I backed up, took a running start, and, with surprising agility, sprang up onto the seat. The biggest challenge was finding a spot near the front of the seat where it was narrow enough to accommodate my two webbed feet but wide enough to let me pee without getting it all over the place. With a marksman's aim and a magician's focus, I unleashed my stream, tickled to hear it splashing into the water in the bowl. I was a champ!

When I hopped back down, not having the patience to figure out how to flush, I had a new realization:

I wanted sardines! Wait, I wanted *what*?

I hate sardines. Julia's the one who loves them. And anchovies too.

Oooo, yum ... anchovies! I would've literally killed for some of those babies in that moment.

What? Why? Oh yeah.

I was a penguin.

A penguin that still needed to open the damn bedroom door.

Think! Think! Think!

Oh my God—I suddenly knew what I needed to do.

Man, life is funny. Ever since I'd started to have these periods of high anxiety and massive stress, Julia had been buying me random gifts she hoped would help to ease my tension. Most of the time, they were incredibly well intentioned but totally useless. I mean, did she really think the healing crystal was going to pay the mortgage? But then I remembered one of those opened-and-cast-aside presents that could potentially be the very thing to spring me from my current cage.

I toddled to my nightstand, tugged the drawer open with my beak, then used said beak to push aside a few random, scribbled future-book ideas and homemade birthday cards from the kids.

Voilá!

There it was: a head massager made of metal prongs that looked like a medieval torture device. I snatched it in my bill and returned to the door.

It was designed to expand to the size of whatever head it was pressed down upon, but its pre-use position had the prongs close together, so it resembled a resting octopus. Carefully maneuvering the handle with my mouth, I fitted the claws over the doorknob and very slowly ... oh-so gently ... gave it a twist.

Tears of relief sprang into my penguin eyes when I heard the catch finally release; the door popped open.

Free at last. Free at last. Thank God Almighty, this hyperventilating spheniscid was free at last!

Bless you, Julia. That ridiculous head massager saved the day. And I was goddamn Aquatic MacGyver for figuring it out.

The good thing about a refrigerator door is it's so much easier to open than a shut-tight bedroom door. It's more about leverage than popping a release.

Realizing that, I darted to the step stool we keep under the built-in kitchen desk and, using my head, pushed it over to the counter. I bounced up its steps, snatched the knife-sharpening tool from the butcher block on the counter, and then slid its metal pole between the refrigerator handle and door. Push ... pry ... *POP!*

With my penguin tummy grumbling loudly enough to register on the Richter scale, I dove headfirst into the blissfully cool shelves, pushed aside jars of pickles and bottles of condiments, and found the unopened tin of sardines I knew had been lurking somewhere in the forgotten recesses. Thank God for Christmas gift baskets filled with things no one ever wants or eats. I snatched that can in my beak and yanked it out.

(Okay, I might also have knocked a bottle of Trader Joe's balsamic-vinaigrette salad dressing and a jar of capers onto the floor in my haste, and maybe they did both shatter and make a gigantic mess, but I defy you to do better operating with a beak and two flippers.)

I waddled away with that prized tin in my maw and slapped it down onto the kitchen table.

(Yes, I suppose I did leave the refrigerator door open, but I'm telling you, I was insane with hunger and clearly not thinking straight.)

I pecked, pecked, and pecked at the top of the tin with my surprisingly sturdy beak and punctured the lid. Turning that small hole into a larger one with repeated jabs of my bill, I created a wide enough opening to suck out that first salty little fish. It slid down my gullet, and I immediately dove in for another. And another. Before I knew it, I had orally vacuumed that dented tin until it was empty.

It was a stellar start, but I was far from sated. I toddled back to the open refrigerator and dove in once more on another reconnaissance mission. I pushed things aside with my penguin head, searching for anything that struck my fancy.

Leftover pizza, probably from Charlie's Pepé's hit the previous weekend? No thanks. If only he'd ordered it with anchovies ….

Julia's skinned-and-cooked chicken held no appeal. The horseradish squirt bottle was useless to me. *Oh shit. Did I knock that whole bottle of Perrier onto the floor too?* It didn't break, but it did spill everywhere because somebody—my money's on Katie—forgot to screw the lid on tight. How many times had I told that girl that bubbly water goes flat really fast unless you cap it properly?

Oooo … what did I happen upon next? Thank you, wife! I might be one who's never been a fan of leftovers, but that plate of two-day-old trout on the middle shelf was suddenly looking like a godsend. I tugged it out. *Fuck!* I was salivating so much, I lost my grip on the plate, and it dropped on the floor, exploding it into shards. That sure didn't stop me from swiftly separating the fish from the china and gobbling it down in three or four bites.

Have I mentioned I'm a mighty fine chef? Even forty-eight hours later, my Trout Almondine was about the most delicious treat I could've imagined.

Between the trout, the sardines, and the fact that I had only recently been liberated from sequestration, I had developed a potent thirst.

Water. I was craving cool, quenching water. But from where? Even as a penguin, I had my pride. Just because our late, great dog, Abby, used to drink out of the toilet, that didn't mean it would work for me.

I could've lapped up the spilled Perrier, but there was too much broken glass from the salad dressing and caper bottles mixed in with the water; in fact, that mess on the kitchen floor was beginning to look like news photos of the Deepwater Horizon oil spill. Probably better to steer clear of the entire thing.

Momentarily stumped, I turned and gazed out the kitchen window into our backyard. I had to admit it: I was an idiot!

Staring back at me was our pool, shimmering in the afternoon sun.

I cannot tell you how swiftly I was learning to hate doors, all doors, but especially ones that happened to be locked.

The door from the dining room into the backyard, and the one in the family room, were safely secured with no way for me to possibly undo them. The door from the laundry room hallway into the garage was slightly ajar, but then there wasn't an option for me to escape from the garage if I used that route. The garage door opener buttons were up way too high, impossibly out of my reach.

Damn it!

That pool was beckoning me like a sly seductress.

I returned to the kitchen to contemplate. I spied a kitchen window opened wide. Sure, it had a screen on it, but maybe I could use my penguin head to ram it out and exit that way. It was worth a shot.

Bang. Push. *Bang.* Push. Push. *Riiiiiipppppp.*

The screen tore before it came loose, but I had my opening. I flailed at the tear with my flippers, ripped it wider, and dove outside. A whole new level of freedom was mine.

With a fleetness I never would have guessed a penguin possessed, I made a beeline for the pool steps, hopped up, and dove into our saltwater lagoon pool. (Who could have ever imagined Katie's chlorine allergy would have an unexpected benefit now that I'd become an aquatic bird?)

I took a long, satisfying drink, delighted to realize ingesting salt water was perfectly fine for a penguin like me.

I paddled through the water; I reveled in that water. I flipped onto my back and floated.

I was one happy, well-fed, cooled-down, black-and-white bird.

JULIA

I'm sure you've heard it said that toddlers and old people have so much in common because the arc of a life tends to bring you back to where you started. Well, that couldn't possibly be truer when we're talking about my mother. No matter what the situation might be, that woman can ask more questions than the most curious three-year-old, and I have to tell you, it's exhausting.

That was one of the many reasons why there was no way in hell I could let her see or learn that my husband had morphed into a penguin. (I'm not suggesting I was fully prepared to embrace Katie's theory, but she *had* laid out a fairly compelling case that morning before heading off to school.)

Mom and I were coming back from her doctor's appointment, entering from the garage into the laundry room the way we always did, when I happened to glance into the kitchen.

Oh my Christ, what the hell happened in there? Were we robbed?

The refrigerator door was wide open. Covering the floor was shattered glass, spilled food, and a broken plate surrounded by an oily puddle the color of aged whiskey. I gripped my mother's arm and swiftly steered her into the hall, blocking any possible view of the disaster zone.

"C'mon, Mom, you look exhausted. Let's get you upstairs for a little nap."

Although she'd lived in Los Angeles for half a century, my mother had somehow managed to retain her pronounced Boston accent. She cocked her head at me in her patented look of righteous indignation.

"What are you talkin' about, de-ah? I feel fine."

"You were complaining all the way home about how exhausted you are." She tilted her head once more in blatant bewilderment. "Was I?"

(Maybe she hadn't exactly *said* she was tired, but I certainly wasn't about to run the risk of letting her have a close encounter with a rampaging penguin.)

Retaining my grip on her elbow, I steered her toward the staircase and up to the second floor. "Go on—take your shoes off, stretch out on the bed, and I'll bring you a nice cup of tea and some toast."

"I don't want you waitin' on me, de-ah. This is why I never should've moved in with you in the first place. I'm ruinin' your life. Ach! Why am I even still here? I should do everyone a fav-ah and drop dead."

"Mom. Please. You should most definitely *not* drop dead. You should just be resting."

With a resigned sigh and a hapless shrug, she took off her spangled Donna Karan jacket, threw it over her arm, and slowly shuffled into her bedroom.

Thank God.

I'd barely made it into the kitchen when a fluttering, rippling motion outside captured my attention. I dashed to the window to gaze out.

Wait, are you kidding me?

That penguin was in the pool, swimming, splashing, diving, gliding—seemingly having the time of its life. I dodged the oily puddle on the kitchen floor, bolted into the adjoining family room, unlocked the door, and sprinted outside.

"Um, excuse me, what do you think you're doing?" I practically bellowed.

I truly wasn't expecting a response. In fact, I have no idea what I *was* expecting, but seeing that stupid bird frolicking in the pool had truly popped my cork.

It flicked its head up and gawked at me, effortlessly treading water. We became locked in an unflinching staring contest. The jumble of emotions I was feeling made me want to scream, but I was too afraid of alarming or alerting my mother.

I felt absolutely insane. Apparently, that had become that week's default emotion.

I nearly had a heart attack when from behind me I heard, "Radical! Where'd we get a penguin?"

I spun around to discover my grinning son.

How had he suddenly appeared? How did I not hear him? What was he doing home at this hour?

"It's Thursday," Charlie said. "Remember? I have the last two periods free. I came home to get something to eat before I gotta go back for rehearsal. But screw all that—how come we have a penguin in our pool? It's so awesome. Are we keeping him?"

I have no idea why this was the next thing that came out of my mouth. I told you, I was feeling crazy. It also might have had to do with the fact that in that moment, I was locked on to the bird's eerily distinct blue eyes.

"It's not a penguin—it's your father."

Charlie chuckled. "Mom, I know Katie says you've been bugged at Dad lately, but that's no reason to dis the poor guy. He's been working out. He looks good. You don't need to be calling him a penguin."

"I'm not calling him a penguin—he *is* the penguin." I thrust my arm sharply toward the water. "That bird in there is the man formerly known as your father."

Charlie issued his superior, snorting cackle that always makes me want to smack the smug right out of him. "Oh, okay. If you're not going to tell me what's really going on, I'm heading inside to grab some food."

After Katie had also gotten home, she, Charlie, and I were sitting at the kitchen table.

Katie wailed, "The worst part of this whole thing is that Dad was supposed to help me study for my AP Chemistry test tonight!"

"Are you seriously serious right now?" Charlie asked. "Our dad has, for absolutely no fucking logical reason—"

I warned him to watch his language, but he just kept ranting.

"—decided to become a penguin, and you're worried about a stupid test? You're unbelievable."

Katie whirled toward her brother. "Okay. Not everybody wants to be a so-called"—she flashed air quotes, guaranteed to set Charlie off—"*filmmaker,* you know. Some of us want to go to college to get a degree that can actually get us a job to earn a living! Just because I care about my tests and my grades and take classes other than ceramics and drama, it doesn't make me a freak."

"You're right," Charlie retorted. "You've been a freak since the day you were born!"

"Ma-ommmmmmm!"

"Stop!" I snapped. "Don't you think this ... situation ... is stressful enough without you two tearing into each other? We need to figure out what we're going to do about ... *that!*"

I sharply pointed my extended hand and arm to the kitchen window. Outside, the penguin was still merrily gliding and diving in the pool.

"If you ask me, he seems pretty happy. So what's the problem?" Charlie shrugged. "Oh, by the by, it's cool if Amy sleeps over tonight, right? I asked Dad yesterday, and he said it was fine."

I don't know if this was even possible, but I swear I could physically feel the color draining from my face. My blood was pounding in my ears. Clark's idea of coparenting was to "good cop" me into a corner so any tough decisions regarding setting boundaries for our teenagers regularly fell to me. I asked Charlie why on earth Amy would need to sleep over when she lived only a few miles away—and, on top of everything else, it was a school night.

"After rehearsal, we still need to work on the cover design for the *R. and J.* program. The school gets locked up as soon as we're done, and we can't go to her house 'cause her parents are really light sleepers, plus they have that totally small house, and you're the one who's always saying you don't want us hanging around in parked cars where we can get robbed or shot or both."

"So? Come here, work on the program, and when you're done, you can drive her home."

"I still have my conditional license, duh! I'm not allowed to have anyone under twenty-five with me in the car after ten. Do you want me to break the law? Or would it be better if I woke you up at midnight and had *you* drive her home? She'll sleep on the family room couch, Mom, I swear. Don't turn this into some big fucking deal."

Again with the mouth!

I hated that even though he could opt to be an absolutely brilliant trial lawyer, Charlie's sole ambition was to conquer the entertainment industry. He so easily could have been looking at a life with a potent, steady income and beautiful three-piece suits. From the time he was in middle school, whenever he'd had an argument to make, he came at Clark and me armed with compelling facts, wrapped in talking points, and backed up by preemptive counterpoints.

I jumped out of my chair and stormed outside. Both kids trailed me. I stomped to the edge of the pool and loudly clapped my hands to capture the penguin's attention. It spun around in the water and aimed its bobbing head at me.

"Did you tell Charlie it was fine for Amy to spend the night here tonight?"

The bird stared at me, issued two slow, guilty blinks—and then nodded.

Charlie slapped his hands together and bounced into the air. "Holy shit! He nodded. It totally *is* Dad. And see? Told you he said it was okay!"

★★★

An hour later, Charlie, Katie, and I were again seated at the kitchen table, attempting to formulate a game plan. For the time being, it didn't really seem like we had any choice other than to accept the premise that the penguin was indeed Clark.

It was getting increasingly more difficult to deny what I felt when I gazed into that stupid bird's face.

In times of stress, some people get ulcers. Some people have a nervous breakdown. Others self-medicate.

My husband? He turned into a penguin.

I honestly don't think I'd ever given enough consideration to the fact that living a freelance life with no guarantee of a regular paycheck had been taking quite a toll on Clark. I always told him we could move at any time; I repeatedly stressed that I cared much more about keeping our family intact and our children happy than I did about needing a walk-in closet or a pool with a waterslide. I had truly meant it when I said I could live anywhere as long as we were all together.

But he's a man.

And men have egos tied to achievement and being the primary breadwinner; they need to fight back the darkness while protecting us from marauding invaders—like cable guys and insurance salesmen. They need to win.

"Okay," Charlie said, snapping me out of my reflections. "I have'ta get back to school. So can Amy spend the night or not?"

"You're sure it's all right with her family?"

"Mom, they live in Topanga. They'd be fine if we built a yurt in Taos, sold all our clothes, and spent the next ten years howling at the moon."

"You know what? I don't have the strength to fight about this. But you have to *swear to me* she'll sleep on the family room couch."

"Of course!"

He was up and out the door before I could change my mind. It was one of the things you could always count on with my son: as long as his needs were being met, he'd be totally fine with having his father be a penguin. It only meant he could borrow Clark's favorite gray suede jacket without any pushback.

"So what are we going to tell Nonnie?" Katie asked.

"We're not. When she asks where Dad is, we'll say he had to go to New York to meet with his editors. And we will do absolutely everything in our power to make sure she and the penguin never collide. You have to trust me on this, Katie-Lady—my bandwidth for any more hysteria is all used up."

Outside the window, I saw the penguin swiftly glide to the steps of the pool; he hopped up each one in succession, and then jumped onto the deck before shaking himself off like a dog. A moment later, before Katie or I had a chance to react, he darted to a chaise outside under the window, bounced up onto it, and slid through the hole in the screen. He plopped awkwardly onto his belly on the tile floor and sprang back up onto his webbed feet. He stared at us with mournful, pleading eyes and patted his belly.

"I think he's hungry, Mom," Katie said. The penguin adamantly nodded.

I looked to my daughter. "So what do I do? What should we feed him? Too bad there's no such thing as Purina Penguin Chow."

"Don't we have some fish?"

I stood at the counter, flaking canned tuna into a bowl while Katie had her books spread across the kitchen table to start on her homework. She's the type of student I never was. Translation: she actually gives a shit. In my humble opinion, she cares *too* much. From third grade on, she's always been incredibly hard on herself. She creates stress and pressure by competing with her peers in a way that feels wholly unnecessary.

While Clark and I certainly wanted her to do well and to acquire a useful base of knowledge to help her through life, we were never those parents who set up rewards for good grades or made threats about anything less than a B being "strictly unacceptable." You might not believe this, but that distinction set us apart from most of our friends and neighbors. We were much more concerned about teaching our children to be kind, compassionate, and generous human beings than we were about making sure they could identify all the provinces of Canada.

Katie and Charlie went to our perfectly decent local public schools with a wide range of students from different ethnic and socioeconomic backgrounds; most of our immediate neighbors were paying more than $60,000 a year to have their kids in white-walled, private schools filled with white-bread peers with bleached-white polo shirts, dazzling vanilla smiles, and high-end name-brand tennis shoes that cost almost as much as my first car. No thanks.

But I digress.

As I was preparing the tuna, Katie was making color-coded flash cards for her upcoming AP Chemistry test. The penguin was plopped on his belly beside Katie's chair, sound asleep on the floor.

"Awwww, look at him," my daughter cooed. "He pooped himself out playing in the pool like a little boy."

Yeah. Great. Glad somebody's enjoying this wretched day.

It was the slapping of my mother's slippers on the tile down the hall that snapped me back to our current reality. I whirled toward Katie and hissed in a panicked stage whisper, "Nonnie's coming! Hide your father."

Like a champ, Katie sprang out of her chair, bolted into the adjoining family room, and snatched a black throw blanket off the couch. She dashed back and swiftly shook it out to cover the dozing penguin.

Thankfully, Mom's eyesight was pretty awful. She had cataracts we hadn't had time to fix, and her glasses were thicker than a bulletproof windshield. She shuffled into the kitchen with a sleepy smile, declaring she had just woken up from "the most mah-velous nap." She wanted to know what we were doing for dinner.

"Haven't decided yet," I replied.

"Who's that tuna for?" Mom asked.

I gawked at the bowl in front of me and the empty can in my hand like they had magically appeared. I stuttered and stammered and finally blurted that Katie needed a little fortification to make it to dinnertime, so she'd be able to concentrate on her studies. I told Mom I'd start focusing on our main meal in a minute.

"What can I do to help, de-ah?"

My glance was magnetically drawn to the blanket-covered mass on the floor. Aware of my mother's presence, seasoned enough to know it would be best if she didn't discover him, the black lump was ever-so-slowly inching its way toward the family room.

"What's that?" Honey asked.

My heart clogged my throat. We were busted. My voice was a raspy squeak.

"What's what?"

My mother pointed to the moose-shaped pepper grinder on the counter; our next-door neighbor had recently brought it back to us from a trip to Maine. I was suddenly breathing again.

"It was a gift from Carol for taking in her mail. It's cute, right? Listen, Mom, if you really want to be a help, why don't you grab me a diet soda out of the garage. I'm parched!"

"Ma-ommmm!" Katie scolded. "You have to stop drinking so much cancer in a can! How many times do I have to tell you?"

I did not need my daughter foiling my diversionary tactic with a lecture. "Not now!" I snapped and whirled toward my mother who looked startled by my outburst.

"Mom, please, I'm worn to a frazzle. I'd really love a cold drink."

My mother turned and wordlessly shuffled toward the garage. I dashed to my daughter with the bowl of flaked tuna in hand.

"Katie, really? Now? You had to do your diet-soda dance *now*? Get your father into the family room closet and give him this before Nonnie gets back."

Oh my God, there was no way I was going to survive.

The stress of trying to keep all life's logistical and emotional balls in the air had sparked a brand-new epiphany. I suddenly gained a much greater understanding of, and empathy for, all the pressure Clark was grappling with. I mean, I'd always been aware of the financial burden he was carrying, but I'd never put too much thought into everything else he had to navigate daily. Most of the time, he made it all look so easy. His calm nature and innate optimism gave him the air of someone who had it all wired.

But, of course, that couldn't be true. He had to deal with editors and publishers weighing in on his creative process. He had to worry about how his books were selling and what his competitors were doing. He had to take notes from people he didn't respect. Plus, he carried with him the endless expectation to be profound and productive and prolific on demand. He also managed our money and did upkeep on the house. Jesus, no wonder the man turned into a penguin. Who wouldn't?

Back when I was teaching full time, of course I'd had idiot principals and brainless bureaucrats to contend with, but I never was the sole breadwinner. When I retired, it was because we both thought it was best for me to be home with the kids while they were young. It was a mutual decision, right? Clark was fully on board. Right?

Oh God, it suddenly occurred to me: *What if this is all my fault?*

I needed to renew my credentials. I needed to get back to work. I needed to be contributing more. I needed—

"MOM!"

Once again, it was Katie's disbelieving tone that returned me to the present. I looked down to the stove top and saw I had poured nearly half a box of salt into the boiling green beans I was preparing.

"What're you doing?" Katie asked.

"Sorry, I got distracted."

"Obvi," my daughter said with an unvarnished "tsk" in her voice.

Katie, Mom, and I made it through a dinner of pork loin and slightly over salted green beans.

Later, we three ladies watched *The Real Housewives of Beverly Hills* with Mom jabbering through the entire thing. She couldn't stop commenting on the women's duck-billed plastic surgery and their cheap-looking expensive clothes.

Around ten, I helped Honey get ready for bed, said goodnight to my daughter—at her desk, dutifully studying—and went to my room. I forced myself not to worry about what Charlie and Amy would do when they got back. I didn't have the fortitude to fight about who slept where. If they were hungry, they could fend for themselves. Charlie was going off to college soon; I had to start letting him learn how to survive without me.

(Not that I thought for a minute he actually *could*, but I had to fake it.)

When I came out of my closet in the threadbare nightgown I couldn't seem to surrender to the rag bin, I was startled to find the penguin right there in front of me, standing straight up, with those far-too-familiar eyes locked on me.

(Now, I don't know if it was denial or willful amnesia or a self-generated survival tactic, but as odd as this might sound, for the previous hour or so, I had almost forgotten that my husband had transformed into a bird.)

"What are you doing up here?"

The penguin turned his head toward our bed and waved a flipper in its direction.

I let out a stunned laugh. "Oh, you cannot possibly think you're getting into bed with me. Are you out of your mind? You're a penguin."

Wait. Did that black-and-white creature just shrug at me? Is it copping an attitude? No, no. Stop. Get a grip. He is not something out of a computer-generated Disney remake, primed to dance with Mary Poppins. He is a swimming, fish-eating, wild animal that will not be sharing my bed.

"Look, if you want me to get some blankets and make you a … you know, a little nest on the floor over here, I can do that, but there's no way in hell you're climbing in there," I said, poking an uncompromising finger toward our quilt-covered queen.

Goddamn Clark and his sad eyes!

Even the doomed puppies in the ASPCA commercials didn't have that look down as well as he did. But it wasn't going to work on me. I marched out of the room to the linen closet at the end of the hall and gathered up an armful of spare blankets and a down pillow.

★★★

Later, roused from a deep sleep by my inflated bladder, I squinted at the digital clock on my nightstand—12:47 a.m. The house was blissfully quiet. I got out of bed, sidestepping the penguin spread out in his roost on the floor, and went to pee.

Remembering that Amy was supposed to be spending the night and wanting to ensure they'd made good on Charlie's promise to have her sleep on the family room couch, I went downstairs to check.

Okay, are any of you actually surprised? The couch was empty. But it was made up with a blanket, pillow, and sheet to facilitate the clearly planned covert predawn return of my elusive houseguest.

I marched upstairs and tapped on Charlie's bedroom door. I knocked again, a bit louder. The door opened a mere crack.

"What?" my groggy and clearly annoyed son asked.

I pushed the door open wider, slipped into the room, and closed the portal behind me. Amy was standing in back of Charlie. They were both fully clothed, but their faces were flushed and sweaty, their hair was matted to their heads like they were a duo of boxers in the eighth round, and their chests were heaving in tandem.

"We're still studying," Charlie said.

"In the dark. Without any books. Nice try."

"I hope you don't mind me saying this, Mrs. W.—"

I already knew I was guaranteed to mind terribly, but I let her continue.

"—Charlie's practically out the door to college, we know what we're doing, and we both know what we want. We're not little kids. And, honestly, if you're worrying about your baby losing his virginity, that boat sailed on Valentine's Day."

"Okay, Aim—" my mortified son said.

I had to hand it to him; it was more than I could muster.

With her beautiful, pitying young eyes trained on me, Amy continued, "You look really tired and stressed. Why don't you go back to sleep?"

I had nothing. I was spent. I threw out both upturned hands in surrender and pivoted to open Charlie's door. As I was exiting, Amy had one last thing to add:

"By the way, sorry to hear Clark turned into a penguin. That must high-key suck for you."

Emotionally liquefied, I floated back to my room in a haze and slid under the covers. I refused to let my mind start spinning because I knew if it did, it would never stop. I sank into the mattress and plumped the pillow under my head. Scooting toward the middle of the bed, I bumped into a solid, unyielding form.

I didn't have to turn over to know it was the penguin.

In bed with me.

I wanted to protest; I wanted to shove him to the floor, but I couldn't. I didn't have the will. Instead, I simply let out a long, anguished sigh. This only compelled the bird to scoot closer. He threw a flipper over my back.

Please don't ask for a rational explanation. I'd really appreciate it if you didn't judge me. Instead of lunging away from him, I nestled into him, spooning.

The contact was cold and clammy yet inexplicably comforting.

CHARLIE

I woke up that next morning wondering what could I possibly have done to deserve the hell that was my current life. Seriously. What the actual fuck? Why did the universe despise me?

After five weeks of intense rehearsals, I was supposed to be opening in *Romeo and Juliet* that very night. In case you didn't get the memo, I was Romeo. Ya know, kind of, like, the star.

D'you think it was easy learning all those lines and working to have them make sense to a bunch of lame-ass high school kids who would rather be watching porn on their phones? I actually *cared* about making the play good. I wanted to be great, a legend. I wanted people to still be talking about my performance years after I'd graduated. But that takes a shit ton of concentration. You'd think there would have been at least one person in my pitiful life who would've been able to understand that—but guess again. I swear to God, they were all conspiring to rattle me into being a colossal failure.

The downward spiral started bright and early that morning. Since Mom had already busted us, Amy didn't see any point in going down to the couch to perpetuate some charade, so when my alarm went off, she slipped out of bed and went to the bathroom at the end of the hall. I got up, made the bed so Mom wouldn't be ragging on my ass, and then got my clothes together. I couldn't figure out why Amy still wasn't back. Darting to the can, hoping to avoid Mom or Katie, I tapped on the door.

"Everything okay in there?"

The response was a choked sob that sounded like a cat with hiccups. "Aim, what's going on?"

"You can't come in."

"Okay ... can you come out? We're gonna be late for school."

"I want to die."

"Please don't."

A moment later, I heard the door unlock. She opened it just a hair and tugged me inside. I had to jump back to avoid stepping into a nonmetaphorical puddle of shit. Amy was perched on the back of the toilet with her knees drawn up. She looked like a Buddha on a porcelain pedestal.

Apparently, she had done her morning business, flushed ... and then it all decided to come pouring back out, flooding the floor in a chocolate sea of turds and tattered toilet paper. Can you say *disgusting*?

"You have to tell your family it was you, okay?" my loving girlfriend begged.

"What? No!"

She claimed that's what I'd do if I really loved her. She insisted it was much less humiliating for my mother to think I had dropped a giant doodie than to let Mom know it was my delicate, green-eyed lady. Seriously? What kind of sexist bullshit is that?

It was all so illogical and bizarre that I was starting to feel like Brad Pitt in *Once Upon a Time in Hollywood*. Remember how he was tripping balls when the Manson family broke in, and he couldn't tell what was reality and what was the drugs?

I swear to God, that's how I was feeling.

Wait ... twenty minutes before I was sound asleep, and now I'm literally in deep shit. What the hell?

Before we could even begin to get the issue resolved, I heard my endlessly annoying sister wailing from downstairs, crying out for Mom. Katie was yelling that the toilet in the family room was overflowing, and she hadn't even gotten anywhere near it. Moments later, I heard Mom bursting out of her room. I sprang out of the bathroom and swiftly closed the door behind me, leaving Amy stranded on the shore of Lake Toxic.

Wanna know the real problem with living in a house with so many bathrooms? If something messes with the main line, you've suddenly got a quartet of toilets spewing out a shitstorm in four-part harmony.

"What do we do?" my frantic mother asked.

"We do what we always do? Get Dad on it."

"Oh really?" my mother snarled in an unsettling mix of anger and irritation. "Do you know a lot of penguins that happen to be competent plumbers? Because I'm sorry, darling, but I *don't!*"

"Well, jeez, calm down. It's not like Dad actually fixes these things himself. He's the *president* of the Call the Man Club."

"Okay ... what man? What plumber? Do you know who we use? Who we gonna call?"

I started to open my mouth, but Mom immediately preempted me. "And, I swear to God, if you say *Ghostbusters* right now, I'll knock your head off."

As we stood glaring at each other in a silent standoff, my Nonnie came out of her bedroom across the hall. Her hair was mashed to one side of her head, her eyes were barely open. She greeted us with a half-whispered "Good mornin'" and shuffled toward the closed bathroom door. Mom barked at her to halt. Nonnie stopped, startled, and announced she had to pee.

"You can't," my mother insisted.

"What d'ya mean I can't? I have to."

Mom explained that all the toilets in the house were overflowing, and Nonnie was just going to have to hold it for a while.

"De-yah, I'm eighty-five years old. Holding it is not an option."

My mother whirled to me and ordered me to go downstairs to fetch the old plastic pitcher from under the bar. Shocked, I told her there was no way Nonnie could pee in that. My adorable grandmother with the smashed hair and sleep-encrusted eyes turned to offer me her sweetest smile.

"Sure I can, love. I once peed in your Grandpa Johnny's martini shaker on the turnpike near Mashpee when our car broke down goin' to Provincetown."

There you had it. I guess you really do learn something new every day.

I ran downstairs, grabbed the aforementioned pitcher, and raced back up. The scene I encountered stopped me in my tracks. Mom, Nonnie, and Katie, who had joined them, were all frozen in the hallway, gaping at the penguin that had emerged from the master suite. Nonnie blinked a few times, as if trying to confirm what her cataract-shrouded eyes were seeing.

"Who's this?"

I'm not sure how it's possible, but the silence grew even louder.

They all looked like something out of that Ben Stiller movie *Night at the Museum*—ya know, when they have all those shots of frozen tableaus from history?

It was Katie who finally piped up.

"Okay ... actually, Nonnie ... please don't freak out, but Dad's been under a humongous amount of pressure lately and, well ... yesterday he ... see, it's kind of hard to explain, and I know it sounds crazy, but he ... well, see, he just ... he spontaneously turned into a penguin."

More contemplative blinking from Nonnie. A few moments to digest. Then: "Interesting." She exhaled deeply, collected herself, and continued. "I always pictured Clark as more of a jackrabbit."

With that, Nonnie snatched the pitcher from my hands, spun on her calloused heels, and returned to her bedroom to pee.

Finally liberating Amy from the bathroom, I told Mom she had to figure out the plumber situation because we had to get ready for school. When Amy and I came downstairs a short time later, Mom and Penguin-Dad were in his office.

Looking like some '50s kid bobbing for apples on Halloween, he was dunking his head into a box of business cards, sorting through them with his beak, flinging several aside in pursuit of one in particular. When he at last found what he was after, clamping it in his bill, he extended his neck to Mom, inviting her to take the card:

Kummerow and Son. Certified Plumbers. Next, Dad waddled toward the front door, swinging his flipper in a gesture to Mom, indicating she needed to follow him. He led her outside and pointed to a spot next to the front walkway where the lid had blown off an access pipe. Shit and toilet paper were spilling out of it. Dad pointed at it adamantly. Registering Mom's confusion, I stuck my head outside.

"I've heard Dad talk about that thing before. I'm pretty sure it's called a clear trap. I guess that's what you have to ask the plumber to come clean out."

Looking like a trained seal, Dad clapped his flippers together and pointed at me; I'm guessing it was the penguin version of "Attaboy."

You're welcome.

While I was making protein smoothies for me and Amy—gotta get your energy up on a performance night—Mom got off the phone and announced the plumber would be there before noon. I told her I'd be staying at school straight through; the cast was planning to grab dinner together before the show. I advised her to get there early, well ahead of the eight o'clock curtain.

"You guys are probably gonna wanna grab seats in the front row. Otherwise, Dad might not be able to see over everybody's head."

Mom gawked at me like I was the village idiot.

(I'm not.)

"Are you out of your mind, Charlie? He can't come. I'm quite sure the school auditorium has a strictly enforced 'no penguin' policy."

Oh my God. A righteous epiphany suddenly slammed full force into my brainpan: *Dad ... hates ... Shakespeare.*

Despite being incredibly well read, and acknowledging that he kicks ass playing along with *Jeopardy!* every night—not to mention he has a ridiculously expansive collection of movie and TV trivia stored in his noggin—he's always had a bug up his ass when it comes to the Bard. Was it possible this whole penguin-transformation thing was an elaborate ploy to get out of having to sit through my play?

The penguin was standing innocently in a corner of the kitchen, waiting patiently to be fed, when I whirled on him, erupting in fury.

"I can't believe you'd do this to me, Dad! I can't believe how much you hate me! Turning into a penguin just to get out of sitting through *Romeo and Juliet*? That's cold!"

All I got back in return was a startled stare.

Okay, so all that wasn't bad enough, right? I mean, so much for preparing. So much for being able to get my head in the game.

Fuck me.

I was driving Katie, Amy, and me to school. Amy's body language was unmistakable; she had transformed into a block of granite. Her arms were folded tightly across her chest, her head was pointedly turned to stare out the side window. She was radiating such a chilly vibe, I'm surprised I didn't need to turn on the defroster.

One of the things I really hate about women is when they do this: the Tenth Avenue Freeze-Out. If something's wrong, tell me. Just so ya know, I flunked out of mind-reading school. Katie, acting totally oblivious to Amy's mood, was chattering about a history quiz she had first period, stressing that she was going to be late even though we were completely fine on time. I asked her calmly and politely if she could please shut the fuck up.

Suddenly, Amy spun in her seat and started spewing dragon fire at me.

"Charlie Whitaker, I cannot believe this is how you talk to your little sister!"

Things only escalated from there. She went on to say she was outraged at me for not telling Mom I was the one who made the toilet overflow. She was hurt and humiliated that I left her stranded in the bathroom for fifteen minutes while we were all outside the door, debating where Nonnie should pee. She didn't care if we had a shitty opening night. She didn't give a crap if the whole run of the play was a disaster. It was all idiotic and ridiculous, and she hated me for never once validating her belief that *she* should have been playing Juliet instead of that no-talent Melissa Milligan.

"All you care about is *you*. I'm sick of it. It's all about you. Always." Then she turned in her seat to enlist the support of my startled sister. "It's true, Katie, right? Charlie only cares about Charlie."

Knowing I was fully capable of crashing the car into the nearest lamppost if provoked, Katie drew a hand across her mouth in the universal sign for zipping her lips. Undeterred, Amy turned back to me, bursting into sobs. She said I had better watch my back during the final act tonight—I'm not even kidding about this; she seriously threatened to fill my little bottle with a dram of real poison. And, just in case that wasn't bad enough, she told me she wasn't going to put up with any of my bullshit for one second longer.

"We're done!"

Once again, my pinwheel brain started spinning out of control.

Ya know what, I thought, *I hope she does poison me. I hope I do die onstage. My life is total crap. Pitiful doesn't even start to cover it. What's the point of any of it? I swear to God, nothing would make me happier than to get through tonight's show, go home, go to sleep; and then tomorrow morning, I seriously hope I wake up dead.*

KATIE

As much of a pain in the ass as he can be, I love my brother. I do. But Amy was right: most of the time, he's totally a self-centered dick. He's an actor, ya know? It goes with the territory.

But, OMG! What happened on their opening night? Nobody could possibly have wished that on their worst enemy. Straight up.

Mom, Nonnie, and I got Penguin-Dadda settled outside in the pool. We left a dish of sardines and tuna on the deck so he could eat whenever he got hungry. I even found an old blow-up beach ball for him to play with. You should have seen him with that thing: he was like that Cristiano Ronaldo dude, flipping it up into the air, bouncing it off his head. So cute.

Anyway, we took Charlie's advice and got to school early to get great seats. Whenever he's in a play, I always try to sit where I know I'll be in his eyeline so I can try to make him laugh while he's performing. He's usually so focused, it's hard to do, but the one or two times I've succeeded, it's straight fire.

So … remember Amy was playing Lady Capulet, Juliet's mom? Well, she was doing the scene with Juliet where she has her big speech about Romeo being such a villain and needing to die for killing Tybalt—who I think was Juliet's cousin or whatever; who can really keep it straight? Anyway, when Amy's going on about wanting Romeo dead, she was just *spitting* those words. I mean, *so* hostile. And, of course, having been there when she broke up with Charlie, I got all the subtext, but everybody else just thought she was this fabulous actress. (Trust me, *she's not*.)

Now I'm pretty sure it was after Juliet's already doing her fake-dead thing, but I spaced out thinking about the leftover cold spaghetti I was gonna eat when we got home. Charlie was back on stage, doing another huge monologue. He was carrying on about needing to see the Apothecary, and right in the middle of some line about, "And if a man did need a poison now," he totally burst out crying! I mean, like, big-time. Since it wasn't a particularly emotional moment, everybody was giving each other these *WTF?* looks, and Charlie was working to pull it back together but no luck. Finally, he just went running offstage. Awkward much? *I* wanted to kill myself, and I wasn't even the one who lost it.

Dylan (who was playing the Apothecary) was like a rock star; he improvised the whole next scene, acting like he was putting together the poison for Romeo—ya know, like Romeo had phoned in a prescription or some shit, which you fully couldn't do in ye olden times.

Dylan completely saved the day, and eventually, Charlie showed back up, and it all went ahead but ... crushing, right? Oh my God. It's a full year later, and when I think about it, I start *totally* dying for the poor guy all over again.

When the play was finally over—it seriously felt like we were in that auditorium for a decade—Mom told Nonnie and me to stay in our seats while she went backstage to find Charlie. She told him he had to leave his car at school overnight and come home with us because he was in no state to drive. He didn't even have the strength to argue. He just grabbed all his shit and got out of there as fast as he could, so he didn't have to deal with the rest of the cast.

That car ride home was like being sealed in a rolling tomb with a mummy that used to be my brother. Oblivious to the breakup, Nonnie was chattering away about how adorable Amy was and how lucky Charlie was to have someone so sweet in his life. Mom kept trying to change the subject, but when Nonnie gets going, good luck to anybody trying to snatch the verbal bone away from that old dog. Charlie seriously looked like he wanted to yeet himself out the car window.

Trying to help my brother out, I told Nonnie she should know that he and Amy had broken up, and it was all for the better because Amy was a little too nuts. Charlie chimed right in to fully agree. We talked about the fact that she had a different hair color, like, every other day, and sometimes it was five colors at once. I mean, making your head look like the LGBTQ+ flag is just blatantly unnecessary. Why does she always need to be so extra? Then I went off on a rant about the rag doll of herself she made and gave Charlie for his birthday. That thing creeped me out from the moment I first saw it. I said, "I mean, the fact that she made an Amy ragdoll with boobs? It's so unsettling. You don't see Raggedy Ann going around flashing big tatas. Plus, have you ever really looked at the smile on that doll? She's up to no good—like, she's just waiting for the perfect moment to go full Chucky on your sorry ass while you're sound asleep."

I was on a roll. I even got Charlie to laugh, which was a huge accomplishment. We started saying he should go right home and rip the stupid head off that stupid doll, screaming *Screw you, Amy!* while he did it. I said he'd be way better off without her because he was gonna be leaving for college in the fall while she still had another year of high school. I said he'd obvi get some East-Coast-college hottie to fall in love with him, so he should be 100 percent thrilled that he got to be free of Amy—starting then and there.

In case the night hadn't already been insane enough, you will not even *believe* what happened when we got back to the house.

Charlie immediately went up to his room and slammed the door. I made a beeline to the refrigerator to lay claim to that leftover spaghetti and meatballs. (What's better than cold spaghetti when the sauce is all, like, stuck on and chilly but so delicious? Heaven.)

Anyway, I was staring into the fridge, and I heard Mom start screaming like a maniac. She was at the kitchen window, staring into the backyard. I raced over to see what was up. (Thank God Nonnie had gone up to her room to watch *Touched by an Angel* reruns so she didn't see any of this.)

There on the deck near the deep end of the pool was my poor Penguin-Dadda surrounded by three mangy-as-fuck coyotes.

They were snarling and slobbering, fully looking like the hyenas in *The Lion King*. Can you say *terrifying*? I, of course, did what I always do in situations like that: I burst out crying. But Mama, she ... I mean, I don't even know who she turned into in that moment, but she went flying into the garage, grabbed a big-ass broom, and charged outside to kick coyote butt.

She started swinging the broom, yelling and yipping like a cowboy on a cattle drive, telling them to "back the fuck off." Those flea-bitten fuckers knew a crazy lady when they saw one; let me tell you, they were not about to mess with her. It didn't take more than thirty seconds for them to turn their ratty tails and haul ass back up the side of the hill at the edge of the yard, jumping over the rear fence and disappearing.

When I came outside a second later, I could totally hear Penguin-Dadda heave the hugest sigh of relief. There was a big pile of penguin poo right underneath him. He'd clearly shit his tuxedo, but wouldn't you?

Mama was shaking and doing that heaving, nervous-laughing thing that happens when you have a major adrenaline rush; she looked astounded by what she'd done.

"Mama," I crowed, "you were such a total badass! My hero. Julia, Warrior Princess. Where did you get the balls to do that? I love you so much. What if we hadn't gotten home in time, and Penguin-Dadda got totally eaten?"

My mother's chest was still heaving. It was difficult for her to catch her breath.

"Oh my God. What was I thinking? They could have turned and attacked *me*. Was I insane? But I could *not* let them mess with your father."

"No. Of course not. You're a full-on superhero-boss-bitch."

The panting penguin gave a hearty nod in absolute agreement.

Later, once we'd managed to calm down, we couldn't wait to tell Charlie and Nonnie the whole story. I completely made Mama sound like some Marvel megastar: Wonder Woman meets that character ... I think it's the one Scarlett Johansson plays ... but ya know why I had to fully pump her up? Because she *so* deserved it. Seriously.

Take a lesson here, people: nobody (not human, not coyote) fucks with my mama's man—even if he happens to be a penguin.

After I got ready for bed, I went into Charlie's room to see how he was doing. The first thing I noticed were these huge tufts of cotton all over his bedroom carpet. He'd done it! I was so happy. Raggedy Amy was in shreds all around the room. Her rainbow-colored yarn hair and cotton boobs looked like remnants of a roadside bombing in Toyland. I don't know if it's a hereditary thing or what, but the men in my family sure seem to like ripping the stuffing out of anything and everything they can get their hands on.

Around midnight, when I was reading in bed, Mama came in to say goodnight. I wanted to tell her one more time how stellar she'd been. See, sometimes she gets into this thing where she thinks she's fully not capable of taking care of things, but she *so* is.

My dad has a big personality, and he makes the money and takes care of a lot of stuff while Mama has been more of a traditional, stay-at-home Earth Mother. It's been wonderful for me and Charlie, but on some days, she gets into this whole "I never finished my master's degree ... I stopped working outside the home after I got pregnant with Charlie ... I'm not smart, I'm not interesting ..." and I constantly tell her none of that's true. She's amazing.

Meanwhile, *Charlie* tells her she needs to finish sewing his costume for whatever-the-hell show he's doing next.

Anyway, I went: "Mama, I hope you realize that if Dad wasn't a penguin, and you saw those coyotes attacking Millicent-next-door's dog or something, you definitely would've run to Dadda to take care of it. But look at what you did tonight—*you handled it yourself!* Totally and beautifully. You are such a capable woman, and I need you to know that. This is huge. Let it be a lesson, okay? Will you promise me?"

She just gave me the most precious smile and kissed the top of my head. I'm pretty sure I saw tears welling up in the corners of her eyes.

★★★

The next morning, which was a Saturday, I came upon an unexpected scene—okay, go ahead and judge me if you must, but I couldn't help hovering out of sight to eavesdrop.

It wasn't even eight o'clock. Penguin-Dadda was back in the pool; I guess he truly needed to stay cool. Early June in Southern California can sometimes be way foggy and gray—remember I told you before about the famous June Gloom? But once it clears around noon, it often gets hot and almost muggy, not exactly the most hospitable climate for a bird that comes from Antarctica.

On that morning, it was full-on sunny right away. So there was Dadda in the water, and Charlie was sitting at the edge, feet dangling in the pool, having, like, this serious heart-to-heart. (*Wait. Can you have a heart-to-heart if only one person's talking? Whatever.*) He was giving Penguin-Dadda a total data dump. (*Dadda-dump?*)

Charlie was talking about his breakdown on stage, saying he was humiliated and embarrassed, but at the same time, he didn't really give a shit. He said he knew he was weird. He never felt like he fit in. He'd spent his whole life so far trying to teach himself how to not care what other people thought.

Then he said something so clear and emotionally open that I was thinking, *Wait, who are you?* I'm used to my brother solely being an egomaniac actor, but he told Dad he really appreciated how Dad and Mom had always let him be exactly who he was. He loved that they didn't try to force him to play soccer or take karate lessons or do Outward Bound to toughen up. Other kids teased him for being gay even though he knew he was straight, and as confusing as it all was, he loved that he could always count on knowing Mom and Dad supported him. It was very sweet.

And then the penguin, bobbing in the water at Charlie's feet, reached up and put a flipper on Charlie's knee. My brother put his hand over that wing, and they just stayed like that until I had to turn away from the kitchen window because it was, like, ya know ... too intimate. I would've felt like a major-league creeper if I'd kept on spying on them for one minute longer.

JULIA

Do you ever have those days where you sleep a full seven or eight hours but still wake up exhausted? The morning after my epic Coyote Smackdown, that's exactly how I was feeling. I'd only been awake for an hour, but the whole "my husband's a penguin" thing was starting to get more draining than you could possibly imagine.

I was sitting at the kitchen table, having my first cup of coffee—my entire family knows not to get near me until after that happens—when the penguin came waddling up to my side. He was clutching the *Romeo and Juliet* program in his beak and then gently set it down beside my mug. He stared at me with the saddest eyes you can imagine. He cocked his head to one side and, don't expect me to tell you how, but I knew exactly what he was asking. He was so bummed that he wasn't going to get to see the play. He couldn't handle the fact he'd have to miss it.

Since the show was way too long to record on my phone, I went and found Charlie to ask him if he knew where we kept the old video camera.

Of course, he did.

I asked him if he could teach me how to work it.

Of course, he could.

I told him his father really wanted to see the show, so I felt like I needed to attend the night's performance to record it for Clark.

"Unless that's going to add extra pressure on you," I quickly added. "I know you're going through a rough patch here, pal."

My heartbroken, humiliated son lit up like George Clooney on Oscar night. The opportunity to be on camera and stage simultaneously? He was all in.

A few hours later, I found Katie curled up on the family room couch, watching *Real Housewives*. I told her I was surprised to see her there; I thought she'd planned to spend the whole day studying for her upcoming AP History final.

My type-A, superstudent daughter just gazed up at me and yawned. "I'm not taking it."

I could hardly believe my ears.

Katie went on. "I'm boycotting to protest the systemic elimination of the Black experience from the history they force us to ingest while pretending it's an accurate depiction of the American legacy."

"Oh really," I replied.

Katie continued. "When do we ever hear about the Tulsa Race Massacre or Juneteenth? Whoever talks about the decades of voter suppression and the incarceration rates for Black men? American history is a literal whitewash, and I am not going to allow this injustice to be perpetuated by bowing to the pressure to take some test that only reinforces this skewed representation of our past."

"Well, that's great and noble and all, but how are you going to feel when ditching this exam means you're not going to get the college credit you've worked so hard for?"

"I don't want to talk about it," my daughter pouted. Then she turned her body and mind back to the TV, pointedly avoiding eye contact. She declared that she seriously needed her full focus to be on the upcoming moment when she knew Kyle was going to flip out over not being invited to Kim's birthday gala.

Since my life was obviously destined to be a series of endless crises, while my penguin husband was floating on his penguin back in the pool, Charlie came to find me in the laundry room; he was in a frenzy.

"I just got an email from Hartford saying the down payment for my dorm is overdue. If they don't have it by Monday, they can no longer hold a room for me. What the fuck? Why didn't you guys pay this?"

I was forced to confess I had no idea. Bill-paying was Clark's terrain. I stopped folding freshly laundered T-shirts and underwear and darted outside with Charlie at my heels. I captured the lolling penguin's attention.

"Did you pay the bill for Charlie's dorm room?"

The penguin just stared at me. No nod, no headshake, just a wide-eyed stare. He clearly had no idea. I turned to Charlie and told him we needed to go scour Clark's desk. We bolted into the office and with very little effort, we found the bill buried in a substantial stack of other bills. All of them unpaid.

Shit.

"We have to take care of this right now," Charlie wailed. "*You* have to do it, Mom. *Right now*, okay?"

I looked around but couldn't find Clark's checkbook. I didn't have enough in my checking account to cover it, so I grabbed the family Visa and phoned it in. Do you know how humiliating it is to have some kid in the bursar's office be the one to tell you that your card's been rejected because you're substantially over your credit limit? And she said it with such an attitude! So judgy.

"Now what?" Charlie wailed.

"I'll use my Bloomingdale's card and figure out how to pay it off when the time comes. It's how the rest of America lives—why shouldn't we?"

***

In the early afternoon, I was sitting alone at the dining room table, working hard to keep from hyperventilating. How had we gotten to this place? Why were the credit cards maxed out? Why was there a stack of unpaid bills on Clark's desk?

Inhaling and exhaling, trying to employ the yoga breathing techniques that had worked for me so well in the past, I had a sudden realization. I was a terrible listener. I had been in deep denial of all the things Clark had been trying to tell me over the last few months. I hadn't heard him because I didn't want to.

When he would complain about being "stuck" because his editor was rejecting all his current ideas for the next book, I assumed it was the typical "creative differences" he'd always faced; in the past, he'd proven quite adept at managing to surmount these occasional impasses. When he'd go off about how he was sure he was getting screwed out of royalties he was owed, I figured he'd work it out like he always had. I had no idea we were so financially stretched and strapped. My husband might have been a penguin, but I was an ostrich with my head buried deep in the sand.

I needed to get more involved in all this. I needed to be more helpful to him. He liked being in control. He loved being in charge. But now I was starting to see that the pressure of it all was slowly killing him.

As I sat, mentally flogging myself, my mother shuffled in and pulled out a chair to sit kitty-corner to me.

She gently took my hands into hers. "What's the matter, de-yah?"

I told her I was the world's worst wife. I confessed that I was sure I was the one who'd driven Clark to turn into a penguin as his (albeit odd and unique) means of self-preservation.

"I don't listen to him. I don't help him. I'm oblivious. I'm horrible. I have no idea why he even puts up with me …."

"You make him laugh, my de-yah. And you love him fiercely. Don't ever underestimate the power those things hold." She gave my folded hands a gentle pat, stood, and shuffled back out of the room.

That evening, I returned to the kids' school for the second night of *Romeo and Juliet* as planned and recorded the entire thing for Clark. Charlie gave an incredible performance, fully charged up and determined to erase the previous evening's humiliation. I know he's my kid, but I can objectively tell you he was fabulous. It felt great to have a rush of parents surround me after the show to tell me how much Charlie had knocked it out of the park.

Leaving those wonderful moments of light, why wasn't I wise enough to know they'd never last for very long?

As I approached the house, humming some silly Britney Spears song that had popped into my head, I saw the porch light, the front hall light, and a visible light from upstairs blink, flash ... and then go out.

While every other home on the block was lit up, my house was suddenly bathed in blackness. I went to open the garage door, but the clicker wouldn't work. The door didn't rise. Even I could figure this one out: we had lost all power.

I parked on the street, used my key to go in through the front door, and went in search of Mom and Katie, who I found darting around the kitchen like a pair of Ms. Pac-Mans.

"Power's out, huh?" I said.

"Two points for Captain Obvious," my smart-ass daughter quipped.

When I asked what had happened, Katie said they'd been watching *Queer Eye*, my mother's current favorite show, just a few moments earlier, when every light and appliance in the house did a dipping, blinking thing and went ... poof.

"We must've blown a fuse or something," Katie grumbled. "Is this gonna be another thing only Dad can fix?"

"Where is your father?"

"Somewhere around. I didn't wanna risk breaking an ankle going to look for him in the dark, and all we've been able to find are some stupid Hanukkah candles that aren't worth a shit for shedding light."

I stalked to the desk in the corner of the kitchen and snatched up the blue, plastic cylinder sitting there. I marched back to my daughter to wave it in her face.

"You could try this, darling. It's called a flashlight. And I believe you also have one on that phone of yours that's never more than six inches from your fingertips."

Setting off in search of my husband, flashlight beam guiding my way, I got less than a foot into the master bedroom and froze in my tracks. Splayed on his belly on the carpet, looking very much like one dead penguin, was Clark.

I let out a sharp scream and ran to him. I gently rolled him over. He felt cold and clammy. *But then again*, I thought, *isn't that how a penguin is supposed to feel?*

My scream was enough to summon Katie; before I knew it, she was at my side.

"Oh my God. What happened?"

Going full Sherlock Holmes, I swung the flashlight beam around to see an electric fan on the carpet not far from where Clark had fallen. The cord was stretched toward a nearby socket. I moved the beam back to the unconscious bird and noticed a black, charred smudge around the tip of his beak.

While I was lost in detective mode, Katie nudged me aside and sprang into action. She laid her penguin father flat on his back.

"Give me space," she said. "I've got this. They made us do CPR training at school."

She began doing vigorous chest compressions. She was muttering a count, pressing, pausing, pressing again. She was frantic but controlled, fighting hysteria but completely in charge.

Keeping up the rhythmic chest pummeling, she bent her head to the penguin's bill and began to breathe her young and vibrant air into him. In less than fifteen seconds, he sputtered, made a strangled coughing sound, and began to breathe on his own.

"You did it!" I yelled. "Oh my God, you saved him!"

The penguin slowly staggered to his webbed feet, looking stunned and slightly off-balance.

I couldn't help myself. The fear mixed with anxiety caused me to bellow in the revived bird's face, "Were you trying to plug this fan in with your beak? What were you thinking? You almost killed yourself—not to mention the fact that you blew out all the power in the house. You need to be more careful, Clark. Honestly! My heart can't take it."

The penguin momentarily hung his head in apologetic shame and then waddled off to lead me to the power box in the garage. Thankfully, living in a wind prone canyon, this was hardly the first blackout we'd experienced. I knew we had circuit breakers and not fuses. I maneuvered myself to the box, opened the panel, and began flipping the black switches. Before hitting the final one, I turned to Katie and my mother hovering in the doorway from the garage to the laundry room. I threw my arms wide open and declared, "Let there be light!"

And there was.

Rest for the weary? Not a chance. About one o'clock the next morning, I was sleeping soundly. The penguin was stretched out on his stomach on top of the blankets on the floor. Slowly, I came back to consciousness, pulled awake by the sound of stifled yet heaving sobs. There beside my bed, illuminated by the filtered moonlight seeping in through our white plantation shutters, was Katie. My maternal adrenaline launched me straight up in bed.

"Honey, what's happening? What's wrong?"

"Mom, I messed up. Totally."

"Why? What—"

"I can't skip my AP History final. If I do, there's no chance I'll get into Berkeley. I'm an idiot. And now I haven't studied, and the test is on Monday, and I'm so gonna fail. Hard. I know I am."

With that, any ability to control her tears vanished; Katie began to wail. The penguin bolted up to gape at her.

"I mean," my daughter said between heaving sobs, "I care about the despicable omission of Black history and all that, but—" She emitted a hiccup and a choking sob before pausing to take a breath. I told her to calm down, take her time.

"The real reason ... I freaked out ... is because Dadda's ... the only one who can help me study ... for tests like this. Especially history. He knows all this material, and he knows how to ask the right questions to get me prepared and ... without ... when I ... I mean, knowing he couldn't help me, I just ... I was, like, paralyzed. I panicked. And now I've sabotaged my whole future."

"No. No, you haven't. It's not too late. I can help you. We can start studying right now."

The penguin was nodding adamantly, and I knew he had an idea. He jumped off the bed and raced out of the room. I asked

Katie how her dad usually helped her prepare for exams like this, and she explained their system: Clark would create a series of color-coded file cards containing different bits of data. Blue cards were facts about people, pink cards focused on dates, the yellow ones covered locations, and green cards pertained to an event's historical significance. Since Katie is a visual learner, seeing the color of the card and linking it to the factoid she was digesting helped her to keep things compartmentalized; that made it easier for her to call them up when Clark quizzed her.

"Well, I can do that," I said. "Go and get your textbook. I'm going to go downstairs and make us a giant pot of coffee. We're pulling an all-nighter!"

As I was dashing down the stairs, I ran into Clark waddling back up with a pack of multicolored highlighters clamped in his beak. He bounced past me to return to the master bedroom.

A short time later, I came back in, toting the coffeepot in one hand and a pair of mugs in the other. On the bed, Katie sat cross-legged with a stack of empty multicolored file cards in hand. Penguin-Dad had the textbook open in front of him, and with a green highlighter clutched in his bill, he was furiously underlining various lines and paragraphs that had to do with the meaning and context of specific events.

I don't know how he and Katie had done it so quickly, but the two of them were already working with an established rhythm. He'd spit out one highlighter, look to Katie, and she'd cap that one and uncork another. He'd move through the same page, using the next color to underscore the subsequent category, color coordinated by dates, locations, and principal players.

"Okay," Katie said to me, taking the offered cup of coffee, "this is how we do it: as Dadda finishes one color on one page, you take a card of the same color and start writing up the things he's highlighted—one fact on each card—and then I can begin studying them as you pass them on to me, okay?"

"Sounds like a plan."

The three of us were working in seamless harmony when Charlie wandered in. I glanced at the bedside clock—1:37 a.m. My son's hair was swept up into tufts like he'd been sleeping in a blender. His eyes were hardly open.

"What the hell's going on?"

"Teamwork," I announced. "We're saving your sister from having a nervous breakdown."

When Charlie asked if there was anything he could do to help, all three of us—the penguin included—gawked at him in disbelief. I sincerely think my son was offended.

"Why're you all looking at me like that?"

"Ah," Katie scoffed, "maybe because that's, like, the most unselfish thing you've said in ... I don't know ... probably a kabillion years."

"*Sor-ree* for trying to be of service."

"No," Katie quickly retorted, "you can absolutely help. While Dad highlights the text and Mom makes the flash cards, give me a few minutes to study the first stack, and then it would be great if you could start quizzing me."

For the first time in ages, the four of us were united in a common cause. Throw in every cliché you can conjure. We were a synchronized History-Fact-Generating Bucket Brigade. A well-oiled Quiz-Making Machine. Clark was highlighting, I was card creating, Katie was studying, and Charlie was doing a reverse Alex Trebek, asking the questions instead of reading the answers. We worked furiously until six thirty the next morning, fueled on caffeine and comradery, when a quartet of growling, rumbling tummies told us it was time to take a break.

Miraculously, that spirit of cooperation carried right over into the kitchen.

Charlie offered to make shrimp omelets so the penguin could enjoy one too. Katie said she'd fry the bacon, and I volunteered to make papaya-and-blueberry fruit cups. Laughing, Katie turned to the bird on the stool at the kitchen counter.

"Guess that means you have to do the dishes, Dadda."

I swiftly kiboshed that idea. "He's dangerous enough with two hands—can you imagine those flippers trying to load the dishwasher?" I glanced at my penguin husband. "You get a pass."

As we moved around each other, twirling and dodging so we could all work simultaneously, Charlie chuckled. "Wait, isn't this like a scene from every '80s and '90s movie ever made where they're suddenly dancing around the kitchen, singing Motown into wooden spoons, banging on pot lids?"

"We can do *much* better than that!" I said. Without needing another moment of prompting, I burst out singing "My Humps" by the Black Eyed Peas.

"Please no," Charlie begged.

"What's the matter? You don't want to hear your old ma, at six forty-five on a Sunday morning, singing about the junk in her trunk and all that ass in her jeans?"

Katie took that as her cue, and the two of us began to sing louder and more vigorously, getting right in Charlie's face as he scrambled the eggs, onions, and shrimp. Waving his spatula at us like a toreador fending off a pair of raging bulls, he was also laughing. Not wanting to be left out, the penguin came darting toward us, clapping his wings together as we sang.

"Aw, poor old-man Dadda," Katie cooed. "Even when he's a penguin, he still can't clap on the beat."

Katie and I sang on about our trunk junk.

Charlie tried to shout above us. "Ya know, you guys, as adorable as you think this is, you probably don't want to wake Nonnie."

Instantly, Katie and I went silent. The three of us cocked our ears.

And there it was, the distinct, slightly disturbing sound I'd lived with since I was a kid: the jet-engine roar of my mother's black-bear-in-hibernation snoring.

CLARK

Hold up. Can we take a brief time-out here, please?

Alone with my thoughts that Sunday morning, while the rest of my sleep-deprived family was taking a much-needed nap before Katie would wake up and spend the rest of the day continuing to cram for her AP test, my head was spinning.

Why am I a penguin? Or, more importantly, how long am I going to be a penguin? How long do penguins live anyway? Am I my actual age, except in penguin years? Are penguin years like dog years? Am I gonna drop dead any day now? What if I die a penguin without ever getting the chance to be me again? Seriously. I cannot even begin to tell you how intensely that would suck.

As my anxiety spiraled, a single, simple word flashed onto my internal movie screen: *internet.* I gamboled into my office, hopped up onto my desk chair—damn, my penguin body was nimble—and used my whole head to draw the keyboard closer.

Luckily, the office computer is on pretty much twenty-four seven, so I began a slow hunt-and-peck with my beak, methodically tapping out "How long is an emperor penguin's life span?" While the information was loading, I found my atheist ass getting lost in silent prayer: *please let it be more like a tortoise, less like a fruit fly.*

When the response did finally load, after one agonizingly long minute, what I saw was less than comforting. It was right there in bold black letters: **15 to 20 years.**

Not exactly what I was hoping for …

I kept reading and did find a wee bit more comfort in the news that some of my species lived to be forty.

Okay … so I obviously wasn't my human age, or I'd already be maggot meat.

But I gotta say, given it was still a pretty short life span, it did nothing to quell my terror.

I know I told you earlier that I wasn't worried about turning fifty, but that's bullshit. Death doesn't scare me; I'm just terrified by the prospect of not being alive.

It's impossible to get to this age and not be confronted by the fact that so many of the chapters that lie ahead are guaranteed to be punctuated by loss.

My father-in-law was already gone. Charlie would be heading to college in a few months. He wants to be an actor, and most of the industry is here in Los Angeles, but what if Broadway beckons? Hartford's only a few hours from the Big Apple. I knew he and his soon-to-be college pals would be making regular pilgrimages there. It's a seductive city; what if he fell in love with it and never came back? He might end up getting cast in a show opposite one of Sarah Jessica Parker's twin daughters, begin a torrid affair, get married, and decide to stay there because who wouldn't rather hang out with SJP and Matthew Broderick than with me and Julia?

And then there's Katie. The way that kid's going, she could wind up being president. Even if that happens, there's no chance I'm moving to Washington. Searing summers, snowy winters. Forget about it. That's the reason I moved west from Rochester in the first place. You can keep your damn changing of the seasons. I'm fine with the perpetual L.A. sunshine.

But I digress.

Loss. Losing my grip. Losing my credibility. Losing my relevance.

With my mind continuing to race out of control, I had another stark realization: I was sweating like a hog. I needed to get outside. I needed to get into the pool. I needed to cool down.

After bouncing up onto the aboveground rim of the pool and diving in, I surfaced with yet another startling discovery: as a by-product of our unseasonal heat wave, the water was at least eighty-five degrees. Fabulous for humans—if Julia had her way, we'd keep it at ninety—not so great for a creature designed to reside in Antarctica. How could I possibly lower my body temperature in there? I could practically feel myself shriveling up from the inside out. If a fifteen-to-twenty-year life span was the norm for my kind in their native habitat, how severely was that life expectancy being reduced for a Brentwood penguin living north of Sunset?

Oh shit. There was one more thing I hadn't really thought about. Charlie was graduating the following Friday afternoon, and I was most likely going to be forced to miss that too. He even had the honor of being one of the kids who would be giving a speech. He wasn't the valedictorian—I think, for that, you need to take classes other than drama, ceramics, and Introduction to Coding—but he had entered an essay contest sponsored by the English faculty and was picked to read his winning entry; it was about why we all need a little of the arts in our lives.

Okay, see, the whole situation was truly fucked.

It was fine that Julia got to tape *Romeo and Juliet* for me; there would be hundreds of other opportunities for me to see Charlie perform in person over the coming years. (Assuming I'd one day be myself again.) But he would only graduate from high school once. And I was not going to be there. Chalk it up as one more enormous, soul-sucking loss.

I dragged my soggy-but-still-overheated penguin butt out of the pool and sulked my way back into the house. Katie was waiting with a wide grin and a bowl of fresh panfried trout, but I had no appetite. She coaxed and cajoled me to eat, but I couldn't get up for it. What was the point? I was going to miss my son's graduation. I was going to drown in a monsoon of my own sweat. I was going to be dead soon.

I shuffled off to the family room's adjoining bathroom where the white tile floor was usually the coolest spot in the house. I stretched out and went to sleep.

***

The sun was already beginning to set when I was roused by a trio of voices whispering in the bathroom doorway. I kept my eyes tightly clenched; I didn't feel equipped to deal with them.

"I think he's depressed." (That was Katie.)

Charlie asked how long I'd been there on the bathroom floor. Katie told him and Julia it had been hours. She told them I hadn't eaten or had anything to drink since noon. She'd spent the afternoon studying on the family room couch so she could keep an eye on me.

Julia chimed in. "What if he's ill? How would we know? What does a sick penguin look like?"

"Dad," Katie said in a gentle but slightly urgent whisper, "you need to wake up."

I didn't budge. I didn't have it in me. I was a penguin playing opossum. I just wanted to be left alone.

Later, I learned that minor miracles do happen.

While I remained engulfed in my floor funk, Charlie volunteered to help Katie review our homemade flash cards she'd been studying all afternoon. They worked together in copacetic harmony until nearly midnight as he grilled his sister on the dates, places, and personalities of American History, 1860–1945.

The next morning, Julia packed lunches and pushed a breakfast that could provide more fuel than the doughnut and caffeinated soda Charlie preferred, while Katie did her last-minute cramming. She looked up from her file cards to glance over her shoulder to the family room bathroom floor. There I remained, safe under my shroud of depression.

"Mama, you have to figure out what's wrong with Dad today. He can't stay like that, or he's gonna die."

Juliet's retort was swift and adamant. "He won't die because I will not allow it. Now go to school and don't worry about anything except doing great on your test."

"Maaaa-om!" Katie wailed, "why are you putting extra pressure on me?"

My normally patient-to-a-fault wife had no time for this. "Oh, for Christ's sake, Katie, what do you want from me? If I don't encourage you, you tell me I don't care, and when I do, you say I'm pressuring you. Do whatever you need to do. I have to go wake up your grandmother and get her to Kaiser."

With a huff, Julia bolted out of the room.

Katie went off to tackle her rigorous exam, and Charlie went to the ceramics studio to make sure his orc-head sculpture got its turn in the kiln. Julia took Honey to get a routine cardio workup and returned to find me right where she'd left me, still there on that cool bathroom tile floor.

She stared at me for a long moment, then began to breathe in and out with each breath getting slightly louder than the last—like a locomotive picking up steam. All at once, she exploded.

"I cannot believe I'm going full Cher in *Moonstruck* on your penguin ass, but, Jesus Christ, Clark, SNAP OUT OF IT! We can't do this right now. I need you here. I need you well. I need you to be my partner in this shitstorm that's now our life."

Although she had somehow managed to remain incredibly strong and stoic through this whole strange ordeal up until that moment, suddenly the tears came with a hurricane-force vengeance. Julia's shoulders were heaving, her sobs were guttural, and her face looked the Halloween-mask version of my beautiful wife.

I hopped up, waddled to her, and wrapped my flippers around the top of her legs, administering the best hug I could muster. We remained like that for several minutes as she continued to cry, slowly getting herself under control. When I released my grip and waddled back a few steps to gaze up at her, she was staring down at me with the most heartbreakingly vulnerable face I'd ever seen.

"What's going on here, honey?" she asked me. "I don't understand why you're so depressed."

With vigor I didn't know I still possessed, I darted out of that bathroom and toddled my way into the kitchen. I hopped up onto the stool at the built-in desk and began to pick through the important papers stored in Julia's plastic slotted letter holder. When I found what I was after, I clamped it in my beak, jumped down, and returned to my waiting wife. I held my bounty up to her. She snatched it from my bill.

It was the invitation to Charlie's graduation.

JULIA

After that moment with my poor penguin husband, I had a calling, and there was absolutely nothing that was going to keep me from bringing said goal to fruition.

Katie told me—after my run-in with the coyotes—I was a strong and capable woman. She was right.

My husband's a good man. He's been an incredible father. He works his ass off for us. Sure, he can have his cranky days and his condescending days and his moments of being a real asshole—he's human—but, on par, he truly doesn't ask for much. When he does ask, and when it's possible, it really should be up to me to make that desire happen.

He desperately wanted to be at Charlie's graduation. He absolutely deserved to be there. I made a vow to him that he *would* be there.

My next mission was to figure out how to pull it off.

In the meantime, there was a more pressing matter that needed to be dealt with first: we had a growing stack of unpaid bills. Clark clearly wouldn't be able to write or turn in book proposals anytime soon, but he was sure his publishers were holding on to royalties from the previous books which he should have gotten months ago. Something had to be done, and the only one available to do it was *me*.

Have you ever had one of those out-of-body moments where you know objectively it's you doing and saying certain things, but you can't believe it's actually happening? Feeling pushed into a suffocating corner by every aspect of my life, I marched into Clark's office and grabbed his phone to search his contacts. Moments later, I was on the line with his agent, Lester Beckwith.

"Julia, what a pleasant surprise. Is everything okay?"

"No, Les. In fact, it is 100 percent the *opposite* of okay. You have Clark so stressed out that he's sick in bed, he can't write, we can't pay our bills, and he says you have done less-than nothing to force his dickhead publisher to cough up the back royalties they owe us so we can cover our goddamn mortgage and send Charlie off to college."

"Oh, is that all?" Lester replied with an uncomfortable chuckle that confirmed his latent guilt.

"I'm not screwing around here, Lester. Will you get into it with Sunshine Press, or should I? I am happy to call them the instant I hang up on you—"

Les leapt in and urged me to calm down and to let him handle it. He promised to get back to me by the end of the day and told me to, instead, spend my formidable energy nursing Clark back to health.

How I wished I had the power to do that.

"I want answers. I want results. I want a check," I barked.

If we were having this encounter in person, I know Lester would have signed off with a military salute. I could feel the vocal equivalent in the sigh that accompanied his goodbye.

Unbeknownst to me, the penguin had been eavesdropping on my entire conversation. When I put the phone back into its cradle, he tottered toward me, raised his right flipper into the air, and slapped me a slick and slimy high five.

When Charlie and Katie came home from school, and Mom woke up from her afternoon nap, I called them to the kitchen table for a family meeting. I told them Clark's depression was directly linked to the fact that he couldn't bear the thought of missing Charlie's graduation.

Ever the can-do optimist, Katie saw no problem at all. She reminded us that the ceremony was going to be held outside in the football stadium. She talked about the fact that, in our current world, people had all kinds of emotional support animals. "One idiot even tried to take her support ostrich on an airplane."

She declared that we could get one of those little red vests, strap it on Clark, and tell anyone who wasn't happy to have a penguin in their midst that he was saving Nonnie's life. If they didn't like it, they could eat shit and die.

"Oh, de-yah," my eighty-five-year-old mother responded, gazing at her granddaughter, "I really don't approve of that language. How about if we just tell them to go screw themselves?"

I wondered aloud where we could possibly get an Emotional Support Animal vest, but Charlie was already on the dark web ordering one. (It wasn't exactly the government-sanctioned kind, but, you know, desperate times and all that ….) He happily announced, "It'll be here day after tomorrow, then we'll be all set."

When my kids were little, one of their favorite books was Laura Numeroff's *If You Give a Mouse a Cookie.* Then it evolved into a whole series with follow-ups like, *If You Give a Moose a Muffin.* Well, I was suddenly living my own live-action sequel, *If You Give a Mom a Mission.*

For this plan to work, it pretty much had to be our personal D-Day. (Dad-Day?) Given his condition at the time, I knew we couldn't have Clark out in the afternoon sun any longer than was absolutely necessary. That was pretty much true of my mother, too, so we decided Katie would go to the school ahead of us and stake out seats in the bleachers; then Mom, Clark, and I would come in moments before the ceremony started. I also realized it would be vital to provide the penguin with as much shade as possible.

Instantly, Charlie was back to cruising the web.

"How about this?" he asked with a wide grin. He swung his laptop around to show us his discovery: it was one of those umbrella hats. I know you've seen them—the ridiculous multicolored umbrellas on a headband you wear like a visor? I always wondered who would order such a thing, and now I knew; they were perfect for any woman whose husband had decided to spontaneously poof into a penguin that needed to be taken to an outdoor graduation.

Later, as Katie, Charlie, and I were working together to prepare dinner, Katie gave her brother a hip bump, accompanied by an approving grin.

"I've gotta tell ya, Brother Bear, I am so glad you and Amy broke up. I didn't wanna say anything before, but ... she's *awful*. Just so 'on' every minute. Gawd, can't the poor thing ever relax? Plus, don't you hate it when she tries to act like she's so much cuter than she actually is?"

Charlie stared at Katie for a moment, blinked a few times, and then said, "We're back together."

Without skipping a beat, Katie's voice went up two octaves as she enthusiastically declared, "Great! What I meant to say was you two are perfect for each other."

As I was smearing my face with Pond's cold cream before bed that night—you can never start moisturizing too early, girls, trust me on this—Katie wandered into my bathroom. She watched me do my slathering routine for a few moments before she piped up.

"Oh my God, can you believe they're back together? Why didn't he say something before I stuck my stupid foot in my mouth?"

"You covered pretty good, I thought," I offered.

"No, I didn't!" Katie wailed. "I said she was awful!"

"Well, she kinda is," I shrugged.

"Obvi. But Charlie doesn't think so. What am I gonna do?"

"You're going to look on the bright side—now you'll have somebody to help you save seats at graduation."

As much as I was anxious to fall asleep that night, my mind was a blender of whirring thoughts. Clark was in his blanket nest beside the bed, but from the pattern of his breathing, I was pretty sure he was also wide awake. With a bone-weary sigh, I sat up and looked down at him.

"Mom and the kids are clearly down for the count, and I can't get my brain to stop tumbling; I need to slip outside and catch a buzz. You're welcome to join me if you'd like."

He instantly bounced up on his webbed feet. A moment later, I swiftly extricated my stash from the safe inside my closet.

With the stealth movements we'd perfected over the years, slipping down the stairs like a pair of Navajo scouts on a recon mission, my penguin husband and I made our way out the family room door and retreated up to a darkened corner on our backyard's upper deck.

I dug a prerolled joint out of my cheap, silk Chinatown coin purse, fired it up, and took a luxurious hit, pulling the smoke deep into my lungs. As I emitted a long, slow exhale, I glanced down to see Clark tilting his avian head up toward me with a look of expectant anticipation. He titled his flippers skyward and then folded them in to point at himself, very clearly sending me the message that he, too, wanted a hit. I asked if he thought that was a good idea. I wondered what affect pot might have on a penguin.

"Are you sure?" I asked.

He nodded his head adamantly.

As I contemplated how I might accommodate him, I remembered a story he'd told me years before about how he and his idiot college friends used to get their dog stoned. One of them would hold the pup's head, and the other guy would shotgun smoke directly up the dog's nostrils. Why they thought it was funny to get a cocker spaniel cockeyed, I have no idea, but I've learned over the years that while I went to college to get a degree that might help me secure a good job, my husband's prime four-year goal, night after night, was to fry as many brain cells as possible.

So it was my turn to aid and abet his mission once more.

Taking great care not to burn myself, I turned the joint around and put the lit end inside my mouth, then knelt in front of Clark and blew two or three hearty smoke streams directly into his face. Knowing exactly how to respond, he inhaled deeply. In very short order, his eyes glazed over, his beak hung slack, and he stared up at the moon, transfixed. His wings dangled limply at his side, and he settled into a seated squat, mesmerized by the world. Staring at him with his silly, stupefied expression, I started to giggle.

"Oh my God, look at you! You're your own next-best book series: *Pothead Penguin!*"

I started laughing even harder until I was completely out of control.

"Oh no, oh no," I gasped, "I need to stop; I'm gonna wet my pants."
And then I did.

Ever since I was a little kid, if I get laughing too hard, I almost
inevitably pee my pants. One time in a hotel, Clark was killing me
with a spot-on impersonation of a crazy Russian woman we'd met
at our nephew's rehearsal dinner earlier that evening; before I could
make it to the bathroom, I unleashed such a forceful stream, Clark
blurted out, "Are you fucking kidding me? Who the hell are you?
Regan MacNeil?"

Of course, that only made me laugh even harder.

(It was one of the many bonding things between Clark and me—
there was hardly a TV or movie reference, no matter how obscure, we
didn't have a mutual connection to—so, naturally, I instantly got his
Exorcist nod.)

Turning away from my stoned penguin husband, I struggled to
get myself in hand, but it was too late. My underwear was soaked. I
swiftly slipped it off and flung it into the deepest recesses of the upper
deck. Clark just looked at me and slowly shook his head. It was weird,
but in that moment, his disbelieving yet slightly amused expression
was so familiar, it was almost like he was himself again.

Except he wasn't.

I was snapped out of my kaleidoscopic reflections by a glimpse
of movement in the family room adjacent to the lower deck. I snuck
closer to see what I could discern.

Wait ... what?

Charlie was down in the family room turning on the TV. Why?
What was he doing up so late? He never came out of his room once
he went to bed. I angled myself into a low crouch and crab-walked
to peer through the upper deck railing so I could fix my eyeline on
the TV.

Oh, Jesus! The logo I saw was for the channel he and Gregory
covertly referred to as Skinemax. Was he about to watch porn? If so,
did that mean he was going to end up ...

Stop, my internal voice screamed. A mother doesn't want to know
these things. A mother certainly doesn't want to *see* these things. A

stoned mother with a whirling mind was suddenly imagining all kinds of scenarios that were absolutely, 100 percent, unequivocally *not* okay.

I darted back to the far corner of the deck where Clark was still fixated on the moon with a placid, beatific expression filling his black-and-white face.

"Charlie's down there watching Skinemax! What if he … do you think he might … how do we? He wouldn't—" Before I could spit out a full sentence, the situation escalated.

Charlie, my firstborn, my Virgo, the one I had trained to always think Safety First, spied the unlocked family room door. Probably assuming we'd inadvertently forgotten to secure it before going up to bed, he hopped up off the couch … and took care of the problem. *Click* went the lock. Our only way back into the house was now barred.

Fantastic.

We were high, locked outside, and our son was about to do God knows what, watching heaven only knows, clearly looking for his own adolescent way to relieve whatever stress he was feeling about the following day's graduation.

I wanted to panic. I wanted to cry. I wanted to flip the fuck out, but instead, I just started laughing again. It was simply too absurd. And I was high as hell. Clark came waddling over to me as I fought to get my giggles in check.

"He just locked us out, Clark! And you know we can't go down there and knock on the family room door without giving him a heart attack. Plus, we'd be so busted. Are we going to have to spend the night out here? We can't—hold on!"

I suddenly had a realization. "Don't we have a spare key in that little magnetic box inside the air-conditioner control panel?"

Clark nodded.

I finally stopped laughing. I exhaled to calm myself down.

"All we have to do now is figure out how to get to it without Charlie seeing us; then maybe we can sneak around to let ourselves in the front door while he's still down there doing … watching …"

Oh God. Stop. Bad visions.

Clark hopped up from his nestled squat and darted for the stairs. In an urgent stage whisper, I asked where he was going, but he simply turned toward me, gave me a swift "I got this" salute with his wing, and went silently hopping down the steps to the lower deck.

Watching in awe, I saw him launch into warrior mode. Although he had to pass by the glass family room doors to get to the AC unit, he dropped onto his belly and went gliding along in a way no human would have been able to accomplish. It was as if the paved deck were suddenly made of ice. He was totally below Charlie's eyeline, even if our son had happened to glance in Clark's direction.

I remained crouched upstairs, observing through the bars of the railing. In a few minutes—although, in my stoned state, it felt like he was gone for half an hour—Clark was back at my side; he was clutching our spare key in his beak, looking incredibly proud of himself.

"Good work, pal. If the kids'-book thing ever flames out, maybe the Navy SEALs are looking to recruit a Navy Penguin."

Back in superstealth mode, we made it down the steps, staying in the shadows, moving an inch at a time to avoid catching Charlie's attention. Of course, if he was doing what I suspected he was doing, we probably could have set off a hail of fireworks, and he wouldn't have noticed.

Reaching the front door, I carefully slipped the key in the lock. "Okay," I whispered to Clark, "now we only have to hope Charlie's not heading up to bed, or the jig is up."

After an eternity of silent, creeping moves, we got in without being detected and made it back up to bed. I had the sneaking suspicion that falling asleep would no longer be an issue. I was stoned, exhausted, and thoroughly worn out from the never-ending absurdist comedy that had become my life.

I don't know how or when he did it, but when I woke up the next morning, I discovered Clark had pulled our old Scrabble game out of the closet in Katie's room and used the tiles to spell out a message for me on the bedside table: STILL A PRETTY GREAT TEAM.

It was Culmination morning, and Charlie took off early to hang with his friends and practice his speech. One thing I love about my boy is he's never suffered even a hint of performance anxiety. Truth is, he feels most at home in front of an audience. Clark has often said he can't wait for the day when Charlie learns how to be as comfortable in real life as he is onstage. Charlie was completely unfazed by the fact that he'd be speaking in front of close to a thousand people. What did worry him was that, despite all our precision planning, we'd somehow blow our intention of having his penguin father in attendance for Charlie's momentous day.

Katie insisted on packing a cooler of ice chips she could feed her dad to keep him hydrated. We had his support-animal vest, his umbrella hat, and even a pair of bright-red children's sunglasses to shield his eyes. I had a whole other backpack loaded with meds and snacks for my mother. Along with her heart condition and high blood pressure, she also has type-2 diabetes; the very last thing I needed was to have her go into a low. Oyster crackers and a Baby Ruth were the tools du jour in case of trouble.

Continuing to work on making amends with Charlie, Katie reached out to Amy and asked her to sit with us during the ceremony. Once Amy agreed, Katie recruited her to come early so they could stake out seats together; it would be easier if the two of them served as bookends with the reserved spots between them. They would meet up at the Starbucks in the village to avoid the mob scene on campus, and then walk to the school more than an hour ahead of the scheduled start time. Amy said she also wanted to make a stop at the florist on Swarthmore to get an orchid lei for Charlie—with a matching one for herself. (Katie confided that she thought this idea personified Amy's "turbocharged Ick Factor," but she had at least learned to share such opinions only with me.)

The ceremony was slated to begin at three o'clock. At noon, Katie, Mom, and I reviewed our checklist. We nailed down the exact location Katie would aim to stake out, and once she and Amy were seated, they'd take pictures of where they landed and text them to me so we'd all be in sync.

We each selected outfits that were light colored and sleeveless so we could ward off the afternoon heat as much as possible. Even though the kids' high school was just a few blocks from the beach, it was still supposed to reach almost ninety degrees by late afternoon. Accordingly, we lathered on the 50 SPF sunscreen. We made sure Clark was well fed. (As soon as he'd learned we'd be bringing him to graduation, his depression lifted; he'd spent the remainder of the week being back to happily gorging on sardines, shrimp, and seaweed snacks. He was also spending a lot of time in the pool.)

All the plans were in place. All the provisions were packed. Our phones were fully charged. Penguin-Dad was happily going to be present at his son's graduation.

What could possibly go wrong?

KATIE

Here's the thing: everybody was so convinced Amy and Charlie were such great actors, but what about me? Seriously. You should've seen me with Amy, being all low-key sweet and so nice, kissing her ass and telling her how happy I was that she and Charlie were back together. I swear, I fully deserved an Oscar. Bottom line is, as much of a narcissistic pain in the ass as he can be, I care about my brother, and like I told you before, I truly do love him. I want him to be happy. And if his terrible taste in women was bringing him joy, who was I to poop all over that?

Once I learned Amy wanted to stop by the florist to get them (such a *Love Island*, cheeseball move) matching leis, I asked her to meet me a half hour earlier than we'd originally planned. We rendezvoused at the Starbucks in the middle of the village, and being in full suck-up mode, I offered to pick up the tab.

Okay, do you want one more reason to hate her? I was a kid surviving on an allowance—not some corporate-millionaire, baller chick—and what did Amy do? She ordered a Pink Drink with six pumps of Cinnamon Dolce Syrup, 2 scoops of frozen strawberries and salted caramel cream cold foam, blended! And then, when the zit-infested kid behind the counter asked what size she wanted, that bitch said, "Trenta." Um … excuse me? *You want a what now?* I know Tall, Grande, and Venti but what the heck is "Trenta"? Oh! Apparently that's the one that's a size bigger than the human stomach. I'm so sure! Who's even ever heard of that? I definitely hadn't. But I ended up paying for it anyway. Because I love my brother.

I got myself a Tall Iced Tea, and we were out of there.

Not only were we going out of our way to do Amy's extra errand, but I had to do it while schlepping the small cooler loaded with ice chips because I wanted Mom to have one less thing to worry about. It wasn't big, but still, that shit was heavy.

Next stop: the florist. I swear to God, this is when I seriously wanted to do a full Walter White on Amy's ass because she had to look over every single orchid lei in the whole place … and then go back and look at each of them all over again even though (duh!) nothing had changed.

They had pink ones and purple ones and a few that had both colors, and she's all, "Which one should I get?" So indecisive, like it was her chance to cure cancer if she made the right choice. I was checking my phone for the time, freaking out that we were going to be too late to get five seats together, and I asked her to please hurry up. She gave me her pouty face that's even gross on a five-year-old. Finally, she decided to get one purple one and one pink one—and then she'd let Charlie pick the one he liked best because, "It's his special day, so he gets to choose." Then she snickered and said, "And this won't be the only time he gets leid today."

Ewwwww! TMI, woman. Seriously!

Did she for one second think I needed the deets on my brother's sex life? (See? I told you she's gross to the tenth power.)

We went up to the register to pay, and Amy whipped out an American Express Gold card. How the hell does *she* have a card like that? It's not like her parents are rich or anything. They're a pair of burned-out hippies living in Topanga Canyon. Her mom works for some theatre in Santa Monica, and her dad sells vintage movie posters online. I swear, they are living, breathing, personified Topanga clichés. So wait, this bitch has an American Express Gold card and I paid for her super deluxe, extra everything Trenta Pink Drink? *What the actual fuck?*

Finally, we made our way to school. A total shit show! Cars were streaming in, there were nowhere near enough parking spaces, and families were overwhelmed and confused and trying to mow down any pedestrians in their way so they could park and get seats before it was totally packed. Thank God Amy and I were on foot so we could head directly into the tunnel that leads to the football bleachers. It was time to stake out our seats.

I told Mom we'd try to get on the north side of the stadium so Nonnie didn't have to walk too far from the parking lot, and that's exactly what we did. We were able to find room about six rows up on the side facing the lectern, allowing for a clear sight line to Charlie when he gave his speech.

(Side note: I know directions in a way Charlie's never learned because he totally relies on his phone for absolutely everything. I tell him, "If you know the ocean is to the west, it's simple to figure out the rest because it goes 'WE' for west to east and then north is up and south is down," but he just goes, "Who cares?" He acts like there will never be a day when he doesn't have his phone with him, or he can't get perfect service. I hope to God he never gets in a plane crash where he winds up alive in the ocean but then dies because he's unable to find land since he couldn't be bothered to learn how to navigate.)

Anyway ... I had Amy stand up so I could take a photo to text to Mom, putting the press box and hot-dog stand in the frame so she could easily pinpoint our location. Then we used the jackets we brought to spread over three spots between Amy and me. We had to tell people over and over again that those seats were saved. (See, this is why I *hate* people. Wouldn't you think the jackets alone would be enough to clue them in? Fools.)

Amy and I were making inane small talk, chatting away as more and more people were streaming in, still asking if the seats between us were taken. Out of the blue, she goes, "I know you really don't like me," and I'm all, like, "What? Of course I do." But she said there was a difference between "liking" someone and "tolerating" them, and I honestly didn't have a comeback because I was too busy trying to figure out how she could sense my disdain when I was sure I was rocking full Meryl Streep status.

Thank God Mom (and posse) came to my rescue.

I felt them coming before I ever saw them because there was this murmuring ripple going through the crowd; it was like the soundtrack of some dumb teen movie where the ugly girl is suddenly pretty (usually because she let her hair down and took off her glasses—so stupid) and everyone at the prom is whispering about her as she arrives.

I stood up, turned, and there they were, coming in from the back.

Trying to look like she was the coolest customer in town—but not coming even close to pulling it off—Mom had Penguin Dad wearing our dead dog's collar clasped to the leash she was holding. He had on the red, Emotional Support Animal vest, the striped umbrella hat, and the red plastic sunglasses held on to his little penguin head with the "Hang Ten" elastic band Dad uses when he swims in the ocean. Looking so pleased with himself, he was hopping down the bleacher stairs. Nonnie was moving slowly and carefully behind them in a wide-brimmed straw hat, the kind "genteel" Southern ladies wear to church, along with giant movie-star shades. Whatever the exact opposite of "low profile" might be, that was my family coming down those cement steps. I jumped up to help Nonnie navigate; it was impossible not to feel like every eye in that packed stadium was trained on us.

As we slid into our row where Amy remained, holding the seats, a chorus of comments was ringing in my ears: "Holy crap, is that a penguin?" "Oh my God, look at him!" "He's so cute." "I *so* have to get a picture with him." "What the hell is a penguin doing at graduation?" "Are you sure it's a penguin?"

Penguin Dadda remained standing in the aisle with me sitting on one side and Mom on the other. Amy was next to me, and Nonnie sat down next to Mom. We were a sideshow unto ourselves.

There's this girl in my grade named Megan Canterbury, and we're kinda friends and kinda not, but she's convinced we fully are. All of a sudden, she was right there in my face, and she goes, "OMG! I can't believe you guys have a penguin. How lucky are you? Can I get a selfie with him?" This is one reason I hate her more days than not: don't use text speak when you're talking out loud. "OMG"? Shut up. To me, that's like people say, "LOL." *What*? If something's funny, I have an idea ... *laugh*! I mean, seriously. What the hell, people?

Anyway, she was practically pushing herself into my lap, leaning in and taking a stupid selfie with Dad. He had to lean so far back, the corner of his umbrella hat almost poked Mom's eye out. She reflexively dove out of his way and crashed into Nonnie who was taking a drink of water. The water bottle got knocked up into her lip and splashed all over the place. Nonnie got soaked, but at least it didn't smash into her dentures and knock a tooth out because then, for sure, I would've had to kill stupid Megan Canterbury.

The ceremony was getting ready to start with the parade of graduates streaming onto the football field from the school, but everybody was still freaking out about Dad. A lot of them were trying to play it cool, acting like they weren't taking pictures; they'd lean down the aisle or whip around for a quick snap and then turn right back, but even Helen Keller would have known what they were up to. The penguin, looking like RuPaul at Wimbledon, was causing a sensation. The professional photographer down on the field turned around with his humongous, long lens and took a bunch of shots of Dad in the stands. I knew right in the moment the photo would end up on the front page of the *Palisades Post*, and that was exactly what happened. At least they had the sense not to add some lame-ass headline like: The Only One at Pali Graduation in a Tuxedo.

Feeling how happy Dad was to be there, seeing the sparkle back in his eyes, I honestly didn't care how anybody else was reacting; I was just glad he got to join us.

Mom was squirming in her seat, hating all the attention. I was preoccupied with feeding Dad ice chips so he didn't overheat. Nonnie seemed perfectly content to be watching the kids march in, wearing their caps and gowns—which, of course, had to be black on a ninety-degree day! Feel sorry for them much?

Amy was fully fixated on trying to spot Charlie. The graduates were coming in alphabetically, so she was all busy looking for him at the back of the line with the other *W* kids, but her dumb ass forgot he was one of the speakers, so he was with the first group in, already sitting right up front. I could've told her, but it was much more fun watching her try to figure it out.

Principal Clyburn made her welcoming remarks, and then Corey Kline came up to the mic and sang "The Way We Were." She has an amazing voice and had been the star of our high-school musicals every year since she was a freshman, but what's the deal with choosing a song that's, like, a million years old? I know in *her* head, she's the clone created from the mushed DNA of Barbra Streisand and Idina Menzel (news flash, Corey Kline: Lea Michele already nabbed that slot), but still, something from this century might have been more meaningful to the graduates.

Or … maybe that was just me.

But, and I seriously mean this, she does have an incredible voice. I've always made a point of being super nice to her, so when she inevitably ends up on Broadway, I can text her and get her to give me house seats. Always thinking, right?

After Corey, there were speeches from a pair of lame-ass kids I didn't care about, and then, finally, they announced it was Charlie's turn to speak. Penguin-Dadda, who had remained standing in the aisle since he couldn't actually sit, wanted a better view.

The guy in front of him had a huge head, and his wife or lady friend was wearing a sun hat, so Dad hopped up on the bench seat we'd saved for him to have a more direct eyeline to the lectern. As soon as Charlie started to deliver his speech, this total dickhead behind us thumped Mom on the shoulder and goes, "Your penguin's blocking my view. Can he at least take off his umbrella hat?"

I very calmly and politely told him Dad couldn't do that because the sun was fully dangerous for him. Mr. Dickhead replied, quite loudly, that maybe then we shouldn't have brought a penguin to an outdoor summer graduation in the first place. Still keeping my cool, I patiently explained he was providing emotional support for my Nonnie who had a heart condition, diabetes, and extreme high blood pressure.

So you know what Dickhead said next? He goes, "Well, Einstein, then maybe you and your mother should have left the penguin *and* the old lady at home."

Mom shushed him and told him her son was the current speaker; she said she'd appreciate it if Dickhead would let her focus on Charlie.

Apparently, he couldn't do that. Things only went south from there.

Dickhead called Mom "a self-centered bitch." Penguin-Dad whipped around, raised a flipper, and slapped the man right across the face. I don't even know how it got so out of hand, but everybody around us was reacting and raising their phones, aiming them at Dickhead and Dad. It made such an obvious disturbance that, down on the football field, Charlie stopped speaking. Ever the great improv actor, he calmly leaned into the microphone and said, "Apparently some of our audience has more important things to do than to listen to me, so I think we can just wait until folks simmer down."

From two rows below us, this kid I didn't recognize—but who instantly catapulted to the top of my "You're Dead to Me" list—cupped a hand to the side of his mouth and yelled at Charlie, "Hey, man, it's your own damn family."

Without even pausing for a breath, Charlie fired back, "Well, at least they're here. Unlike your dad who's probably glued to his favorite barstool at the Gaslight."

A roar of "Wooooooo" ricocheted around the stadium, and suddenly the sedate graduation had turned into one of those *Real Housewives* reunion shows.

Dickhead stood up and puffed out his fat chest like he was about to say something way insulting, but then, seeing the battalion of cell phones pointed at him, he let out a huge, loud "harrumph." I swear, that's exactly what it sounded like; ya know, like some character in those lame comic strips in the newspaper when they express total exasperation. Who does that in real life?

Then, opting to take the literal high road, he grabbed his cooler—probably filled with tall cans of malt liquor—and stormed up the steps to exit the bleachers. The penguin gave an audible sigh. Mom took my hand and patted it. Pretty oblivious, Nonnie asked why Charlie had stopped talking. Amy was annoyed that this whole dustup had interrupted Charlie's speech, but then she was gushing about how cool he was to just stand there and wait it out.

Charlie glanced around the stadium, looked directly at us, and went, "We good?" Half the audience yelled out in total sync like it had been rehearsed, telling him to continue. So he did.

He was funny and passionate and amazingly articulate. That's one thing I can say for my brother: his vocabulary really rocks. Whenever he makes any kind of speech, there are always at least two or three words I have to go home and look up afterward. I think it's because he reads like a maniac. Plus, he memorizes Shakespeare—for fun!—and actually *understands* it. As my relatives in Boston say, "He's wicked smahht!"

When Charlie finished, getting *so* much more applause than the other boring speakers—and (big surprise) a whooping standing ovation from Amy—next up was the marching band doing Katy Perry's "Firework." They were at the front of the field, behind the lectern, facing the graduates. Oh my God, I can't even tell you how close I came to wetting my pants. (A tendency Mom tells me I inherited from her.) The band had to perform without the seniors (obvi), so it was like the JV team being called up to the majors way before they were ready for prime time. The trumpet players were the most confused, totally forgetting all the proper turns, so they were crashing into each other, and then Tommy Hamer, the guy with the huge drum strapped to him, started laughing so hard, he got half the other kids laughing, making it impossible for the horn players to puff out the notes between their guffaws. Classic.

They left, laughing all the way, and then it was time for the valedictorian. Griffin Papadopoulos? He was the kind of kid you could tell in first grade would end up being valedictorian—and there he so was. The hilarious thing is his younger sister Gina is the exact opposite. Trust me, I am a mad-dog feminist and *so* not into slut shaming, but you can't have a different boyfriend every fifteen minutes and then act all offended when people call you Gina Drop-Your-Topoulos. You know what I say? If it's your thing to dole out BJs in the back of the school bus, own it, girl. Let it be your superpower.

Anyway … Griffin was doing his speech, and the thing about high-school valedictorian speeches is they're all exactly the same—the world's facing terrible troubles, it's a totally tough time to be entering into adulthood, but with hope and optimism and the "can-do" spirit that built this country, anything is possible.

I call bullshit.

Just once, it would be so cool to see someone get up, all serious in their black robe and that stupid hat, and say, "We're fucked; we're all going to die; what's the point of any of it? Thank you and good luck." Seriously. How great would that be?

But that wasn't Griffin Papadopoulos's style. He was brimming with hope and possibility. He even has those earnest red cheeks like Adam Schiff. I pretty much tuned him out, thinking about the big-ass shrimp burrito I was going to order at Casa Escobar once graduation was over.

There I was, lost in my burrito daydream. Mom and Nonnie were in love with Griffin. Amy was staring at her phone photos so she could add a rainbow glitter filter to her eyelids on the selfie she'd just taken. (So extra!)

Then, out of nowhere, right at the end of our aisle, Dickhead reappeared … only he wasn't alone. There were two animal control officers in official vests, cop hats, and with Tasers and other junk hanging off their belts. The one officer, who looked way too much like John Cena—only without the cute sense of humor—was carrying a metal cage with handles. His partner was this lady who for sure was a retired marine. She leaned toward Mom, trying to keep her voice down, and told us they were there to remove the penguin. They quoted some "section this" of "ordinance that" and said it was illegal in Los Angeles County to keep a penguin as a domestic pet.

We were seriously trying not to make a big scene (again) and arguing that they had no right to take our penguin, but these two were fully by the book and not messing around. The John Cena guy stepped right past Nonnie and Mom, grabbed Dad up in a bear hug, and scooted back out of the aisle so fast, it was kind of impressive. Dad was flapping his wings and making this strangled squawking sound I'd never heard before, but Cena wrangled him into the cage and slammed its wire door shut. In the melee, Dad's umbrella hat got knocked off his little penguin head; the sunglasses remained in place, thanks to the trusty elastic band. I jumped up to grab the striped hat off the ground and held it out to the female officer.

"Please," I pleaded. "Take this for him. He really needs it if he's out in the sun."

The mucho macho Marine Mama snatched it from me without a word, but I could tell from her kind eyes that she wouldn't let Dad be out in the elements without it.

The whole time, Dickhead was standing there with his hands on his hips and this hateful shit-eating grin plastered on his ugly face, so proud of himself for getting Dad arrested.

Everybody around us was jeering and booing, and once again, they had to hold up the ceremony so the entire crowd could gawk at us. For me, the whole thing became one gigantic, horrific blur.

The next thing I knew, me, Mom, and Nonnie were gathering up all our stuff as the animal control officers were carrying the cage holding Dad back up the stairs. Amy said she'd stay behind to be with Charlie; we told her we'd text them when we knew what the hell was going on. It was a humongous nightmare. Seriously.

Mom and I parked Nonnie on the first bench we found at the edge of the parking lot so we could run after the officers; we were shouting at them to tell us where they were taking Dad. They had lapsed into full stone-faced professional mode and were no longer saying anything. They put the cage—kind of roughly, if you ask me—into the back of their official truck, climbed into the cab, and drove off.

Wait, were they serious? Where were they taking my dad?

CLARK

When they slammed the back doors of that Los Angeles County Animal Control Department paddy wagon, I couldn't help but flash back to spring break my freshman year of college. I was eighteen; the drinking age in Florida was twenty-one. I was sharing a single hotel room with fourteen of my best college buddies, and we were practically required by law to act like idiots. We were all hanging out over every inch of our beach-hotel walkway, pounding back beers, working to chat up the girls from a wide swath of colleges up and down the East Coast. The cops showed up, started asking to see IDs, and began hauling away anyone who had a beer in hand and couldn't prove they were of legal age.

Being young and stupid, I didn't follow my roommates' leads and duck into our room; I just kept talking and drinking and thinking I was far too slick to be taken into custody.

Boy, was I wrong.

The truth is, arresting kids for underage drinking, keeping them in jail overnight, and then releasing them once they paid the hundred-dollar fine was an enormous source of revenue for the city of Daytona Beach during spring break. That April night, I became one more unwitting donor to the municipal coffers. What I remember most was the journey to the downtown jail in the back of the police wagon—I was drunk; starting to get chilly; wearing only a tank top, cutoff jean shorts, and sandals. Throughout the ride, I was having tremendous difficulty getting my alcohol-soaked brain to process the fact that I was a prisoner of the state of Florida.

Being held captive in that animal control van, I was experiencing major déjà vu. Peering out of my wire cage, I made a startling discovery: instead of being accompanied by an inebriated group of rowdy peers, this time, my fellow prisoners were a snarling raccoon and an opossum, each in cages of their own.

Yup. That's right. In the wire box directly across from me, an ugly-ass raccoon was up on its hind legs, gripping the cage-door bars with unnervingly humanlike hands. His stare was fixed directly on me. He clearly aspired to be our prison-gang tough guy, aching to make me his bitch. But let me ask you this: If he was so smart, why didn't he think to take off his bandit mask before the cops nabbed him?

(Do you suppose this is an occupational hazard of writing children's books for the past two decades? I was only capable of seeing the world through the filter of someone hoping to conjure up my next potential blockbuster franchise.)

The opossum, on the other hand, didn't give a shit about either of us. He was on his belly in the corner of his cage, flaunting his spooky opaque eyes and garbage-eating ass, silently daring anybody to get close enough to mess with him.

I lost all sense of how long we were in that van and had no idea where we ended up once we stopped moving. The male and female Animal-Control Officers who had taken me into custody carried the three cages inside, one at a time.

They temporarily stashed the raccoon and the opossum, but that wasn't where they left me. They brusquely scooted me out of my cage, slapped the umbrella hat back on my head, adjusted my crooked sunglasses, and snapped the leash back onto my collar. It was late afternoon; I was feeling clammy and light headed. I knew I needed water—to drink and to dive into—but the officers didn't seem to care about any of that.

"C'mon, buddy," the square-headed male half of the team said, "you're coming with us." (I wondered if anybody had noticed that the guy could be John Cena's younger brother.) He gave my leash a tug. Trailed by his lady partner—whose name tag said Officer Brenda—he dragged me through a door leading from the brick-and-cement-cage storage area to the wood-paneled front reception room.

Behind the brightly lit counter, a jovial desk sergeant had his head down with his full focus trained on the day's *New York Times* crossword puzzle.

"Hey, Dodenhoff," the John Cena guy chortled, "check this out."

Dodenhoff's head snapped up, and his jaw dropped down. He was acting like he'd never seen a penguin before.

... Okay, I get it. Chances are he *had* never seen a penguin in a striped umbrella hat, wearing an Emotional Support Animal vest and red sunglasses, waddle into his shelter on a leash.

"What. The. Hell?" Dodenhoff queried.

Officer Brenda spoke up. "We were called to remove him from the Palisades High graduation where, apparently, he slapped one of the fathers with his flipper. Can you believe this shit? Westsiders with too much money and too much time on their hands are the only people on God's green earth that could think it was a wise idea to keep a penguin as a pet in Southern California."

Cena wanted to know what they were supposed to do with me.

Dodenhoff seemed to get a tremendous kick out of the question. "Well, unlike most of the critters we rescue, you can't exactly release him into the wild—unless you're in the mood to drive him up to Alaska and set him free in Sarah Palin's backyard. I heard he'd have a great view of Russia."

"Can't do that," Officer Brenda said with a completely serious tone, "or Sarah and Todd would probably mistake him for a Soviet spy and shoot him dead."

"Todd won't be a problem. They're not married anymore," Dodenhoff said.

"Of course they are!" Officer Brenda insisted. "People like that stay married forever. No matter how miserable they are, they don't quit. It's the redneck code."

"Hate to burst your bubble there, Brenda," Dodenhoff said, "but I'm quite certain they got divorced. Most of their kids did too. Some of them more than once. Shit, for my money, you can keep the whole dumbass pack of 'em."

Officer Brenda whipped out her phone to look up "Sarah Palin's marriage" while I stood there, growing more and more parched and feeling faint.

It was Cena who chimed in next. "Well, I'm sure as hell not driving to Alaska. And here's one more thing I know: we are *definitely* not equipped to keep him here."

That was the last thing I remember hearing before my penguin body went rigid, and I crashed to the linoleum floor.

JULIA

"Mom, STOP! You're totally spinning out and not helping anything."

As much as I knew Katie was right, that didn't keep me from feeling a hot flash of anger mixed with shame at having been called out by my fifteen-year-old.

While the graduation ceremony was proceeding without us, I was behind the wheel of my Lexus SUV with Katie in the passenger seat. My mother was in the back seat, devouring oyster crackers to stave off a diabetic low. I told her she was absolutely forbidden from having any kind of a health crisis. All our focus had to be on rescuing Clark from …

Oh no.

That was my next horrible realization: How the hell could we get on the road if we had no idea where they had taken him?

"Oh dear God," Katie suddenly blurted, "do you think they're going to euthanize him?"

I whipped my head toward her and gawked. Why in the world would she say something like that to me? Doesn't she know who I am? I'm the queen of dark visions. I am the keeper of every Worst-Case Scenario ever imagined. I see danger and death in a dish of pretzels. But euthanizing an innocent penguin? Even I hadn't managed to go there yet. However, I sure *was* there after that—stuck there—the instant Katie had brought it up.

We had to get moving. Quickly. Thank God we were in a handicapped spot using the placard I had for Mom. What if we had been in a normal spot that day? What if we had been totally boxed in, unable to go anywhere until after the graduation ended, and everybody finished taking pictures and making small talk and offering congratulations—

"MOM!"

Once again, it was Katie who pulled me back to the present. With her face glued to her phone, she announced that there was an animal control shelter in Carson and another one in Agoura, but neither of them specifically mentioned serving the Pacific Palisades.

"What about Santa Monica?" I asked. "They must have a shelter. They have everything."

"Yeah," Katie responded, "but they're their own city, and the van that took Dad away was marked Los Angeles County Department of Animal Control."

God bless my crackerjack, A+ student—always paying attention, always picking up on the details. I asked her what she thought we should do.

"I'm going to call the Carson one to see if they got sent out on a call about a penguin, but in the meantime, I think you should start heading that way. We might not have a lot of time to fuck around."

"Oh de'yah," my mother piped up from the back seat. "That language!"

"Sorry, Nonnie—we're in crisis mode. I'll clean up my act tomorrow."

I was making a slightly shaky beeline for the southbound 405 freeway; Katie was on what seemed to be an endless hold as she tried to call the shelter.

Of course, we were heading into rush hour.

On a Friday.

In June.

The traffic was in that speed-up/slow-down/accelerate/brake pattern that's never fun but takes on a whole other level of "let me rip my hair out" when you're trying to save your penguin husband from dying in some animal cremation oven.

Exasperated, Katie put her phone on speaker so we could all "enjoy" the Muzak version of "Stairway to Heaven" serving as their wait-time tune. Do you mind if I go on the record here? *Muzak Led Zeppelin?* I'm sorry. Some things are just plain wrong.

We were halfway to Carson before a chipper male voice finally came on the line.

"Los Angeles County Department of Animal Control. This is Sergeant Dodenhoff. How may I help you?"

Katie was breathless. "Yeah ... um ... see it's my ... well, no ... we ... I mean, he ... it's—shoot—by any chance, do you ... do you have a penguin there?"

"Well, as a matter of fact, young lady, we do. He was brought in moments ago."

"Oh thank God! He's ours."

"Pardon me for asking this, little darling, but what were you people doing taking a penguin to a public graduation?"

"First of all, you really should *not* be calling me 'little darling' like you're stuck in the fifties, but let me stay on point. He really wanted—no, forget it. I just need to know: Is he okay?"

There was an excruciatingly long and stilted silence from Sergeant Dodenhoff.

And then I was rattled to my core by a terrified shriek from Katie. "MOM! What are you doing?"

I looked up just in time to see the way-too-close rear bumper of the pickup truck in front of me. I jammed the brakes to the floor. The Tesla behind us had to make a sharp swerve into the next lane to avoid rear-ending us.

It was all right. We were all fine. A few of Mom's oyster crackers got smashed to sawdust when she was sent lurching forward, and they collided with the back of the seat in front of her, but that was the extent of the damage.

Sure, *we* might have been okay, but I had no idea about Clark.

When we arrived at the shelter fifty minutes later, we rushed into the lobby and were greeted by Sergeant Dodenhoff. Katie darted forward ahead of her grandmother and me.

"Hi," she breathlessly blurted, "we're the penguin people. I called … you said he was here—"

"Yup. He's here. Although, I gotta be honest with you folks, he was in pretty rough shape last I checked."

I let go of Honey's arm and raced to the desk. "What do you mean, 'last you checked'? Who's with him? Where is he now?"

"In the clinic," Sergeant Dodenhoff replied, "with the vet. But let me ask you something: You folks knew Todd and Sarah Palin got divorced, am I right?"

I could hardly believe my ears. Why was he talking about the idiot Palins, and more importantly, why would we possibly give a shit? Katie said she had heard about their split, but so what? We needed to see our penguin ASAP.

"Where is this clinic? Is it close?" Katie panted.

"Real close," Dodenhoff said. This fool was so laconic he was making the Marlboro Man look like a speed freak.

"Great," Katie said. "Just tell us how to get there, and we'll go."

Dodenhoff reached under his desk, clicked a button, and the heavy metal door behind him slowly swung open.

"Straight back past the cages, make a right."

Katie whirled toward Mom and me. *Hallelujah!* Clark was right there in some rear room. We didn't have to get back into that nightmare traffic.

The three of us followed Dodenhoff's directions, passing through the door into an enormous room with stacked cages lining the central passageway on both sides. Maybe I've seen one too many jailhouse movies, but as we made our way past those cages, I kept expecting the critters being housed there to start banging on the bars with tin cups. There were dogs, cats, terrifying-looking opossums, mangy coyotes (like the ones that had tried to devour Clark), and even one creepy raccoon standing up on its hind legs, gripping the cage bars with his nasty leathery hands. I really did *not* like the way he was following me with his beady little eyes.

Finally reaching the end of that long corridor, we saw the clinic door and hurried into what looked like a standard veterinarian examination room. A short skinny doctor in a white lab coat was sitting at the desk, writing up a report. I stopped and gaped at Katie, knowing we were both thinking the exact same thing: there was no penguin in there. What had they done with Clark?

I was having trouble breathing. It took me a minute to find my voice. "Excuse me ..."

The miniature man snapped his head up. (He had almost certainly been a jockey in a former life.) He refocused, as if this were the first moment he'd noticed other people were present.

"Yes?"

"Did you have ... were you ..."

I couldn't finish the question because I was so terrified of the answer. Katie moved past me to confront the jockey more directly.

"The guy out front said you were treating our penguin ...."

"Yes. That's a true fact. I sure was."

"Where is he? Can we see him?" Katie asked.

I was positive she was going to burst into tears at any moment.

"I can't imagine why you wouldn't be able to see him."

"Great. *Now*, please?"

"No, that probably won't happen. More like tomorrow I'm guesstimating."

"What? Why? Why *not* now?" Katie pleaded.

He looked up at her over the edge of his round John Lennon glasses.

"Well ..." He paused and glanced at his watch. "It's five thirty. On a Friday. In June. In Carson ...."

"Okay, but what does any of that have to do with us getting to see my ... our ... our penguin?"

"Even if the traffic gods happened to be smiling on ya—which they almost never are, especially not on a Friday, in June, in Carson—by the time you got there, it'd be closed."

Now I was the one who was fighting to keep from getting hysterical. My voice was locked in a high, tight octave I hardly recognized. "*What* will be closed?"

The jockey shook his head like we were the densest people he'd ever encountered. He had the nerve to unleash a condescending chuckle.

"Do I look like I'm set up to care for a severely ill penguin? Does it honestly appear to you people like we could nurse an aquatic bird back to health right here in this little room?"

"All right, so where is he? Where did you send him?"

"After I—quite heroically I hasten to add—got your penguin hydrated, cooled him down, and managed to get his heartbeat back into proper rhythm, I had him transported to where he belongs: the Aquarium of the Pacific."

I wanted to be more controlled. I wanted to be more dignified. I just was incapable of stopping myself. "I'm so very sorry, sir, but where the fuck is that?"

CHARLIE

That went well. (Read acute sarcasm here.)

Who else but my family could have turned a high-school graduation into a near riot? I still didn't know all the details of how and why everything went sideways. I did what I could to get through my speech, fighting like a maniac to keep focused, and then the next time I looked up to where they'd all been sitting, everybody but Amy was gone. It was like in *Back to the Future* when Marty's family members started fading out of the picture, only with a penguin replacing wacky Crispin Glover.

I couldn't believe I had worked on that stupid speech for a full month, rehearsing it a million times like a crazy person. What was the point? Mom and Dad never even got to hear it.

After the faculty did their handing-out-the-fake-diplomas thing, and the Madrigals (our show choir) came out to sing "Time of Your Life" (such a cliché), it was finally over.

Amy met me on the field and tried to fill me in, but all the kids were crowding around, giving me crap, yelling about how they couldn't believe my mother had brought a penguin to graduation. A bunch of them were blaming me for wrecking the whole day. But not my buddy Dylan. That kid—he's just happy all the time. He busted through all the crap givers, raised a high hand, and with this huge grin on his round face, he goes, "Up top, my man—that was LIT!" I'm asking ya, how can you not love a guy like that?

There was so much input and noise that I couldn't make sense out of any of it. Amy said our celebration dinner had been canceled because Mom, Katie, and Nonnie were off trying to get Dad out of some sort of penguin jail. What? *No comprendo.*

Around six thirty, I got a text from Katie, saying they were on the way home, and I should meet them there. Mom was going to stop at Casa Escobar and pick up take-out Mexican food so we could at least have a semicelebration at the house.

It turned out that Dad was being held hostage at the Long Beach Aquarium which they also call the Aquarium of the Pacific. Feeling like he needed to be in an environment more equipped to deal with a sick penguin, the animal control doc had him transferred there. The vet told my family that if those guys were able to nurse him back to health, he'd be temporarily housed in the aquarium's June Keyes (whoever she is or was) Penguin Habitat. Then whenever it could be arranged, they'd transport him back to Antarctica where he belonged. It's illegal to keep a penguin as a pet in Los Angeles County, so there was no way they were going to let us get him back.

Oh ... kay. Sorry but ... NO. Did you think for even one second we were going to let them ship Dad off to Antarctica? This was *not* going to be like in *The Searchers* when Natalie Wood got kidnapped by the Comanches, and they opted to raise her as one of their own. Those aquarium dudes were leaving us no choice. We needed to strap on our inner John Wayne and rescue Dad's black-and-white ass, PRONTO.

One thing I knew for sure was that you can't go to war without a battle plan.

Before we could begin to formulate one, Nonnie announced that her nerves were shot. But not so shot she couldn't first down two dry gin martinis before she toddled—or more accurately *wobbled*—off to bed.

I thought it made the most sense for me to be the general of this operation, but Katie strongly disagreed. She said as someone who was positive she was going to receive a 5 (top score) on her AP History test, she had the better grasp on previous successful battle campaigns.

Therefore, she reasoned, she deserved to be in charge. It might've been nice if she'd at least taken a minute to thank me for all my excellent tutoring that had helped her to potentially earn that 5, but what the hell? I guess sharing credit isn't her style.

She dictated that I should handle role-playing rehearsals and any wardrobe choices we needed to make; we made Mom the getaway driver and chief lieutenant. Now all we needed was a workable plan.

One thing my sister and I quickly agreed on was we couldn't possibly stage an effective raid without first setting up a recon mission. Neither of us had been to that aquarium since we were little kids. If I'm remembering it right, the East Coast cousins had been in town, it was raining, and we needed something to do so we didn't destroy the house. Dad and Uncle Mark got stuck taking us all there, while Mom and Aunt Susan went off to get pedicures.

★★★

When I rolled downstairs around eight thirty the next Saturday morning, Mom was at the kitchen table, staring off into space like she was stoned; her hands were wrapped around her giant coffee mug. At first, she didn't even register I was there.

"Mom?"

She slowly turned to gape at me with glazed, unfocused eyes and a raspy exhale.

"I had a *horrrrr–ible* night."

When I asked her what had happened, she confessed that she'd hardly slept; when she did sleep, she was inundated with nightmares. I encouraged her to tell me more, but she declined. (Hey, you never know where your next great horror-flick screenplay inspiration's gonna come from.) She said she didn't have the strength to talk about it; she was so exhausted, she felt like she was getting sick.

What she *did* want to talk about was being terrified that we weren't ever going to be able to get Dad back.

"Look, Charlie, I don't know why he turned into a penguin," she finally said. "I have no idea if he has any intention of ever turning back, but ... I love that man. He's been my whole world for more than twenty years. What if we get there and can't find him? What if he's fallen in love with some cute lady penguin and decides he doesn't want to be married to me anymore?"

Her face did that crumbling, trembling thing that happens when she's trying not to cry.

I'm sorry, but ... I've never been very good at the emotional comforting stuff. In that moment, I was willing Katie to appear so she could take over. This was much more in her wheelhouse. Hey, sorry. Cut me some slack. I'm working on it ....

"Mom. We're going to find him. We are going to rescue him. He loves you. He loves all of us. It's gonna be okay. It's like in *Indiana Jones and the Temple of Doom* when Mola Ram makes Indy drink a potion, and he goes all zombie while they're getting ready to sacrifice Willie, but then Short Round brings Indy back to his senses so he can save Willie in the nick of time, right? And ya know what Spielberg did after that movie wrapped? He married Willie—it was Kate Capshaw, remember?—and they've been together ever since, so there you go."

I don't know if I should have hugged her or what. Even if I'd wanted to, it would have been totally awkward because she was sitting down, and I was standing up, so I just reached across the table and patted her right hand still clutching that big coffee mug. In return, she gave my hand a squeeze.

Thank God. Katie must've gotten my telepathic Bat Signal because, suddenly, there she was. She was holding a copy of an Aquarium of the Pacific map she'd printed off the internet. Plus, she had a whole pile of other shit tucked under her arm. Even though she was still in the ancient Springsteen-tour T-shirt Dad had given her years ago to sleep in, she had Grandpa Johnny's bird-watching binoculars hanging around her neck.

"All right," she said, doing her best to sound like George C. Scott in *Patton*—even though I knew she'd never seen the film and probably had no clue who George C. Scott was, but still ... "Here's what we need to do. The aquarium opens at ten, so I say we take off as soon as we can pull it together. The less crowded it is, the easier it'll be to suss out what we're up against."

Mom, Katie, and I arrived at the aquarium only a half hour after they began admitting the day's visitors. There were more people than I would've expected, but it wasn't nearly as packed as I knew it would be later. We made an immediate beeline for the You Are Here map near the entrance and quickly found our way to the penguin habitat.

There were two ways to access it: 1) from an eye-level view on the upper deck, or 2) from a crawl space below that let you look up into the environment or from side to side into their pool, almost like you were immersed in it. Katie said we needed to start up top to get an overview of the whole exhibit.

A placard on the wall announced that these were Magellanic Penguins, native to South America, breeding in places like Chile, Argentina, and Patagonia. (Wait, is that where the jackets come from?) The environment was built with a rocky shoreline bordering a deep blue pool. At that moment, most of the birds were swimming in one big follow-the-leader circle with their faces in the water, so it was impossible to tell if Dad was among them. I thought he was bigger than those guys, but it was tough to be sure from our vantage point.

I looked over at Mom; her eyes were brimming with tears as she frantically scanned the area.

"Where is he? How come I don't see him anywhere?"

"What if the other penguins didn't like him? What if they did some, ya know, like, 'gang up on the new guy,' *Lord of the Flies* bullshit?" Katie asked. "And—"

"What if he's sicker than we thought, and they haven't released him yet?" I interjected. "Didn't you say the vet guy said they needed to get him fully healthy before they could cut him loose?"

The three of us were on the verge of flipping out, working hard not to escalate each other. One of the penguins popped up out of the water and shook himself off on the cement shore. Suddenly, several other heads surfaced, gazing around like it was imperative for them to know where their buddy had gone.

"Check it out," Katie said, "these guys don't even look like Dad. They all have little priest collars and black stripes under their necks.

Dad's penguin neck has the big yellow-orange patches on either side, plus he's definitely taller than them—it should be easy to spot him."

"Yeah," I countered. "If he's in there."

Katie gave me a swift swat on the arm. She was *not* in the mood for negativity.

As we stood in silence, working to formulate our next move, a young dude suddenly appeared inside the habitat. I have no idea how he got in there, but he was carrying a bucket filled with small silver fish. He wore plastic gloves, rubber boots, an Aquarium of the Pacific T-shirt, and white shorts that, if you want my opinion, should have been at least three inches longer. C'mon, bro, you're at work. Look professional. He also had a *serious* man bun.

"Oh my God, how cute is he?"

"Katie," I snapped. "Focus."

"She has a point," my mom said, "he is pretty adorable."

Really? Now, ladies? This is what you're fixated on? Jesus.

While I was unleashing my most exasperated sigh, Bun Boy dug his scooper into the fish bucket. Before he could even begin to deposit his bounty into the pool, the penguins swarmed. They were no dummies. They knew it was feeding time, and they also knew it was first come, first served.

All at once, there was hella squawking and braying as they bounced up out of the water and surrounded Bun Boy. The most we'd heard out of Dad were some isolated honks and clicks but nothing like the noise that crew was generating. I gotta be honest, it woulda totally freaked me out to have those birds all agitated, swarming around me, but Bun Boy was unfazed. He calmly twirled in a full circle as he shook the scoop to distribute his bounty of sardines on the rocky surface. The penguins dove for their breakfast.

Watching them, I suddenly saw something that made me gasp.

"Look, you guys! There in that, like, crack in the cave behind Bun Boy." Mom and Katie turned their heads to follow my pointing finger.

Katie was breathless, clearly about to start crying. "That's him, isn't it? Dadda."

Tucked away so he was almost out of sight, hidden in the cave but peering out at the feeding frenzy at the edge of the pool, was our blue-eyed, yellow-necked penguin father.

"Oh no," Mom lamented. "Look at him. He looks so scared."

"But he's there. He's okay. Now all we gotta do is rescue him," Katie declared.

I looked at the enclosed environment. I looked at the prominently placed security cameras. I looked to my gleefully gaping sister.

"All right, genius. How?"

KATIE

Sometimes it would be really helpful if Charlie weren't so cynical. I swear, he's absolutely convinced the only good ideas in this universe have to come from *his* giant brain. I promised him I'd come up with a rescue plan for Dad, so I did.

After carefully checking out the penguin habitat from every possible angle, using Grandpa Johnny's vintage binoculars, I discovered the nearly invisible door cut into the back of the rock wall. *Aha!* So that was how Bun Boy had gotten in. I also happened to see a girl about my age go rushing by, wearing a T-shirt that said, "Aquarium of the Pacific Intern." *Bam!* I knew exactly what we needed to do.

Before I tell you about that, let me fill you in on the most precious thing that happened while we were watching the penguins.

The three of us were moving from one side of the habitat to the other, making sure we were taking it all in. Using the handy-dandy sketch-pad app on my phone, I was busy making janky maps of what was where and what kind of vantage points each angle had. I heard Mom pant and then make that noise you do when you're trying to swallow your tears but end up almost gag choking on them instead.

I followed her eyeline and saw Dadda with his penguin eyes glued directly on her. He made a waddle-dash to the edge of the pool, dove in, and swam across the water like he was going for Olympic gold.

When he reached the edge nearest to where Mama was perched against the border railing, he raised his head up out of the water, emitted a happy squawk, and ... you're gonna think I'm totally out of my mind, but he was smiling at her. All right, I know, *technically* penguins can't smile. Their beaks don't really change; they only have that one permanent hook shape. But you're gonna have to trust me: he was smiling—or, at the very least, *smizing*. And he couldn't take those happy, smiling eyes off his wife. Melt me like butter; I was *done*.

Then Mom started crying; frankly, she was pretty much out of control. It was sweet. The only trouble is—and this has been a thing since I was little—if Mama cries, so do I. I can't help myself.

Anyway, through her hiccuping sobs, Mom promised Dadda we'd be back. Soon. She promised we were going to get him out of there. We just needed to do a few things first.

I guess he had mad lipreading skills through the glass because as soon as Mom finished talking at him, he gave his penguin head an exuberant and appreciative nod.

On the drive back home, the instant I started to tell Mom and Charlie what I was thinking about our next steps for *Operation Rescue Dad: Phase Two*, Charlie slapped a hand to his forehead.

"How did I not think of this before? My friend Lulu was an intern at the aquarium last summer."

"First of all," I said with a heavy exhale, "you do *not* have a friend named Lulu—and who cares if she was an intern?"

"You know Lulu," Charlie insisted. "She's the one who played Potpan in *Romeo and Juliet*."

"Ohhhhhh," I said with a sarcastic, highly exaggerated nod. "Potpan! That totally clears it up. *Not!*"

"Why do you have to be so ignorant?" Charlie snapped.

"Why do you have to be so annoying?"

"I have an idea," Mom said. "Why don't you both cool it so we can get back to focusing on how we're going to get your father home again."

"Anyway," Charlie sighed, "if your plan requires us to sneak into the habitat through that back door you discovered, it might be a whole lot easier if we were wearing intern T-shirts."

"And you're thinking this imaginary friend Lulu might have a few of them left over from when she worked there?"

"Yes. And she is *not* imaginary. She was Potpan."

Just to get under Charlie's skin—because it's so easy to do—I did a big eye roll and bobbed my head from side to side. "Okay, sure, she was *Potpan*. Are you sure she wasn't Saucepan or Peter Pan or Marzipan? Or wait, I know, maybe you should quit your yammering and get her on the phone to see if she can help."

If I don't end up becoming the CEO of a major corporation, the world will have been robbed of my many gifts. Not only did I come up with a plan, I created an amazing one.

Hillary Clinton nailed it. It takes a village, right?

Charlie got ahold of Lulu "Potpan," and proving there truly is a God, she had two perfectly preserved Aquarium of the Pacific Intern T-shirts she was quite willing to lend us. I have no idea what kind of a story Charlie told her about why we needed them; I didn't ask because I didn't care. He was an actor; he was an improviser. Despite all my complaints about my brother, I knew this was one part of the mission he'd be able to pull off, no sweat.

The next thing we needed was a high-end baby stroller and the most lifelike baby doll we could get our hands on. Thankfully, Mom likes to walk in our neighborhood for exercise, and she's pretty much the mayor of the street. Somehow, in doing her daily ten thousand steps on our cul-de-sac, she knew who lived where and which dog belonged to which family. She knew who seemed to have a happy marriage, who was miserable, and who got more deliveries than anyone else on the block. Obviously, she concluded, those people had to be hoarders because every single time there was an Amazon, UPS, or FedEx van around, it always stopped at the Hoarder House. I'm telling you … my mom? She totally cracks me up.

"I'll go talk to Carla who lives in the Leichman's old house," Mom offered. "She has three kids, and the baby can't be more than two.

The oldest is around six—that's a household that's bound to have everything we need. Plus, Carla's always so sweet when she sees me. Although, I have to say, that husband seems like a big crab. One of those man-o-rexic, mountain biking fools who probably has a secret drinking problem."

"You're basing all this on what, now?" I laughed.

"I know what I know ... you'll have to trust me."

Back at the house, Nonnie was on the couch with a cup of tea, watching reruns of *The Golden Girls*, chortling away.

"These gals crack me up," she said when she saw us. "What did you find out at the zoo?"

I reminded her we'd been at the aquarium, not the zoo, and told her she was going to be playing a crucial role in our rescue project.

"I get a pa'ht to play?" she asked with clear delight. "Did I ever tell ya about the time I was the granddaughta' in the Braintree Community Players production of *You Can't Take It with You*? Everybody said I was mah-velous!"

Normally I love to hear Nonnie's stories, even the ones she's told us, like, a bajillion times, but it was kind of important to get her to focus. While Mom went down the street to see about borrowing the stroller and the baby doll, and Charlie was off rounding up the intern T-shirts, I filled Nonnie in on the precision moves we each had to make to pull off *The Great Escape: Penguin Edition*.

A little more than an hour later, we were back in the car, once again headed for the Long Beach Aquarium. It is so beyond gross we had to make that drive twice in a single day, but that's life in L.A. Thank God it wasn't a weekday, or I seriously might have gone bad. Severely bad. I mean, the weather in Southern California is the best, but if I had a job where I had to be in bumper-to-bumper traffic for two hours, five days a week? I can promise you, you'd quickly find me filed under Next Level Cray.

While I tried to go over the plan again, Charlie was begging me to shut up, insisting everybody knew what they had to do once we got there. Still, I was in total-hyper, Eminem "You-Only-Get-One-Shot" mode. I was a drill sergeant on crack. We couldn't mess up. We could *not* let Dadda down.

Luckily, once you have your ticket, it's good for the full day, so all we had to do was buy a pass for Nonnie, show ours from earlier, and we were in. Mom had the baby doll in a front pack-thingy strapped to her chest and was pushing the empty stroller. Charlie and I were wearing the intern T-shirts—his was too small, mine was too big, so I guess the mysterious Lulu "Potpan" was our Goldilocks; on her, the shirts were probably *juuust right*. Charlie was also wearing a backpack stuffed with a big black blanket.

Even though she doesn't need it most days, we had Nonnie walking with her cane because she was going to be playing the part of the Frail Old Lady with a Medical Emergency. It was cute how stoked she was to be revisiting her thespian past. I guess Charlie wasn't the only half-Kosher ham in the family.

He and I left Mom and Nonnie milling around the penguin environment. We went off to find an intern to tail, hoping one of them would lead us to the door that granted access to the behind-the-scenes area of the park.

We found our perfect pigeon sweeping up around the Shark Lagoon. She was probably sixteen years old and looked like one of those ass-kissing, do-everything perfect girls I hate on-sight. I mean, her shirt was tucked in so neatly, it looked like she put it on and *then* ironed it. Creepy, right? Anyway, I bounced up to her with my brightest fake smile.

"Hiiiiii," I gushed. I stuck my hand straight out like a total dork. "I'm Katie."

She told me her name was Jennifer. (See? Tight-ass—otherwise, she would have called herself Jenny.) I told her Charlie and I had just started working there and got totally turned around, but we were supposed to feed the penguins. I claimed we'd lost our way to the preparation area and wondered if she might help. She was all, like, "Sure. No worries. It happens all the time. This place is a maze. Don't give it a second thought—just follow me."

So we did.

She got us to where we needed to be and used her magnetic pass thing to open the door—so eager to please, she never asked why we didn't have our own passes around our necks. Dork. With an over-the-top sweep of her hand, she gestured for us to enter and then said she had to scurry back to her post to continue sweeping up the spilled popcorn and peanut shells around Shark Lagoon. I swear to God, she actually said "scurry." Isn't that so embarrassing?

When we got into the sterile, white hallway that looked like some convoluted passageway in a video game, Charlie and I understood we had to at least *look* like we knew where we were going so if we ran into anyone, they wouldn't question us. It was a great theory; it had nothing to do with reality.

From behind, I heard a deep middle-school-principal-type voice. "Do you mind if I ask where you're going?"

My brother and I whipped around. Thank God Charlie sprang into improv mode.

"We were assigned to go check the current temperature in the penguin habitat. Are we going the wrong way?"

The guy was as tall as an office building, had jet-black hair and epic dimples. The ultimate '50s sitcom dad.

"I don't believe I've seen you two here before."

I began to burble. (That's a thing, right? Burbling?)

"We only started last week," I said. "It's been my dream to work here since I was a tiny kid. Bindi Irwin is, like, my total hero." And then for a reason I could not possibly begin to explain, I just blurted right in the giant man's face, "CRIKEY!"

It came out horrifyingly loud.

I could feel myself going full-on crimson, from my chest to my forehead, but thankfully he started to laugh.

Charlie tried to rescue me by saying he was working for the summer to build up his college resume. "They really like it if you act like you care about the environment and animals and shit," he said. Hearing himself, he swiftly added, "Not that I don't care because I do. I totally do! So ... about that penguin habitat ..."

Okay, I know everybody says there are all kinds of things wrong with growing up in the current era with the pressures of social media and all the other stuff we deal with, but I'll take it. You know why? Because right then, the Big Guy's cell phone rang, and once he saw who was calling, he totally stopped caring about us.

He pointed down an adjacent hall, told us to make two lefts and a right, and we'd wind up where we needed to be. He hustled off to answer the call. Seeing how distracted and flustered he got, it either had to have been his boss or maybe his totally hot sidepiece he didn't dare blow off.

Following Big Guy's instructions, we got to a door marked June Keyes Penguin Habitat. Jeez, I guess if you give a big enough chunk of change, they slap your name on every possible place—even a dingy back door buried deep in the park bowels.

I felt my heart make this total flutter when we stepped out onto that fake rocky shore where we'd first spotted Bun Boy. Charlie was right behind me. Most of the penguins were back to swimming around in circles in the pool. (Don'tcha wonder why they never get dizzy?)

Taking a quick look into that little crack in the cave where Dadda had been earlier, I saw that, sure enough, he was sequestered there once again. Poor thing. He was like the little nerd nobody wanted to play with. Or maybe he was like that one kid in middle school who was suddenly a foot taller than everybody else, and no one knew if he was a student or a teacher's aide, so it was easier to simply ignore him. I was really hoping it wasn't because Dadda was the only one in there who wasn't South American, ya know? I mean, humans are depressing enough; it would break my heart to think penguins are full-on racist dicks too.

Charlie moved down the rocky shore to get closer to where Mom and Nonnie were sitting on a nearby bench, sharing a box of popcorn. He gave them our signal. We were ready to spring into action.

You've heard people talk about feeling like their heart was totally going to explode out of their chest, right? Please tell me that can't really happen. Because, I mean, I swear that's what I was feeling like. We had almost pulled off our plan, but what if something went wrong?

What if Bun Boy suddenly appeared, or that Jennifer-who-should-have-been-Jenny or the Big Guy came to check up on us? What if the penguins knew we were interlopers and suddenly attacked? I mean, they were obviously shunning Dad, so who was to say they wouldn't go after me and Charlie?

Trying to appear cool, trying to look like we belonged, Charlie picked up the empty feeding bucket and pretended to be inspecting it. I swept some nonexistent dirt off the rocky cliffs. There were about a dozen moms, dads, and kids staring into the habitat, watching the birds, watching us. I was praying so hard that I wouldn't yak from all the tension.

Finally, Charlie gave the "it's on" nod to Mom and Nonnie.

They got up off the bench and took a few steps closer to the edge of the penguin pool. Nonnie made a *GASP* loud enough for us to hear through the glass and then forced her knees to buckle as she sank toward the ground. Mom launched into Helen Mirren mode, shouting out as she grasped Nonnie's elbow to break her fall.

While the folks around them rushed over to see if they could help, I jumped in front of the cave crevice to block the visitors' view; Charlie darted behind me, pulled the black blanket from his backpack, and dashed to Dad, scooping him up and totally enveloping him.

I was staring out at the commotion Nonnie was creating and told Charlie we were in the clear; not one person was looking our way. They were all focused on the old lady who appeared to be having a seizure. I seriously wished I had the power to nominate Nonnie for a Tony Award. (Or maybe an Obie Award since we were pretty far off Broadway.)

Charlie and I went galloping out the back door and bolted into the hallway. I ran a bit ahead of him to make sure no one else was around, promising to signal him to hide if the need arose. As he was running, Charlie kept up a play-by-play for Dad who was buried under the blanket's folds.

"We've got you, Pa. We're almost out of here. You can breathe okay, right? Give me one of your little squawks if I'm suffocating you. Mom and Nonnie are right outside. We're gonna make it. We're gonna get you home."

Suddenly, just a few feet in front of me, I saw something that made me want to sing out "Hallelujah" like in the movies, with an angelic chorus and harp music. There was a glowing EXIT sign off to my right, much closer than having to go all the way back the way we came.

"Charlie! Detour! Follow me!"

A few moments later, we burst out that door into the bright sunshine.

Penguin Dadda was squirming but not squawking. Now all we had to do was get our bearings so we could make our way back to the front of the June Keyes exhibit.

I spied a map and ran to it while Charlie did his best to hoist the penguin, still under the blanket, up onto his shoulder so it looked like he was carrying a hefty sleeping toddler.

I checked the map, figured out our next move, and once again ordered my brother to follow me. When we got to where we needed to be, Mom had Nonnie sitting up on the ground, carefully guiding her to drink from the bottle of water a stranger had purchased for them. Some folks were still hovering to make sure everything was all right, but others had moved on. Once again, several of them were delightedly absorbed in watching the frolicking penguins.

Charlie and I dashed to the bench where Mom had left the stroller. The baby doll was now casually discarded in the bottom basket, still secure in its denim front pack. The stroller bed was empty, except for some rando pink pacifier that must've belonged to the neighbor baby. Once again providing the needed blockage, I stood in front of the stroller while Charlie pushed the pacifier out of the way and carefully loaded Dad in. My brother unwrapped him just enough to allow for easier breathing and then pulled the canopy as far forward as it would go. He bent down to whisper: "Just be cool, dude. Stay as still and quiet as you can, and we'll be outta here in no time."

Mom glanced over her shoulder at us, and, seeing that our part of the plan had been expertly executed, she slowly lifted Nonnie back to her feet. Still playing her role to the hilt, Nonnie pulled a lace hankie from her purse and mopped her brow like a Southern Belle recovering from the vapors. (Whatever the hell "the vapors" were; I only know about them from old movies where proper ladies seemed to faint over everything. What a pack of pussies.)

A very concerned man leaned in, speaking way too loud like he assumed anybody over the age of eighty had to be deaf.

"IS EVERYTHING OKAY NOW, MA'AM?"

Nonnie assured him she was fine; it was just a momentary "spell."

"YOU DON'T NEED ME TO CALL SECURITY?"

"All I need you to do, de-ah, is please lower your voice and back up."

Two minutes later, we were the very vision of a picture-perfect suburban family ending our day of aquarium fun. Charlie was pushing the stroller; I was walking beside him; Mom and Nonnie were bringing up the rear. When a full-on Mormon-looking family was walking toward us ... I'm sorry but I couldn't resist ... I peered into the stroller and then looked to Charlie.

"Well, brother," I said, being deliberately louder than necessary, "as lovely as she is, I hope next time you'll remember to wear a condom."

We were less than a hundred feet from the exit gate when I heard a commanding voice behind us.

"Stop!"

I clenched my lips and whispered to Charlie with my heart once again doing acrobatics. "Ignore him. Keep going."

His voice rang out, sounding more insistent. "Folks with the stroller—stop!"

Mom and Nonnie froze. Charlie and I quit moving. I ever so slowly turned to see a husky guy in an Aquarium of the Pacific Security uniform. I almost started to cry but knew that would be our undoing. Somehow, I kept it together. As we all gaped at him, he stuck out an arm.

"You dropped your pacifier."

Oh, thank God!

Mom dashed to him and snatched the bright-pink rubber nipple from his grip. She thanked him profusely, shoved it in her pocket, and we were on our way.

We sailed out the gate with Dadda in the stroller, once again in our custody.

CLARK

It's difficult to be a good dad. For anybody. But can I let you in on a little secret? It's even harder if you're a penguin attempting to console a human teenager.

After my family's heroic and stunningly successful rescue operation, we all decided what we needed most was a few low-profile days at home. The kids were out of school, I was out of immediate danger, Julia was out of gas. We watched mindless TV, took naps in the middle of the day, and let the kids sleep in as late as they needed to and stay up as late as they wanted to. It was peaceful. It felt good.

It didn't last.

Julia and I have always told both kids we knew it was inevitable that at some point they would drink and probably smoke pot; but we also said that if they ever got themselves into a social situation where they didn't feel safe, they could call us to come pick them up with no questions asked. We thought it was important to set boundaries. We wanted them to know we didn't expect them to be saints—we just would prefer it if they didn't end up dead.

The downhill slide started Monday morning. I was in my blanket lair beside our bed, just waking up. Julia was in the bathroom brushing her teeth when Charlie came bursting in. He was having trouble catching his breath, and everything about his face looked like he should be crying, but there were no tears. Julia heard him wheezing and came galloping out of the bathroom. I bolted upright to gawk at him.

"Charlie, what's wrong? Speak," his mother said.

He emitted a few more strangled breaths and then said a string of rapid words, but the only one I clearly understood was "dumped." Julia tried to put the puzzle pieces into place.

"Amy? Amy dumped you?"

"Again," Charlie exhaled. "A-fucking-gain."

Julia asked why, but instead of an answer, she got a bellowing rebuke. "Who cares why? She's nothing but a fuckwad BITCH!"

He threw up a hand, spun away from both of us, and went sailing out of the bedroom, slamming the door behind him as hard as he could. Julia looked to me with pleading, "what do we do" eyes, but I was incapable of offering anything more than a helpless squawk.

I don't know how she does it but, as usual, it was Katie who had the full scoop. Charlie had barricaded himself in his bedroom, refusing all offers of food or emotional support, but somewhere along the line, Katie had managed to extract the details of the breakup.

Apparently, Charlie woke up to a text from Amy saying that since he was going off to college on the East Coast in a few months, and she was stuck at Pali High for one more year, it made no sense for them to try to sustain a long-distance relationship. She said he deserved his freedom as he embarked on the college experience, and that if they stayed together all summer, it would only make parting that much harder. She even threw in a *Romeo and Juliet* quote, which really pissed Charlie off because he thought she'd totally misinterpreted the line's intention.

(Who else but my son could be in the middle of devastating heartbreak and still manage to critique his now-former girlfriend's comprehension of the true meaning of a specific passage of Shakespearean dialogue?)

"I'll tell you one thing," Katie said to Julia and me that afternoon, "I am not saying one bad word about that ho. You know they'll be back together by next Saturday, and then I'd be stuck issuing rando retractions all over again."

About seven o'clock that evening, Charlie finally emerged from his cocoon dressed in a black satin shirt, tight jeans, and a pair of vintage combat boots. His hair was unusually tamed, and his face was freshly shaved. He had my vintage suede bomber jacket slung over his shoulder; just as Julia had rightly predicted when I first underwent my transformation, that little shit was acting like he now had unrestricted access to my closet.

"I'm going out," he announced, sounding like he was willing himself to appear much more in control than he felt.

When we asked where he was headed, he said Gregory—his best buddy since kindergarten—was on the way over to pick him up and that they were going to a summer kickoff party at Lindsay Wilder's house.

Oh God, the notorious Wilders. All the drama-kids' parents had nicknamed them the "Wilder-by-the-hour" family. Dave and Sue Wilder thought it was their job to buy cases of beer for the pack of underaged kids they perpetually entertained, because at least they'd be drinking at home instead of in parked cars or on abandoned playgrounds. Great for *their* kids, but what about all the others who eventually had to drive back to their own homes?

Knowing this wasn't the night to fight with Charlie, Julia repeated the family mantra of "Call us if you need us" and told him to be careful and sane. She knew he was hurting but didn't want that to be the reason for him to shut off his rational brain and act like an idiot. Speaking to our son in the language she knew he understood, she said, "Remember that scene in *Almost Famous* when Billy Crudup jumped off the kid's roof into the pool and could have killed himself? Don't do that."

"Lucky for you, the Wilders don't have a pool."

But *we* did.

I went for a long swim while Julia and Katie curled up together on the couch and watched one of those hideous *Real Housewives* shows. It was something I never understood: my intelligent wife and my fiercely feminist daughter finding delight in watching Botox-inflated, aging Barbie dolls flip tables and throw wine at each other like a gaggle of angry primates. Julia would often say it was something she *couldn't* rationally explain. For her and Katie, it was their version of being NASCAR fans: they only showed up hoping for a spectacular crash.

When the show was over, Katie went up to her room to call her friend Ori. Julia fixed me a second dinner of leftover salmon and seaweed chips. Honey had been asleep for hours.

A few minutes before ten, the landline started ringing. Seeing Charlie's name on the caller ID, Julia anxiously plucked up the receiver.

"Baby, what's wrong?"

"Don't ask one single thing," our son curtly blurted. "I need you to come and pick me up at the Wilders'."

Julia told him she was on the way and bolted to grab her car keys. I waddle hopped in front of her, jumping up and down to indicate that I wanted to come along. I guess we were getting pretty good at this penguin-to-human ongoing game of charades, because she totally got it and told me to follow her to the garage.

If our kid was in crisis, I wanted to be a part of it—or at least as much as I could be in my avian form.

While we wound through the quiet streets of the Palisades on the way to retrieve our boy, I was once again amazed by how, for all its hype and alleged glamour, most of Los Angeles turned into a ghost town any time after ten.

Nearing the house, I could see Charlie a few doors away from the Wilders', pacing back and forth on the little strip of median grass in the center of the wide street. The instant he spotted Julia's car, he came dashing toward us and dove into the back seat.

"Thanks," he huffed.

Julia asked, "Are you okay?"

"Fine."

Silence. Suffocating silence. It didn't even sound like Charlie was breathing. I knew my wife well enough to know this was absolute torture for her. There had to be no fewer than seventy-five questions she wanted to ask. But we'd always told him we wouldn't do that if he had specifically instructed his mother *not* to probe when he called.

If we wanted to retain his trust, it was vital we hold up our end of the bargain.

For the first time since my whole bizarre odyssey had started, I was relieved to be a penguin. It was impossible to ask a question even if I were tempted to.

Shortly before we reached the house, Charlie's emotional dam crumbled.

"Do you know what she did? Do you know what she's doing?" He started crying, almost howling.

"Take your time, love. Take a breath."

He wailed and forced out more words. "How long ago did she break up with me?" Now he was spitting his words. "Oh, I don't know … what was it … eight, maybe nine hours ago? I walked into the Wilders' kitchen to grab a beer—one beer, so don't go off on some lecture—and I caught her in there making out with fucking Will!"

Julia couldn't keep the shock out of her voice. "*Will Kilmer?*"

"YES! The worst actor in the history of Pali High! Do you know how many hours she and I spent making fun of him? My impersonation of his terrible acting always made Amy lose her shit."

It was impossible for me to figure out if my son was more offended by Amy's betrayal or by Will's apparent lack of talent.

Charlie went on without taking a breath.

"Don't you remember how god-fucking-awful he was in *Mamma Mia*?"

"He was one of the dads, right?" Julia asked with trepidation, afraid of triggering a land mine.

Charlie roared between his tears, "YEAH! The one the director randomly decided was supposed to be from Greece—but somehow stupid Will sounded more like Fievel's friend, Tony Toponi. You know what I'm talking about, right? He had that ridiculous racist accent. 'I'm'a gonna prove'a to you I can be a wonderful'a dad.'"

Julia started laughing and then instantly curtailed herself. She assured Charlie that she wasn't laughing at him or minimizing his pain; it was only that he was doing such a spot-on imitation, it brought back a rush of memories of how thoroughly Will had missed the mark.

"Why would she do that?" he cried. "Why the fuck would she be making out with him when she knew I was right there in another room?"

"I hate to say this," Julia replied, "but maybe you were right this morning. Maybe she's just a bee-atch."

"To be accurate," Charlie snapped, "I believe I called her a *fuckwad* bitch."

Despite my previous relief at being mute, it began to feel frustrating that I was unable to offer my son any solace while he was such an emotional mess. As we walked into the house, I patted his back with my flipper, but I'm not sure that was the kind of paternal support he needed.

Julia bustled around the kitchen, making Charlie a cup of tea with cinnamon toast. He said he didn't want any of it, but she insisted.

"It'll help you to calm down, baby. I promise."

"So would blowing the back of my head off with a shotgun, but I'm guessing that might be an overreaction."

When Charlie moved on to a more catatonic phase, sitting at the kitchen table staring into space, Julia got him to assure her that he was all right and then announced she couldn't keep her eyes open another minute. She gave Charlie a kiss on the top of his head, wrapped her arms around him in a protracted hug (while he remained seated), and then wandered away, leaving me alone with my son.

Not knowing what else to do, I used my beak to pull out the chair opposite him and jumped up into it. I stood on the seat and gazed across at my slumped and sad boy. His swollen face, red eyes, and flushed cheeks made him look like his three-year-old self waking up from a nap. After another long moment of quiet, he started to speak.

"Love sucks," he declared. "I don't know how you and Mom do it. I'm just … I'm done. I mean, what's the point? We were like … two days ago she said she loved me and couldn't wait to visit me in Connecticut. Then out of the fucking blue she's kissing Will-fucking-Kilmer in Lindsay's kitchen. Of all fucking people. Does she hate me now? Was she trying to reach into my chest and rip my heart out with her bare hands? Seriously, Dad; I don't get it."

In my head, I had all these brilliant, wise, and comforting things to say to him, but there was no way to get those words down from my brain and out my beak. I concentrated. I riveted my eyes onto his. I made sure the thoughts were fully formed. I mustered all my willpower to deliver the things he needed to hear.

Squawk.

That was it? That was my best shot? Goddamnit!

My penguin shoulders slumped. I felt totally inadequate. I felt as sad as Charlie looked.

It was then that inspiration struck. For me, whenever I was in a deep, dark funk, there was only one sure way to begin to pull out of it.

I hopped down off the kitchen chair and waddled into the family room. I used my head to push the step stool from under the desk into place beside the shelf of DVDs. With my beak, I pulled down the one I was looking for. I toddled back to Charlie and laid the case on the table beside him.

Charlie looked at me with something that almost came close to a smile. "You want to watch *The Graduate*? With me? Now?"

I gave my head several vigorous, repeated nods.

Charlie nodded back. "Okay, Pops. Let's do it."

As we watched Elaine's face register the stunning realization that her mother was the older woman Benjamin was having an affair with, I wanted to tell Charlie that his life was inevitably going to be punctuated by a series of hurts and disappointments, yet he'd slowly learn how to recover from them.

Later, as Benjamin wandered the Berkeley campus searching for Elaine, I wanted to let my son know that, even though it wouldn't always work out the way he'd hoped, he still needed to follow his heart.

By the time Ben was swinging that cross, pulling Elaine away from her own wedding, I wished I could have warned Charlie that no matter how hard we fight for certain things along our life's journey, they won't necessarily wind up leading to our happy ending.

I wanted to tell him so much, but I couldn't say a word.

Instead, I placed my penguin flipper on his knee, scooted a bit closer to him, and pressed my black-and-white shoulder against his.

On-screen, the bus rolled on down the road as Benjamin and Elaine's faces slowly evolved from pure elation into "Now what?"

JULIA

"Why does it have to be so wicked *hottttttt*? I'm melting."

That was Katie slouching into my bathroom to wail at me before we'd even made it to seven thirty in the morning.

I tried to explain that it was summer in a city built in a desert, but she was in no mood for logic. She berated me for not wanting to turn on the air-conditioning. I reminded her that it was unwise to run major appliances during the peak hours in a heat wave unless we wanted to be complicit in causing a citywide blackout.

"Okay," she grumbled, "so I guess it's better if we all just shrivel up and die. You're gonna kill Nonnie, you know. And probably Dadda too. I hope you'll be able to live with all that blood on your hands. Seriously. Last I checked, 'Save the Planet While You Kill Your Family' is not the motto of the Green New Deal."

I wanted to beg her to let me finish taking my morning poop in peace.

Frankly, I wanted to politely ask her to shut up, but I restrained myself. Charlie was still deep into Mope Mode. I didn't need both my kids melting down at once.

I forced a sweet maternal smile and pleaded with her to chill out with a nice, cool morning dip in the pool.

When I made my way into the kitchen a short time later, my mother was at the sink in her bright-red robe and the green-and-red Christmas slippers she wears year-round. She was singing "Oh, What a Beautiful Mornin' " with robust exuberance (in some hilarious hybrid Boston/Okie accent of her own creation) as she whipped up blueberry pancakes from scratch.

"You're in an awfully good mood," I commented.

"I had the most mah-velous night's sleep! Plus, don't you rememba' what day this is?"

When I confessed I had no idea, she was all too eager to remind me: the pre–Fourth of July sale was starting at Macy's and, apparently, I had promised to take her to replenish her stock of holiday tchotchkes and decorations.

That was one of the most endearing things about my mother: she loved to celebrate any and all holidays. The more flags, banners, ornaments, and knickknacks she had to do it with, the happier it made her.

Entering the kitchen as her Nonnie was making this declaration, Katie asked if she could come along. I told her I was shocked she was volunteering to go to the mall with her grandmother and me.

"I thought you hated shopping with us?"

"I do. But Nonnie always buys me something—plus, unlike some people, *Macy's* isn't afraid to run their air conditioner, so who's the dope?"

Mom told Katie she was "tickled" she wanted to come along, and then she ordered her to wash her hands and take a seat at the table; the pancakes would be ready any minute.

As shoppers, Katie and my mother were two annoying peas in a pod. Both strong-willed Leos, when they were on the hunt for something, they could pore over every single piece of relevant merchandise with the precision of a high-end jeweler in search of a flawless diamond. On mall days with either one of them, I had to put a strict limit on my morning caffeine intake; it wasn't good for anybody if I was a jittery, impatient mess as I watched those two pokey puppies inch their way through every department. You'll have to believe me on this: it was a challenge.

We said goodbye to Lethargic Charlie, asked him to keep an eye on Clark, and went off to do battle with the summer mall rats. As we climbed into the car, I had a flash of an old *Flintstones* cartoon. It was made when credit first became a thing; Betty and Wilma would raise their cards over their heads and, as trumpets sounded, they'd bellow "Charrrrrrge … it," before running into their favorite emporium.

A few hours later—or an endless eternity, depending on who you asked—I staggered back into the house, a defeated and sweaty mess. My mother and daughter, Championship Shoppers Extraordinaire, had done it once again. I needed a nap. I needed to be alone. I needed a Bloody Maria with a double shot of tequila.

What I got was none of the above.

As soon as he heard my car pull into the garage, Charlie was right there waiting for us.

He was worked up, nearly hyperventilating. "There's something wrong with Dad. I think this weather might be giving him heatstroke."

Charlie told us Clark had spent most of the day in the pool but, even in there, he'd reached a point when he just stopped swimming and went into a listless dead-man's float. Due to multiple days in a row of temperatures in the upper nineties, even without the heater on, the pool was currently at eighty-eight degrees.

"That's fine for us," Charlie said, "but I don't think it's too good for Dad. He's a penguin from Antarctica—doesn't he need to be in really cold water?"

I found Clark splayed out on the cool tile on the family room bathroom floor. He was listless like he had been when he lapsed into his depression about possibly having to miss graduation—only now he looked even worse. Thoroughly fried. And considering he was an escaped, illegally kept penguin in hiding, we knew it wouldn't be safe to take him to a local vet.

Charlie was in my face, insisting I come up with a plan; I was pretty much drawing a blank. All my mothering instincts kept leading me back to "sick equals doctor visit" but I agreed it wasn't a viable option. Katie had disappeared the moment she'd had a chance to grasp the dire nature of the situation and was now back to blurt in our faces:

"Lake Tahoe!"

I asked her to please elaborate.

"I checked the internet and Tahoe is the coldest lake in California—even this time of year. We have to go. We have to get Dadda up there. It's our best chance to revive him until things cool down."

I immediately launched into the Practical Mom adjustment, spewing out all the reasons why we couldn't suddenly up and leave for who knew how long. Honey had doctors' appointments. Katie was supposed to start summer school to take AP English so her load would be lighter in the fall. We had to begin to get Charlie ready to leave for college, and he was still nursing a broken heart and needed time to heal. Worst of all—not that I could confess this to the kids—I was almost out of pot and needed to visit my dispensary.

"Mom. Everything you just said is beside the point. Our priority has to be saving Dadda," Katie said.

Knowing that trying to make a spontaneous road trip with Mom along would make everything ten times harder, I had to force myself to pull up my Big Girl panties and call my brother. He isn't an evil guy; he truly wants to do the right thing. He just happens to be afflicted with a narcissistic personality cemented during his early years by my mother's blind willingness to cater to his every whim.

He somehow managed to get three different women to marry him, all of whom were equally unwilling or incapable of confrontation. The first two wives were fine with him until they weren't ... and then they left. No negotiation, no second chances—just over and out—and it would be difficult to say if he ever really noticed. Hence, he's reached his late forties swaddled in selfishness, deluded enough to believe he's one terrific guy. What he fails to acknowledge is that when it comes to taking care of our mother, I'm pretty much an only child.

I don't even know if she was aware that she was doing this, but as soon as I explained to Mom why I needed her to go stay with Tits-on-a-Bull for a few days, she looked like I'd sentenced her to a month in San Quentin. Her eyes got wide and her jowls drooped; her mouth was saying it was fine while her face was saying *Please don't abandon me.*

"Mom, it's only for a few days. I promise you'll be okay."

When we arrived at my brother's house in the dustiest recesses of the San Fernando Valley, I insisted the kids stay in the car with Clark. I could not even begin to fathom what a rabbit hole I'd have to dive into to make Tits-on-a-Bull and his Lobotomized Wife (LW) understand that my husband was a penguin in need of a swift trip to Tahoe. I simply said we had to tend to an urgent out-of-town errand, and we'd be back before they knew it. (It's the beauty of dealing with a narcissist: if it's not about him, he's not inclined to ask questions.)

I handed him a bag of Mom's myriad medications accompanied by a very specific, printed list of what she took when and why.

"Just follow my instructions and everything will be fine. She eats like a bird and sleeps like a bear, so pretend you're a zookeeper. It'll be nice for you two to get some quality time together. But let me warn you, buddy, if you kill her while I'm gone, I will torment you forever—even if I go first, I'll come back from the grave to haunt your ass."

With that, I gave him a big smile and a cheery wave, kissed Mom on the cheek, and bolted out the door.

Katie climbed up into the passenger seat to be my navigator and deejay, running her phone's music apps through Bluetooth. Charlie remained in back with Clark's penguin head in his lap. The bird was stretched across the rest of the seat, emitting a raspy wheeze with each exhale. Charlie had a bucket of ice water at his feet and was continually using a wet washcloth to wipe his dad down in the hope of lowering his body temperature. Of course I was running the air-conditioning, but it was tough to tell how much that was actually helping.

"Hey," Charlie piped up, "I hate to be Debbie Downer here, but once we do get Dad to Tahoe and throw him in the lake ... then what? We're not gonna just leave him there, are we?"

"Of course not, you dork," Katie snapped.

"All right. So what's the play?"

Sometimes I really hated Charlie and his relentlessly logical mind.

"One thing at a time, all right?" I barked. "Our first job is to save your father's life." I gave a hearty exhale and added, "Again."

At my insistence, Katie was curating the most mellow playlist she could concoct. For almost four hours, the hum of the road and the underscore of gentle music lulled me into a blissful trance. It was the first time in ages I wasn't focused on anything other than staying in my lane. Believe me, it was no small feat to maintain a safe distance from whatever speeding asshole continually felt the burning need to careen ahead of me only to cut back in, nearly fusing himself to the tailpipe of the car in front of him. Fortunately, I was able to breathe myself into a meditative state. I became lost in my own head, fixated on maintaining the speed limit, studiously avoiding glancing in the rearview mirror so I wouldn't have to see my poor, withered avian husband.

To borrow a phrase from *The Daily Show*, my Moment of Zen lasted until my phone started ringing; the caller ID on my monitor showed it was my brother.

"Great," I groaned before punching the on-screen button to accept the call. I forced out a chipper, "Hey there," all the while dreading what he was about to tell me regarding Mom. (My brother has never been known for calling just to offer a happy update.)

With no "hello" or "how are you" or "how's your trip going," Tits-on-a-Bull blurted, "Did you pack Mom's reading glasses?"

"I packed three pairs. They're all in her purse."

"She says they're not," my brother said.

I asked him if he'd emptied the contents of that black hole my mother called her "pocketbook," but of course he hadn't. Honey was vehemently insisting that she didn't have her reading glasses and couldn't possibly get by without them. She was badgering Tits to take her to CVS to buy new ones.

I was already operating on my last nerve and had no patience for any of this.

"Dump out her purse, find the glasses, and don't bother me again unless it's an emergency. Take some initiative, buddy. Why don't you see if you can surprise us all and act like a grown-up for a change?"

He started to defend himself, but I did not want to hear it. I made some bogus claim about a terrible cell connection and clicked him off. Katie reached over and clapped me on the shoulder.

"Good job, Mama. He needs to seriously start stepping up."

"Why is he so useless?" Charlie asked from the back seat.

"Because Nonnie always treated him like the Christ child. And he's never gotten over the fact that the rest of the world doesn't happen to agree."

The silence returned and I slowly let my mind drift off to begin replaying one of my favorite fantasies. In it, I'm on a tropical beach with a Bond-era Sean Connery, and Idris Elba—who's dressed only in a tie-dyed sarong. They're fighting over which one of them will have the privilege of carrying me into a nearby thatched hut to have their way with me. Suddenly, they both draw fencing swords and become engaged in a ferocious battle while I stand by begging them not to hurt each other.

Just as Fantasy Sean seemed to be gaining the upper hand, the vivid imagery was dispelled by Katie yelping a frantic, "Mama—LOOK OUT!"

Apparently, her warning came too late.

A jagged piece of rusted metal had fallen out of the bed of a pickup truck in front of us and landed directly in my path. There was a dreadful clunk, then the car took an uneven lurch before we heard a distinct POP. The next sound was the whapping and flapping of a completely shredded tire.

"Oh shit!" Charlie wailed. "Get to the shoulder, Mom. Quick."

The car was listing badly to the right. At seventy miles an hour, it wasn't easy to control, but somehow, I forced myself to stay calm. Everyone around us seemed acutely aware of our misfortune; they were all moving out of my way, creating a seamless path for me to get to the shoulder.

I have no clue how long I'd been holding my breath—I wasn't even aware I was doing it until we parked on the edge of the highway, and I unleashed a tremendous, protracted exhale. Katie squeezed my upper arm.

"Holy shit, Mama. When did you turn into some crazy-ass stunt driver?"

Even though I was finally breathing again, I was having a tough time finding words. I grabbed my water bottle from the center console and rapidly gulped most of it down.

"Does anybody know where we are?" Charlie asked.

Katie squinted and put an open hand over her forehead to block out the glaring sun.

"The sign up there says we're seven miles from Twin Pines. Wherever that is."

Charlie retorted, "I'm betting it's not even a real town."

One thing about being on the outskirts of a place with a total population of 327 people is that you're probably safe to assume the Auto Club isn't going to be coming to your rescue in anything close to a timely fashion. Fortunately, we were at a high enough elevation that the temperature was a very tolerable seventy-five degrees in the late afternoon; it was a saving grace for Clark since we couldn't risk keeping the air-conditioning running and possibly overheating the car or killing the battery.

When the tow truck did finally coast up close to two hours after we'd placed the call, I realized the image of the driver I'd been holding in my head had been smashed to smithereens.

Though I'd been picturing a redneck with a substantial beer belly, a Make America Great Again red hat, and a Southern twang (even though we were in central California), what we got instead was a forty-year-old Dolly Parton doppelgänger. She had enormous breasts, purple cat-eye sunglasses with rhinestone accents, darling dimples, and the most open, joyous face I'd seen in eons.

She jumped down from the cab of her tow truck and swiftly assessed the situation. Seconds later, she had the rear hatch of our Lexus SUV thrown open and was lifting out our luggage and cooler to get to the spare. Glancing up to peer into the middle seat, she let out a delighted giggle.

"Oh for heaven's sake, is that a real live penguin? He is about the most precious thing I've ever seen."

"Actually," Charlie said, "he's not doing too well right now. We need to get him into a cool bath as soon as possible."

Our new best friend, Brenda, said she'd pop on the spare and point us toward town "in two shakes of a lamb's tail, baby boy."

"I hate to say it," she added, "but the spare you have looks like somebody stole it off a Tonka truck. In my professional opinion, limping into Twin Pines is about as far as you folks should go until you can replace that dinky little thing with a *real* tire."

"I'm afraid we don't have time for all that," I told her.

"Well, my love, do you have time to die? Because there's a good chance that's what'll happen if you insist on riding on this thing up through the mountains to get to Tahoe."

CHARLIE

I've said it before, and I'll say it again: fuck my life.

I've got no girlfriend and I'm miserable. I'm stressed as shit about leaving for college in a few months, and now I'm stuck in some piddly-ass town with my mother, my annoying sister, and my dad who's a dying penguin.

Yeah, of course he is! Why wouldn't he be? I mean, shit—doesn't everybody's father spontaneously turn into a penguin? Seriously, people, what the fuck?

I swear to God, this town looks like one long outtake from *Back to the Future III*; that's the one where Marty and Doc Brown got stuck in the Wild West trying to keep Doc from getting murdered.

Twin Pines is basically a single main street with a gas station, a general store, a Starbucks, and two bars kitty-corner to two churches so you can get blind drunk in the night and then roll across the street to seek forgiveness by dawn's early light. Oh yeah, and a diner straight out of an Edward Hopper painting. If you don't know who that is, dumbasses, look the dude up. If nothing else, you've probably seen his work on a postcard at some janky rest stop.

To nick a lyric from *RENT*: "America!"

Like Tow Truck Brenda had warned us, we needed to get a new tire before we could keep going up to Tahoe. Did you for one second think there was any chance the single Chevron station would have the size and model of the tire we needed? Fuck no. If Mom had been driving a pickup truck with a gun rack, we'd have been good to go, but an upscale, suburban Lexus SUV? Not a chance in hell.

The gas-station guys—I swear to God, I'm not making any of this up—they were brothers named Ron and Don. They were like the small-town version of Laurel and Hardy with Ron being tall and skinny, while Don was short and fat and had a moustache that looked like a copper whisk broom. They did this thing, like some unconscious schtick they'd been doing all their lives, where one would start a thought and space out and then the other one would pick right up and keep going like he was the one talking in the first place. I can't recite verbatim how they did it, but it was pretty much like this:

RON: Welp, if we don't have the tire we need in stock …

DON: We're just gonna have to call over to Ridgecrest and see if Six-Pack has one. Of course …

RON: No telling when he'd be able to get it to us unless …

DON: Lorelei might be coming up this way to see her sister who just had the twins.

So wait … the tire we needed was nowhere in Twin Pines, and they had no idea when or where we might get it?

Fuuuuuuck. Me.

Man, if you thought *I* was stressed, you should have seen my mom. I legit felt bad for her. She was trying so hard not to cry, but she knew we were at the mercy of those guys, and we had to do our best to butter them up.

The second Brenda had led us into their gas station, she'd popped out of her truck and told Ron and Don about the penguin in our back seat. You would have thought a whole traveling circus had come to town. The three of them were laughing, asking a million questions, and wanting to pet him like he was a dog; all we wanted to do was get him into some water to save his life.

When it fully computed for Mom that we weren't going anywhere until at least the next morning, she asked Ron and Don if they had a recommendation for a nearby hotel.

"Well," Ron said, taking his sweet time forming the words, "it's not like you got your pick, ma'am …."

Don snatched up the verbal baton. "It's either the Pine Lodge Motel or Brenda's pullout couch in her basement that she's been trying to peddle as one of those Air BeeBee things. Unless, of course, you'd rather shell out for the Ritz-Carlton."

Seeing Mom's face light up, Don burst into an explosive guffaw. "I'm just pulling your leg, ma'am. There isn't a Ritz-Carlton within four hundred miles of this place."

The three of them thought that was the funniest joke they'd heard all year. Me? I was praying Uma Thurman would show up in a yellow tracksuit and slice my head off.

While we left the brothers to do their sworn best to find the tire we needed and get it up to Twin Pines as soon as possible, we drove on the low-rent spare a half block down to the aforementioned Pine Lodge Motel. The entire place consisted of six connected mini–log cabins bordering a horseshoe courtyard; five of them were already occupied.

Terrific.

Okay … I'm guessing I'm probably one of the few people on the planet who knows the 1986 movie *Haunted Honeymoon*. It's got Gene Wilder and Gilda Radner—plus Dom DeLuise in drag playing Aunt Kate. Well, that was exactly what it felt like we'd walked into. The lady at the front desk was a dead ringer for Aunt Kate: quite large with a gray wig that didn't fit right and a rhinestone spider brooch that was almost getting swallowed by her … how do I say this? Her decidedly ample bosom. Plus, she was wearing worn out rubber flip-flops that were so squashed, they were crying out for mercy. Oh, and did I mention she was cranky as shit?

She made a HUGE point of telling us how lucky we were to have arrived when we did because we were getting her very last room. She was sorry but it only had one queen bed. She also apologized that the motel's single rollaway cot was already being used by, and I quote, "the overly tanned couple from Tucson with a ten-year-old daughter who looks like Honey Boo Boo in a strawberry-blond fright wig." May I be honest here, Aunt Kate? TMI.

Then she leaned over the desk so it was impossible not to stare down into the Grand Canyon of her cleavage as she wagged an incongruously bony finger to warn that "this facility is a NO SMOKING, NO PETS establishment. There is a four-hundred-dollar fine and instant eviction for anyone who violates either of those policies."

Lucky for us, Aunt Kate wasn't swift enough to detect the "oh shit" looks Mom and Katie exchanged; if she'd noticed, we would have been so busted. "No pets" obviously meant "no penguins"; once again, Dad was going to have to be kept on the absolute down-low or we'd be screwed.

Terrific.

In case things weren't messed up enough, now I was going to have to spend the night in a probably haunted motel room with my mother, my sister, my penguin-non-grata dad—and *one* queen bed.

Fuck. My. Life.

You already know that if only two people could be in the bed, it was going to be Mom and Katie. My sorry ass would be sleeping on a moth-eaten blanket on the floor. In that moment, only one thought flashed in my head:

Seriously. Kill me now.

Of course, our room had to be almost directly across from the office, right in Aunt Kate's unrelentingly suspicious eyeline. This meant we'd have to be incredibly stealth about getting Dad out of the car and into our cabin.

Katie launched back into her General Patton mode that was quickly becoming her very irritating default affect. "You and Mom need to wrap Dad up in the picnic blanket in the way back while I go ask Miss Titty where we should have dinner."

I snapped back that there was only one restaurant in town so why even ask, but Katie jumped down my throat. She said, of course she knew the diner was our only option; that wasn't the point. She wanted to block Aunt Kate's view while Mom and I lugged Dad inside.

Okay, so maybe once in a while she does know what she's talking about.

Fine.

Katie went off on her diversionary mission. Mom and I found a still-more-faded Dad languishing on the back seat with his tongue hanging out. We quickly let him know why we had to wrap him up like some jumbo pig in a blanket. That's what those cocktail weenies rolled in dough are called, right?

Man ... I would love a plate of those about now. Fresh from the oven. Trader Joe's even makes ones where the dough is like an everything bagel. How mofolicious is that?

Hold on. I'm getting sidetracked ....

Anyway, we burritoed Dad into the blanket, hefted him up, and staggered into the room, knocking his poor bird head into the door casing on the way in.

We set him on the bed, and I unwrapped him while Mom bolted into the bathroom to run a tub for him. I don't think she'd even landed both feet on the linoleum before I heard her scream like she was Ichabod Crane encountering the Headless Horseman.

"What?" I yelled.

She was panting. "There's a spider!"

"So? Grab some toilet paper and kill it."

"Toilet paper?" Mom gasped back. "You're gonna need a bazooka!"

Look, I know my mom is a total arachnophobe, but seriously? *Now?* Our focus needed to be on saving Dad. Just kill the fucking eight-legged menace; how tough could it be?

Not wanting to get into some big back-and-forth with her, I jumped off the bed and ran to be her knight in a Hard Rock hoodie.

Wait, are you joking?

The spider she was pointing to was big enough to need a collar and a leash. It was thick and black and might have been a tarantula, but I didn't have time to launch off on a web search to confirm that. I darted back into the bedroom, grabbed the first weapon I saw (which happened to be an ice bucket), and returned to do battle.

Mom was cowering all the way on the far side of the bedroom when I raised the bucket overhead. I pointed the flat bottom toward the wall where the spider was hanging out over the tub and brought the bucket smashing down into it. Several times. This motherfucker was not going to pull some Glenn Close in *Fatal Attraction* shit and come rising back up out of the dead.

Eventually, I did manage to kill that god-awful spider. But I also put a pretty substantial crack in the plasterboard and a major dent in the ice bucket. It didn't take a genius to guess that Aunt Kate would have a major opinion about both those transgressions.

Shit.

Anyway, I disposed of the hairy spider corpse and Mom filled the bathtub for Dad. The instant Katie came back in, I shoved the dented ice bucket in her hands and told her to go fill it to the brim from the ice machine out front.

For once in her life, Katie followed my command without an argument. (A minor miracle.) When she came back, she reported that Aunt Kate had come rushing out to yell at her to be sure she didn't hog all the ice.

"As I informed you earlier," she'd scolded Katie, "I am running at full capacity this evening. Be nice—share the ice."

Later, Katie asked me not to tell Mom because she didn't want to get in trouble, but she confessed that she'd been so over it, she shot right back at Miss Titty: "Hate to be crass, but kiss my ass."

Nice one, sister.

Ya know, if the old bat wasn't running such a jankified motel, we wouldn't have needed ice in the first place. Even though Mom ran only *cold* water into the tub, it was still lukewarm at best, and we had to get it colder to help revive Dad. I hung around out front of our room a bit, stealing glances at Aunt Kate as she sat at the front desk, guzzling a giant can of some cheap-ass energy drink. I figured she'd have to go pee sooner than later, and then I could make a mad dash for more ice.

Heading out to dinner as the sun was setting, with Dad happily soaking in an ice-water tub, all I wanted was a decent meal and an hour devoid of drama. Did I fish my wish?

Fat fucking chance.

I would love it if somebody could explain to me how you can wreck a burger and fries. I mean, the place was a diner. Isn't that pretty much supposed to be the most basic thing they do? It's the whole reason why that was what I ordered.

From the moment we stepped inside, it was pretty clear there hadn't been a single upgrade in decades. The kitchen equipment, the cracked upholstery in the booths patched with black electrical tape, and the desertscape mural on the wall all looked like holdovers from the days of Annie Oakley. It was clear that this was *not* the place to order the "catch of the day" or the chef's special.

My requested well-done burger was pinker than a piglet's butt, and my fries were undercooked and cold. Katie was served a charred grilled cheese deliberately placed on the plate with the browned side up while its hidden bottom was blacker than Ma Rainey's; of course, this was a fact Katie didn't discover until after she took her first bite. Mom ordered the "world famous" pea soup that she said was mostly flour and cream blended with a pauper's portion of frozen peas.

Sorry but I couldn't help myself. While Mom was at the register paying the check, I pulled out a black marker from my jacket pocket and covertly amended the sign on the front door. As we departed, Katie glanced back at my handiwork and offered me an approving high five.

DIS-COMFORT FOOD SERVED 24-HOURS DAILY.

Walking back into the motel parking lot, we instantly knew our shit day was about to slide deeper into the crapper.

Charging out of our cabin with the fury of Mad Madam Mim from *The Sword in the Stone*, Aunt Kate was coming right for us.

Oh shit. So busted.

Before she even opened her frothing mouth, Mom headed her off at the pass.

"Please, we can explain—"

Aunt Kate interrupted. "You can explain why you nearly burned down my entire establishment?"

Mom blinked in confusion. She had assumed—we'd all assumed—that we were about to be called out for violating the "no pets" provision. We had no idea why she was barking at us about a circumvented conflagration.

"I cannot for the life of me figure out why seemingly intelligent folks like yourselves would head out to dinner with a curling iron plugged in."

Mom's face flushed red. She muttered a quiet, contrite, "Oh dear."

Aunt Kate kept going with unabated fury. "I was just settling down to enjoy my Kroger's chicken potpie, when all of a sudden, the smoke alarm in your room began screaming like a teakettle on steroids. Ya left the curling iron up on the metal shelf over the bathroom sink, plugged in and turned on, and the darn thing overheated."

Mom, Katie, and I were holding our breath, waiting for her to get to the part where she kicked our asses to the curb for harboring an against-her-policy penguin ... but she never mentioned Dad.

Mom apologized profusely for her absentmindedness, tried to plead sheer mental exhaustion from our—shout out to Alexander—"*terrible, horrible, no good, very bad day,*" but Aunt Kate was in no mood to be forgiving. She huffed and puffed and bitched about her, by now, stone-cold chicken potpie and then stormed back to her office.

For a moment, the three of us just stood there, gaping at each other in shock. How had she been in the bathroom and not seen Penguin Pop? Breaking free from our inertia, we bolted into our room.

The curling iron was unplugged. The tub was still filled. The dented ice bucket was on the back of the toilet.

But where was Dad?

Katie looked in the closet. Mom looked under the bed. Even though it made no sense, I dashed outside and checked the car. No penguin.

"Oh my God," Katie gasped. "Do you think she called animal control and had Dad hauled away?"

I shook my head at her. "This town doesn't even have its own cop car. I seriously doubt they have animal control."

While Katie and I continued our oral sparring, Mom called out from the bathroom.

"Found him!"

We rushed in to see Dad, contorted and trembling, crammed into the fake-wood cabinet under the bathroom sink. He must've heard that smoke alarm going off and been smart enough to know it was time to skedaddle. How he got those doors shut once he'd burrowed his way into the cupboard, I have no idea, but nice work, Dad. Way to save us from an eviction when we had nowhere else to go.

Mom bent down and coaxed him out of hiding. He was still shaking all over; it seemed like it was hard for him to breathe.

Sitting cross-legged on the warped, yellowed linoleum, Mom pulled the traumatized penguin into her lap and gently rocked him back and forth. Ever so slowly, his raggedy breathing began to chill.

With her eyes closed in some sort of a meditative trance, Mom dipped her head, hummed softly, and gently kissed the top of her penguin husband's head.

KATIE

I'm not saying I for sure believe in ghosts, but that first night in Twin Pines was full-on hectic creepy—I'm not even kidding. If there's no such thing as ghosts, then what the hell was making that moaning noise for, like, a full hour around four a.m.? Charlie said it was the bathroom pipes, but it *so* wasn't coming from there—and anyway, what would he know about any of it? He was too busy grinding his teeth in his sleep from his sad little spot on the floor under the window. He was gnashing so hard, I'm totally shocked he didn't wake up this morning with a mouth full of nubbins.

So I said to him, I go: "Hate to tell you, smart-ass, but Mom heard the moaning too."

It was a complete *woooooo* sound like ghosts make in the movies, and then at one point, it even let out a terrifying shriek.

When I was a way-too-little kid, Charlie made me watch this Disney movie about leprechauns with a banshee that came to take away a dying old Irishman and … I can't even remember what it was called but that whole idea of a banshee coming to get you when you're about to die? Um … excuse me? No thanks.

Wait, where was I? Oh yeah, the moaning-shrieking was exactly like the banshee in that movie. I didn't dare to open my eyes 'cause I thought if there was some freaky Irish spirit in the room, he was probably coming to snatch penguin Dadda out of the bathtub, and I wouldn't have been able to handle it.

In case that wasn't bad enough, there were also trains running all night long. For a reason I will never understand, they were *constantly* blasting their horns. Even, like, way before sunrise. Can somebody please tell me why? What, are there, like, hundreds of runaway cows constantly getting on the tracks or something? People are sleeping, train dudes; why in the world did you have to be blasting that loud and horrible horn?

Between Charlie's teeth grinding, a moaning banshee, and the trains, I think that whole entire night I probably slept fifteen minutes. In case you haven't already figured it out, not sleeping makes me a complete bitch.

The *good* news was the banshee didn't take Dadda because he was still there; the bad news was he was looking full-on grim bones. His little downy feathers were suddenly all thin and gray and his breathing sounded like he was a ninety-year-old with asthma or that COPD shit they talk about in those commercials where the kid thinks his grandpa is the Big Bad Wolf. Mom went to the drugstore down the street to buy salt she could add to his bathwater, thinking that might feel soothing to him. I was praying those goofballs at the gas station would track down our tire ASAP. I knew in my heart we really needed to get poor Dadda into that cold lake the first instant we possibly could.

We were all starving after our crappy dinner the night before. The diner was the only option in town and none of us wanted to go back there. Was the sad little general store going to be our savior? Not exactly, but what choice did we have?

If you ever find yourself in a situation like this, let me give you a tip: instead of getting something like an egg-bacon-and-cheese croissant breakfast sandwich that might've been sitting under a heat lamp since dinosaurs roamed the earth, just put a gun in your mouth and pull the trigger. It's quicker and less painful than what I went through.

About an hour after we ate, Charlie and I were back at the room taking care of Dad while Mom went to the gas station to see if our tire had arrived. I was sitting on the bed, watching *Real Housewives of*

Atlanta on my laptop. Charlie was outside on his phone, fighting with right-wing nutjobs on Facebook. He said the sound of those ladies on my *Housewives* shows make him want to "do a double van Gogh and cut his ears off." Does he always have to be so extra? Seriously.

Anyway, my stomach made this rumbling noise—like when you dump a ton of drain cleaner in the kitchen sink, and then a clog instantly clears. I knew it was my cue to make a thundering beeline for the toilet. I'll try not to be too gross and graphic, but let's just say *explosive* diarrhea would be a massive understatement.

Dadda was in the bathtub, fully submerged, but apparently even being underwater wasn't enough to protect him from my assault to his senses. As I continued to evacuate every single thing in my digestive system, he came rocketing up from below the surface, dove over the side of the tub, and made a mad waddle into the bedroom. A moment later, I saw him swing a flipper to furiously shut the bathroom door.

Sorry, dude.

I sat on the toilet until I was so empty I felt like Flat Stanley. Then the chills started ... and the shakes. I had this unquenchable thirst— like a shit salesman with a mouthful of samples. Oh, and did I mention that I also had really bad cramps?

Seriously, where was that banshee when I needed him?

Charlie came back in to find me sprawled out on the bed; I'm guessing I must've looked pretty pitiful.

"Jesus, what happened to you?" he asked.

My answer was somewhere between a groan and a wail. "Breakfast." And then I raced back into the bathroom and threw up.

When Mom returned an hour later—with the new tire on the car, hallelujah—she took one look at me, my pale face, and my pink watery eyes, and declared what I already knew: "We won't be going anywhere today."

I nodded, burst out crying, and then raced back to reclaim my perch on the porcelain throne. I could see on Charlie's face that he was totally hostile and dying to blame me for ruining everything, but even he knew I was too pathetic and weak to be picked on.

Mom told him to go over to the office and notify Aunt Kate that we were going to need the room for another night.

As incredible as this might sound, he came back five minutes later and told us it was a no go. Our room was already rented to someone else for the next two nights. We had ninety minutes until checkout time and the rest of the cabins were fully booked.

Wait, what?

Who were all these ignorant fools clamoring to spend a night in the wasteland known as Twin Pines? Ghosts, a diner serving shit food, and all-night whistling trains? Wow, talk about a vacation paradise!

While I continued to cramp and dump and shiver, Mom sent Charlie back to the general store to buy two giant jugs of Gatorade—one for me and one for Dad. We didn't really know if he would like it, but we all reasoned that if it was good for keeping humans from dehydrating, it might be good for a shriveling penguin too. Since Charlie was going to the store, Mom instructed him to also pick up several cans of tuna and a bunch of tins of sardines, so we could get Dad fed before we got back on the road.

Mom brought my phone into the bathroom and asked if I could "go on the online" to try to locate another town nearby that might have an available room for us. Her thought was that even though I'd never survive the remaining three hours to Tahoe, I could hopefully make it through a short trek to someplace nearby where she could set me up with a bed and a toilet for my much-needed rest and recovery.

Despite my never-ending efforts to convince her she is a strong and capable woman, there's something about trying to navigate an internet search that sends Mom into rapid meltdown mode. Almost all her efforts end the same way: "I don't know what I hit—I don't know what button I pushed. I swear I did exactly what you told me to do, but the computer hates me. It does. It just hates me."

Inevitably these scenarios end with me, Charlie, or Dad coming to her rescue; sometimes it's just easier to take over and eliminate that middleman named Misery.

Reaching my poop-search-poop stride, I eventually found a place that looked like it might fit our needs: Grover's Glen, California. Eleven and a half miles from Twin Pines. Population 276.

Charlie returned a short time later. I downed a quart of Gatorade; Dad wolfed down two cans of tuna and a stack of sardines and actually seemed to rally a little. He apparently was also really into that Arctic Blitz Gatorade, lapping it up with great vigor. When he was done, he had this little turquoise ring around his beak. He looked so precious I just … I couldn't, I couldn't even from him … he just … seriously!

Since absolutely nothing about our trip was destined to be easy, the next challenge was to pack up and straighten up to eliminate any evidence that a penguin had been in the room. Then we'd have to get Dad into the car undetected by the vigilant and ever-snarling Aunt Kate. With me pretty much out of commission and needing to stay adhered to the toilet until the last possible moment, it was on Mom and Charlie to pull this off. The maids had already started cleaning up the adjacent rooms, only making it that much trickier to execute our Operation Am-scray.

As much as he can really bug the shit out of me, sometimes my brother is hella smart. He came up with the perfect plan to get us out of there.

The first thing he did was open the window that faced the backyard patio area of the motel and hoisted Dad outside. He told him to hang on and then Charlie climbed out to join him. There was this setup with a half-dozen Adirondack chairs and a little table on a stone patio beside a natural firepit like you'd have at a campground. I guess it was so guests could hang out there and chill if they wanted to, but we hadn't seen anybody take advantage of it.

Anyway, Charlie posed Dad in several different ways and took a bunch of pictures on his phone. My brother in full director mode? He couldn't have been happier, and Dad was a more-than-willing actor in Charlie's ploy. Once Charlie had what he needed, he lifted Dad back in through the window and then followed closely behind.

I stayed right by the toilet even though I was pretty sure there was nothing left for me to expel from either end. Mom and Charlie loaded the suitcases and all our other junk into the car, then Mom went over to the office to check out—with Charlie's phone in tow. Coached by her son, she had her full routine down pat. The picnic blanket we'd used to smuggle Dad into the room was spread out on the bed with penguin Dad lolling on top of it. Charlie was perched in the open doorway of our room, waiting for the cue to make his next move.

Later, when we were on the road to Grover's Glen, Mom told us how it had all gone down.

Aunt Kate was at her usual post at the front desk. (Did that woman *ever* take a break?) Mom handed over the room keys and told Aunt Kate we were checking out. And then, by her own account, being as cool as a proverbial cucumber, Mom remarked, "How very unusual that you have a wild penguin on the property. I had no idea they could survive in this sort of climate."

Aunt Kate was shocked enough to bounce up onto her Kmart-sandaled feet.

"We have a *what where?*"

Mom pulled out Charlie's phone and flashed the pictures of Dad frolicking out back, standing up on the table, pooping in the firepit, and dragging a rando pillowcase through the mud.

"You know," Mom said, with a practiced innocence, "that could be quite a liability for you. If a guest gets bitten—or contracts penguin rabies—"

Aunt Kate was aghast. "Is that a thing?"

Mom collected her receipt from Aunt Kate and gave a nonchalant shrug. "I don't actually know, but I doubt if you want to wait to find out."

Aunt Kate bolted into the back room and then came charging out a moment later—toting a shotgun! (What?! Where the hell were we?) Mom was already heading back to our room. Around that time, Charlie told me to hurry to the car and I obeyed. Breezing past all of us, Aunt Kate and her rifle disappeared around the rear of the motel.

Mom and Charlie took the opportunity to swiftly roll Dad up into the picnic blanket, dash with him to the car, and load him in. Just before she climbed into the driver's seat, Mom ran to a maid's cart sitting unattended outside of one of the rooms; she swiftly snatched something off the trolley and hustled back to us. Climbing in behind the wheel, she tossed me a roll of that cheap-shit single-ply toilet paper that's one notch up from sandpaper. "For emergencies," she said.

Mom tells us a lot that if she wasn't born a girl, she would've made a great Boy Scout and I totally know why: say what you want, folks, but Julia Whitaker is *always* prepared.

Driving to Grover's Glen with my butt cheeks clenched together so tight it felt like they'd been hit with a double dose of superglue, I was thankful for the dark clouds rolling in, blanketing the sky. Mom was keeping the temperature in the car in the low sixties, which definitely worked better for Dadda. He was standing up on the back seat behind Mom, with a seat belt stretched from his left shoulder, across his chest, and down to his webbed right foot, gazing out the window. His eyes looked brighter, and his feathers had stopped falling out; maybe he *was* going to survive after all.

I had no idea I was into meditation but, I swear to God, the way I made it through those first six miles was pure Zen mastery. I was breathing and focusing, working to convince myself that I didn't need to use the bathroom.

Until I did.

Charlie was yelling at me to "just hold it." Mom was looking for a place to pull over. I was crossing my legs, moaning, doing panting breaths like I was in labor as I prayed for a turnout. At that moment, we were bordered by nothing but the edge of a mountain with absolutely no shoulder. The other side of the road had a sheer drop-off into a canyon.

How could this be happening?

Finally, we rounded a hairpin turn and there it was: a wide shoulder bordering a big patch of green grass and a cluster of tall trees. Mom saw it the same second I did and swerved into the dirt, throwing the car into park. I grabbed the scratchy toilet paper off the floor, bolted into the coven of pines, and got my sweats down just in time. Squatting like a cavewoman, I let loose.

The next five miles were blessedly uneventful. Passing a weather-beaten sign welcoming us to Grover's Glen, Population 275—I guess somebody had croaked since the last time they updated their website (or maybe somebody new had been born since they updated the sign)—we were greeted by a one-lane wooden bridge. It spanned this rushing river, or stream, or whatever-the-hell, and provided the only way in or out of town.

A sign facing us about twenty yards before the bridge gave strict instructions regarding how to navigate it: four cars at a time were allowed to pass in one direction. If necessary, you had to wait for four cars coming the other way first; then the cycle would repeat. Despite my cramps and general discomfort, I had to laugh. We were in the middle of nowhere on a road with a single purpose: to take you in or out of Grover's Glen. Was there seriously *ever* a time when you were likely to encounter four cars in a row in either direction? I couldn't imagine it, but as we approached the bridge, fortunately our Lexus SUV was the only vehicle in sight.

That still didn't keep Mom from being a total nervous wreck. "What if somebody comes from the other direction?"

"As long as you're on the bridge first, you have the right-of-way," Charlie said. "Gun it!"

Of course, Mama did the exact opposite. She inched the car onto those rumbling wooden planks so slowly, it felt like we were barely moving. There was something about rolling so gradually that made it seem even more likely that we were going to be the ones to cause that ancient bridge to finally collapse.

Luckily, we weren't.

We got safely to the other side and found ourselves in a tiny town that was so cute and charming, it was like we'd traveled back in time. (I'm sure Charlie instantly would've had some analogous, obscure movie reference, but I was happy not to poke that cage.)

Keeping my attention riveted on the GPS on my phone, I told Mom that the Enchanted Inn was 1.6 miles dead ahead.

I'm not even kidding: Grover's Glen was the yin to Twin Pines's yang. Wait … that's how you use that expression, right? One is the direct opposite of the other?

Anyway, everything that had felt tacky and tired about our last stop was bright and inviting in this new place. The Enchanted Inn appeared to be exactly what the name promised. It was a bright-yellow, two-story clapboard building with pumpkin-orange shutters on all the windows. The roof was made of bright-green shingles; the sign over the archway entrance was hand painted in a fancy, swirling black font, like something you'd see in New Orleans Square at Disneyland. We'd made a reservation before we ever left Twin Pines and were promised a two-bedroom suite with two bathrooms, a king bed in one room, and a pair of twin beds in the other. Nobody was going to have to sleep on the floor. And, best of all, it advertised itself to be pet friendly!

Mom parked in one of the guest spots near the office, then she and I went in to get us registered. We left Charlie in the car with Dad. As soon as we entered, ever-on-it Mom spotted a bathroom and nodded her chin in that direction to make sure I saw it too. Turning my head from it to the front desk, my jaw literally dropped open; I could feel my face fully turning bright red when I realized I was gawking.

Okay, so if the last place had been run by Dom DeLuise in drag, the guy behind this desk was like if George Clooney, Robert Pattinson, and that dude from *Normal People* all mashed their DNA together to make a baby who was now standing there in front of us. Even Mom was totally giddy trying to talk to him. I mean, it's one thing to see guys like that jogging around L.A., but out here in the middle of absolutely nowhere? Oh, and did I mention his body was, like … how do you say … stunning? Seriously. Plus he had long hair that was pulled back on both sides—Thor status. Then the final little detail to die for? He opened his mouth and out came a deep Clooney voice with a little growl in it.

Are you joking?

After we were signed in and did the credit-card thing, Mom put on her most ingratiating smile. "Now, I know your website says you take pets, but I did want you to know our pet is … well … he's a wee bit … *exotic*."

Sexy Man looked intrigued.

Mom cut right to the chase. "He's a penguin."

Sexy Man laughed and gave a dimpled smile. "A penguin you say?"

Mom nodded and we both braced ourselves for what was inevitably coming next.

"Cool! May I meet him? He sounds awesome. By the way, my name's Archer."

Of course it is.

Archer came out to the car with Mom and me. I could see Charlie tensing up, expecting a whole ration of trouble, but Archer just tugged open the back door next to where Dad was standing up on the seat and gave a throaty chuckle, accompanied by that dazzling, dimpled grin.

"Hey, little buddy." Archer beamed. "What the heck are you doing in Grover's Glen?"

After Archer helped us schlep all our stuff into our first-floor room tucked into a quiet back corner of the place, I told Mom my belly was feeling *so* much better, but now I was starving. Spooked by our twin culinary disasters in Twin Pines, I was understandably nervous, wanting to be sure to chart the best course to reconcile my dueling desires.

Asking a few relevant questions to bring himself up to speed, it was Archer to the rescue once again. I seriously didn't even care if he was offering good advice; I just wanted him to keep talking so I could keep gazing at him.

With all of us crammed in this room and the windows shut tight, don't you think it's getting hot in here, Archer? Maybe you should take off your shirt.

Wait. Easy, girl. Get a grip.

Snapping myself back to reality, I heard him tell Mom that the Wander Inn, a little mom-and-pop café down the street, had the best homemade chicken soup in the state. He looked at me with those perfect brown eyes and said, "I guarantee ya it's the ideal remedy for a recovering tummy."

I believe you, Archer. I so do.

"Listen," he said, "I'll make you a deal."

Yes, please.

He gave another deep-dimpled grin and went on. "Why don't you guys go grab lunch and leave Little Buddy here with me. We've got a pool out back that no one's taking advantage of right now. He can get in a nice cool swim while I keep an eye on him."

When Mom asked how he could do that and still man the front desk, Archer whipped out his phone and pulled up the Ring-camera app.

"Anytime someone steps foot in the office, this baby'll lemme know and I can go tend to them. Your penguin's cool to be alone for five to ten while I do my duty, right?"

We agreed that Dadda would be fine. All Archer wanted in return was for us to bring him back a Reuben sandwich from the Wander Inn.

"Just tell Harold and Phyllis it's for me, and they'll put it on my tab."

Jeez, this place really was straight out of a fairy tale. "Harold and Phyllis." "Put it on my tab." Had we gone over the rainbow?

The next thing I was expecting was for him to tell us that we'd better look out for the troll living under that rickety one-lane bridge.

We went around back with Archer to get Dad situated in the pool and told him we'd return in about an hour.

"Hey, by the way," Archer called out to us, "does this little guy have a name?"

We all hesitated for a beat before Mama piped right up. "We call him Clark. Like Clark Kent 'cause he's our little Superman."

Damn, Mom. Smooth.

Like Twin Pines, everything in Grover's Glen was within walking distance so Mom, Charlie, and I ambled off to grab a late lunch.

Okay, so when you first heard me mention Harold and Phyllis who run a mom-and-pop café called the Wander Inn, I'll bet you were picturing a couple that looks like those farmers in *American Gothic*, right? Ya know, the granny-bun-and-pitchfork duo? But that's not what you get in Grover's Glen.

I swear to God—Harold and Phyllis? All I could think about was Jon Hamm and Gal Gadot in that movie where they play married spies who move in next door to Zach Galifianakis. (By the way,

did you know her name is pronounced "ga-*dot,*" not "ga-dough?"
Weird, right?)

*Oh God, I really had been spending way too much time with Charlie; I was
literally turning into him.*

Okay, so seeing them there behind the counter, standing next to
each other to greet us with the warmest and sweetest "Welcome" (him)
and "How are you today?" (her), I turned to Mom and whispered,
"I'm sure! What is this, Village of the Hotties?"

In-sane.

Not surprisingly, the chicken soup was beyond delicious and the
exact right thing for my recovering tummy. Charlie had a bacon-
mushroom-swiss cheeseburger that looked like it was crafted by the
gods; Mom had a chorizo-and-black-bean salad that smelled like
heaven on a flour tortilla. Harold and Phyllis were adorable and
hilarious. They got the biggest kick out of the fact that we'd been
requested to bring a Reuben back to Archer.

"That boy could charm the rust off a weather vane," Phyllis said.

I don't know what got into me, but I blurted out, "Is he married?"

Charlie sneered and then embarrassed me so bad I could've died.
"Even if he's not, you dumbass, I'm guessing he's probably not into
fifteen-year-olds."

For the second time in a few hours, I blushed from my toes
to my topknot. I swear to God, if I hadn't been so weak from my
massive blowout, I would have lunged across the table and smacked
Charlie stupid.

While Phyllis was waiting on a cute teenage couple in a corner
booth, Harold hung around, chatting with us. He told us about the
Fireman's Carnival that would be happening that evening at dusk in
the church parking lot; he practically insisted we check it out.

"It's our biggest charity event of the year, raising funds for the co-
op preschool that most of our town's kiddos attend. I gotta tell ya, we
really do it up right: carnival games, a Ferris wheel, Tilt-A-Whirl,
pony rides for the tots …."

Phyllis reappeared beside our table to gleefully add, "And best of
all, the clown in the dunk tank is this guy right here. What could

be more fun than throwing beanbags at a target if you know you're gonna get to drop his pretty butt into a tank of freezing water!"

Harold laughed and gave her a sweet kiss on the cheek.

I was dead. Seriously. I couldn't even handle it. The whole place was totes adorbs.

We finished up, collected Archer's "to-go" Reuben, paid the check, and promised Harold and Phyllis we'd see them at the carnival that night.

"Save your appetites," Harold called out after us. "Phyllis will be serving her famous fried chicken and sweet-potato fries; nothing better on the whole West Coast."

By the time we got back to the hotel, the temperature had climbed into the low eighties; Charlie and I hurried to get into our bathing suits so we could join Dadda in the pool.

You know that old saying "Be careful what you wish for?" Well, let me add this to that: *no shit!*

Archer was stretched out in a chaise with his shirt off, acting like a lifeguard for the frolicking penguin in his pool. I couldn't look directly at him for fear I'd turn into a pillar of salt like that lady in the Bible. I'm not even joking. The man was so perfect it was unnatural.

Mom gave him his Reuben, which he happily devoured while Charlie and I got into the water. Mom said she was going back to the room to give Nonnie a check-in call. I tried to tell her that no news was good news and that she should just let them be. She nodded like she agreed and then went back to the room anyway, obvi blowing me off.

There was a pink rubber mat in the pool that I stretched out on so I could float with my eyes closed to keep from giving Archer my thirsty stare. Charlie was doing laps, furiously trying to burn off the energy that used to get consumed by smashing with Amy. Dad was bobbing and splashing, repeatedly diving for the floppy rubber fish Archer kept throwing for him. The way the two of them were playing together was precious to the tenth power and beyond. Seriously.

I heard Archer call out to me. "So how is it you guys came to be in possession of this penguin anyway?"

Oh shit.

What was I supposed to say? I couldn't exactly tell him the penguin was my dad.

This was when I really needed Charlie and his improv skills. "Actually, we didn't find him—he found us."

Okay … and …

I rolled on the rubber float like I was turning to face Archer and purposely made myself spill into the water, so I could buy some time to concoct my story. When I surfaced, grabbing for my sunglasses and slapping them back onto my face, I smiled in Archer's general direction without making exact eye contact; ya know, so his beauty didn't melt me.

"He … we … you see … apparently his family abandoned him, and he was feeling lonely and neglected so he … he must've escaped from his habitat and, we … well, we just sorta found him and took him in. Who wouldn't, right?"

When I get nervous, I start talking a million miles an hour and hope nobody notices.

"He's been with us since the end of May, but we know he needs a cooler climate and a place to really thrive so there's this … it's … it's like, um, you know … a penguin habitat-slash-shelter in Lake Tahoe that we found and that's where we're taking him so he can … you get it … be happy and not die from heat exposure."

Right then, a little kid, about six or so, and his mom came into the pool area and, thank God, shifted the focus to save me from any more questions. Not surprisingly, when the boy saw Dadda, he went wild. He raced to the edge of the pool, dancing and clapping as he cried out, "Penguin, Mommy! It's a penguin!"

The mother looked to Archer and began to ask fifty questions at once. She wanted to know if the penguin was friendly, if it was safe to have him in the pool, if it was sanitary, how did Archer know he wouldn't poop in the water … on and on. The boy, whose name was Ralph—hilarious for a little kid, true?—didn't care about any of her questions or the answers. He just took a leap into the water and made a splashing, dog-paddling beeline for Dad.

To no one's surprise, Archer had a whole bucket of those rubber fish. For the next hour, Ralph, Charlie, Dad, and I played a rowdy game of toss and catch, flinging the colorful fake flounders back and forth until we were all exhausted.

The sun was shining, the water was warm, and my tummy had completely settled. Dad was energized and clearly having a blast.

It turned out that the Enchanted Inn in this enchanting village was exactly what the doctor—veterinarian?—had ordered.

JULIA

I can already hear your next question: How did we end up in this tiny town, bringing a penguin to a Fireman's Carnival?

The answer is simple: Archer.

He absolutely insisted that his friends and neighbors would love having my penguin husband there; he didn't see any reason why Clark should be stuck alone in the hotel room while the rest of us went off to have fun. To be supersafe, he lent us a collar and leash that belonged to his hound dog, Elvis, and suggested we keep the penguin tethered so he didn't get lost or freaked out by the crowd.

Inspired by Karamo from *Queer Eye*, Katie took her favorite bright, purple L.A. Dodgers cap and tugged it onto the penguin's head. When I asked her why, she responded like I was an imbecile.

"What do you mean, why? Check out how insanely cute he looks."

Hearing this, the penguin waddled over to the mirror on the wall, gazed at himself, puffed out his chest, and then turned to slap a high-five flipper into his daughter's raised hand.

Charlie emerged from the bathroom a minute later, trailed by the overwhelming scent of Axe body spray that nearly knocked Katie and I off our feet. His sister told him he smelled like a rent boy from Thailand.

"How the hell do you know about rent boys?" he barked.

"You're not the only one in this family who reads, ya know. And I actually read things other than Stephen King novels and Hollywood biographies."

Charlie's sophisticated response was to flip her the two-handed bird. "Hey, you're the one who said we're in the Village of the Hotties," he snapped. "Keep up or shut up, that's my motto."

I don't know why I'm surprised, but the minute we strolled into that gigantic church parking lot with its adjacent wide green lawn hosting a noisy, colorful carnival in full swing, it felt like every eye in Grover's Glen drilled down on the penguin in the purple baseball cap.

Kids, especially, came rushing at him. Phones were flashing, people were laughing and pointing. Charlie and Katie were asking everybody to step back to give him a little air. I was feeling completely overwhelmed, but Clark seemed to be adoring the adulation.

Inevitably, it was Archer to the rescue once again. Since he seemed to know every one of the town's 275 residents, he whipped the unruly mob into a much more manageable state of calm with a few dimpled pleas and throaty chuckles.

"Okay, Clyde, you need to move back and let the bird breathe. You, too, Scooter. I'm watching you, Lola. You want a picture with him, Debbie Sue? Line up behind Ezra and wait your turn."

After the frenzy subsided and the townies began to coo over Clark from a more respectful distance, Archer finally had a moment to introduce us to his girlfriend, Imani. Glancing at my daughter, I could tell she could hardly believe what she was seeing.

Imani was almost as tall as Archer and was—to borrow a trick from my kids—a perfect incarnation of a baby made from the DNA of Lupita Nyong'o and Amanda Gorman. (Please don't show your ignorance; Amanda's the National Youth Poet Laureate who delivered that incredible poem at Joe Biden's inauguration.) Imani's body was the female equivalent of Archer's proportions of perfection, and she wore a white cinched-waist sundress with a matching wide-brimmed hat. To be honest, I had to blink a few times to convince myself she wasn't a page out of *Vogue* come to life. She told us that she and Archer were about to head over to partake of Phyllis's famous fried chicken and sweet-potato fries, and insisted we join them.

Well, why not?

Sitting at a long picnic table covered in a red-and-white checkered cloth, I couldn't figure out how my life had turned into a Norman Rockwell painting. Clark was up on the bench beside me, gobbling down the plate of fried calamari rings that Archer had procured for him. Katie and Charlie were sitting across from me, both face deep in their platters of chicken, fries, and coleslaw, as content as I had seen them in ages.

I forget if I've told you this before, but I've been a devout WeightWatchers member for the past fifteen years. I've struggled with my weight my entire life, but when I lost forty unneeded pounds at the start of my current journey a decade and a half ago, I swore I would never again put them back on. And I haven't.

One of the ways I've been able to have this consistency is to allow myself occasional cheat days: a cocktail or two on the weekends, but never during the week; Saturday-night desserts; and, on very special occasions like that evening at the carnival, I dive into a full-throttle Fuck It Day.

The funny thing is, I honestly don't care about fried food. Clark adores it—fried chicken, fish-and-chips, fried shrimp. To me, it mostly seems greasy and sickening. (If Katie was doing her impersonation of me, she'd tell you I think it's "SICK'ning!") But whatever Phyllis did to that chicken—if I hadn't been seated across from my children, I probably would have unleashed the all-out food orgasm it warranted.

Around us as we ate, families were strolling, laughing, and having picnics on the lawn. Some folks were setting up their folding chairs in front of the gazebo where, soon, the high-school band was going to begin a program of American anthems and show tunes. Kids and their parents waited in lines for the Ferris wheel and the Tilt-A-Whirl, happily chatting with their neighbors ahead of and behind them. The arcade games—balloon darts, a shooting gallery, the ring toss—each had a line of patient patrons awaiting their turn to win a stuffed Daffy Duck or rubber whoopee cushion. The sinking sun was sending streaks of pink and orange across the pale-blue sky, occasionally bisecting a cluster of marshmallow clouds.

After the many months of tension and strain, that truly was a bliss-laden respite.

As we were finishing dinner, literally gnawing on the chicken bones to devour every last morsel of scrumptiousness, Phyllis came floating over to us in her bright-yellow dress dappled with splashes of red like a Jackson Pollock painting.

"I had the most marvelous idea," she said. "Watching the way everyone has been going crazy over your penguin, do you think he'd mind doing a little fundraising for the preschool co-op?"

I asked her what she was thinking, and she gestured across the lawn to where a photo booth had been set up. It was surrounded by bins of funny hats and wigs, boas, and vintage vests, with an old-time background for people to pose in front of. Phyllis thought that if the carnival goers were willing to pay a dollar per picture, certainly they'd pay double that to pose with the penguin.

To Katie, it sounded like a wonderful idea; she volunteered to be Clark's chaperone.

Okay, I'll come clean: my first thought was that this plan could provide me with the perfect cover to sneak off into the nearby glade of trees and catch a teeny-tiny buzz.

Don't judge me!

I had been so good and so stressed and so devoted to my kids and my penguin husband but, c'mon—out there in the middle of that rural paradise with a band about to play "Yankee Doodle Dandy," and "Till There Was You" from *The Music Man*? What could possibly be more fun than getting stoned before listening to that all-American music while eating a bag of cheat-day caramel corn?

With Katie and Clark gathering a flock of fans eager to nab a penguin photo, and Charlie wanting to try his luck at the midway games, I made my move. I told the kids I needed ten minutes to check in on Nonnie, and that I'd find them upon my return. Constantly peering over my shoulder, I did a quick dart across the lawn. Taking one last glance to make sure the coast was clear, I disappeared into the grove of poplar trees.

Secure in my seclusion, I pulled out the throat-lozenge tin that houses the joints I keep rolled and ready. (This was a recent innovation after I realized the little silk coin purse from Chinatown I used to carry was useless when it came to effectively camouflaging the pungent smell.)

I fired up the doobie, got it burning past the paper and glue, and took a deep, luxurious inhale.

Oh. My. God. YES! Thank you, Jesus.

Blowing out the smoke, I hadn't realized how badly I'd needed this chance to unwind. After the second hit, I could feel my shoulders relax and the knot in my neck begin to loosen. I took a few more tokes, then extinguished the joint and stood in silence as the sun sank farther into the horizon.

The sounds of the joy-filled carnival were constant and comforting. There was a warm breeze rocking the branches overhead. I felt like I might burst into tears of joy and gratitude.

I took a glug from the travel-size bottle of mouthwash that also has a permanent home in my purse, then checked in my hand mirror to make sure there was no evidence snagged between my teeth. I inhaled and exhaled a few times to calm my leaping heart.

Preparing to move back out onto the lawn, I suddenly stopped. If my joint had been extinguished for more than five minutes, why was I still smelling pot? I looked up to see a snake of smoke wending my way. I wasn't alone! A fellow stoner had had the exact same idea. I was about to meet one of my brethren. As one who always enjoys communing with fellow lovers of the wacky tobacky, I couldn't wait to make the acquaintance of the Grover's Glen resident who shared my private passion.

I slowly wandered toward the smell that was calling me. Coming around the trunk of a mighty oak thriving amid the poplars, there he was with his back to me. The only problem?

He wasn't some local stranger. He was my son.

"Charlie?"

He jumped so furiously, it looked like he'd been launched off a catapult; he spun to face me, a stubby roach still clutched between his fingers.

"Mom! What the fuck? What are you doing out here?" It was a crossroads moment for me as a parent.

I was perfectly within my rights to come up with some cockamamie lie. But he was a high-school graduate. He was going off to college in a few months. I didn't want to lose my credibility with him. I didn't want to be a hypocrite. (Well, part of me did, but I opted for the truth.)

"I was doing the same thing you are."

I would pay just about all the money in the world if someone had been there with a camera to capture the look on my son's face. It was as if I'd just told him Santa Claus was real. He wasn't shocked. He wasn't angry. He was ... delighted. Absolutely tickled.

"Are you shitting me?" He laughed. "You were out here getting high?"

I nodded.

He rushed at me and gave me a hug. A real hug, a tight and loving hug. I couldn't remember the last time I had felt an embrace like that from my son. He laughed again.

"That's awesome."

"But you can't tell Katie, okay?" I begged. "She needs a few more years to let her brain cells gel. It would be hard to tell her not to do something I do. I mean ... how long have you been smoking pot?"

"Since freshman year. But not all the time. Actually, Gregory and I would rather steal beers from his parents' basement refrigerator. They never keep track. Plus, Amy was totally against booze and drugs. Just so you know, I never drink and drive or drive when I'm high; I'm, like, a responsible idiot so that's one thing you don't have to worry about."

"That's reassuring. Thanks."

I exhaled again and beamed at my boy.

"So what do you say we keep our secret and head back to share one of those big-ass bags of caramel corn?"

Casually strolling into the thick of the action, Charlie and I saw a bunch of people gathered near the Ferris wheel, laughing and pointing into the sky. Following their fingers we spied Katie and Clark, still sporting his purple Dodgers cap, in one of the swaying seats on the ride. They were stopped at the very top as it let off disembarking passengers below. The penguin's flippers were curled around the safety bar, but he was gazing out over the area as Katie leaned into him. She was laughing as she pointed out various sights around the grounds; I knew she was most likely making fun of everyone in range with the kind of hilarious social critiques that always enchanted her dad. When the ride started up again with a disconcerting jerk, she screamed, he squawked, and then my daughter was once again laughing hysterically. Spotting Charlie and I down below as they made their rickety descent—I couldn't even start to let myself imagine how unsafe these ancient rides probably were—Katie blew us kisses as Clark waved his wings.

"Well, *they* obviously couldn't be happier," Charlie said. "So let's ditch their butts and go get that caramel corn!"

★★★

Later, with the band in full swing, the kids wanted to go take a turn throwing beanbags to drop Harold (who was sporting a full, ridiculous clown costume) into the dunk tank. I told them I'd happily take Clark with me over to the music pagoda. It was a plan that worked for everybody.

Finding an open spot on the lawn near the bandstand, stoned, happy, and leading my penguin husband on the borrowed leash, I felt like a character in some turn-of-the-twentieth-century romance novel.

Just so you know, I'm a sucker for marching songs and overblown patriotic anthems. I always have been. Clark and I were married outdoors on the Fourth of July, for heaven's sake. When those young white musicians with their red cheeks and blue balls started playing "Stars and Stripes Forever" and then, moments into it, fireworks began to explode overhead, I was truly in heaven.

I was staring up into the night sky, grinning from ear to ear as tears were freely flowing down my face. The penguin waddled up to press himself against my side and threw a comforting wing across my shoulder.

In my periphery vision, I could see a slew of phone cameras suddenly swing in our direction. Like it or not, I was pretty sure we would be going viral.

Katie and Charlie came back to find us a short time later, giddy with tales of how they'd each hit the bull's-eye more than once, sending Harold, his curly-haired purple clown wig, and his soggy derby down into the tub of cold water; all the while, an adoring yet slightly sadistic Phyllis stood by, cheering them on.

"Oh my God," Katie said, "have you been seeing those ginormous waffle cones going by all night? C'mon, Mama, let's go get some ice cream."

Luckily, Charlie had bogarted the lion's share of the caramel corn we were allegedly sharing, so an ice-cream cone sounded like the perfect nightcap for my Fuck It Day.

Sitting together on a picnic-table bench near the ice-cream stand, the four of us had found nirvana. Not thinking it was fair to deprive Clark, Katie was holding a cone of vanilla for him in her left hand while going to town on her own cone of chocolate in her other hand. Charlie had some double-scoop Rocky Road on top, and salted caramel peanut butter on the bottom—with chocolate sprinkles. I was over the moon with my single scoop of coffee chip in a cup. Even on a Fuck It Day, you don't have to be a total pig.

Archer and Imani wandered up to us, and he instantly whipped out his phone. "Oh, this is an image I have to capture. I don't think I've *seen* four more-ecstatic faces. Seriously. If Clark had a longer tail, he'd be wagging it."

Archer darted out in front of us, dropped down onto one knee, and took a series of shots that, to this day, contain one of my favorite family photos of all time. If you can manage to look past the fact that our patriarch is a penguin, it's the very essence of familial bliss. We're pressed shoulder to shoulder, cones in hand, beaming.

The joy of the moment was disrupted by a sizzling bolt of lightning cleaving the night sky. In my convivial state, I guess I'd failed to notice the billowing, dark clouds that had rolled in. A second flash of lightning was joined moments later by a crashing boom of thunder.

The locals seemed to all get the message at once; they swiftly began making their way toward their cars in the large lot.

Archer looked to us with a knowing smile as an even louder and closer thunderclap drowned out his first few words. He was telling us that in Grover's Glen, it was usually a very short time between the initial warning shots of lightning and thunder, and the inevitable summer downpour. Knowing we'd walked to the church from the hotel, he and Imani offered to give us a ride back. Before we could voice our acceptance, the skies opened up and a pounding rain began. People were darting in every direction. Folks collected their blankets and folding chairs. The rides were shut down. The food stands began packing up. The lightning cracked, the thunder boomed, and the rain bounced back up off the steaming pavement, releasing the heat of the day.

I envisioned us being trapped in the snarl of departing traffic for the next hour or so, but I'd clearly forgotten who was leading us. Of course, Archer the Magical had deliberately parked his vintage Jeep on the shoulder of the road outside the parking lot so he wouldn't be hemmed in. Soaked to the skin, we piled into his waiting chariot and were back at our room five minutes later.

We thanked him profusely and then, getting drenched even more, made a beeline into our room with Clark waddling at our heels.

Once inside, Katie and I took turns in the primary bathroom to change out of our wet clothes while Charlie went into the second bedroom to put on dry and comfy sweats.

As we caught our breath and towel dried our hair, Katie raced to her open bag across the room.

"I have an idea! Let's play UNO."

She pulled out the specialty deck and scorepad. Charlie said it wasn't fair that Clark couldn't play, but Katie adamantly disagreed.

"Sure he can. I'll draw the cards for him, and lean them up against this without looking." She reached over, grabbed the hardback novel she'd brought along, and set it up, tent-style, as an easel for Clark's cards before she went on. "And then he can use his beak to push out the ones he wants to play each round."

Clark bobbed his head in firm agreement. There was a blindingly bright splinter of lightning and a simultaneous heart-jumping explosion of thunder that let us know the storm was directly overhead. The rain pelting the sidewalk outside our room sounded like the raucous applause of fifty thousand fans at Dodger stadium.

"Man," Charlie said, "I don't think we've had a storm like this in L.A. in ten years."

"Thank you, climate change," Katie added.

While our Uno game progressed, with plenty of trash-talking and ferocious, competitive barbs flying back and forth between my children, I noticed Clark kept taking curious glances out the rear window. He seemed excited, agitated. The lightning and thunder had begun to recede, but the pounding rain wasn't letting up.

Katie's score hit three hundred points, sending her bouncing to her feet, shaking her clenched fists above her head as she did a victory jig. As she proudly and loudly declared herself "the Uno Champion of the Universe," Clark went gliding to the door and knocked a flipper against it, signaling he wanted to go outside.

"Where do you think you're going, Mister?" I asked.

He pointed a wing forward in a perfectly clear indication that he wished to leave the room. I reminded him that it was teeming, but that only prompted him to point more insistently.

I looked to the kids, confused. "It's not like he has to go out there to pee or poop. He's been using the toilet since this craziness started."

Katie reasoned that if he was being that adamant, he probably had a mission in mind; she darted over and opened the door for him. Clark happily rushed out into the rain. Feeling protective, Katie nabbed the courtesy umbrella hanging from the antique coatrack near the door. (No shock there; Archer thought of everything.)

Katie trailed her father outside. Not the least bit invested in any of this, Charlie flopped onto the bed and asked permission to rent a movie.

A few minutes later, hearing Katie's excited voice coming from the rear of the hotel, I dashed to the back window. On the far side of the pool where Clark had been frolicking earlier in the day, there was a small hill with a stand of pine trees at its crest. Down the slope of it, there was some sort of plastic-lined drainage ditch that was now brimming with rainwater and mud. Obviously, this was what Clark had been eyeing out the window; with Katie cheering him on, laughing, and clapping, he was turning it into his own personal Slip 'N Slide.

I called over to Charlie who was already getting sucked into one of those endless *Lord of the Rings* movies he adored. (Why, I will never know.) "You have to come see this," I insisted.

He grudgingly joined me at the window. Clark was waddling back up the little hill, then positioning himself at the top of the drainage ditch. He backed up several steps and took a running start before lunging forward and flopping onto his belly; he went swiftly sliding down with his flippers flapping in unfettered elation. Seconds later, I saw Katie toss aside the umbrella, tug off her tennis shoes, and step out of her sweatpants. In her bikini briefs and T-shirt, she ran up the hill right behind Clark and prepared to take her turn on this improvised ride.

"Holy shit! I wanna do that," Charlie declared. "C'mon, Mom—come with me!"

I told my son he was crazy; he said that was the whole point.

"We're in a tiny town in the middle of Who-Knows-Where-the-Fuck with my father who's a penguin. What part of this is *not* crazy? We might as well make the most of it."

"What if it's freezing out there? What if we catch colds? What if somebody slips and breaks a leg?"

Charlie stared at me for a long beat, shrugged one shoulder, and then looked me directly in the eye. "Or ... what if we end up having a seriously awesome time?"

Maybe it was the weed. Maybe it was the infusion of Americana at the carnival. Maybe it was a pent-up need to surrender control and be spontaneous. Whatever it was, I got undressed and put on my (brand new, really cute) bathing suit and followed Charlie out into the rain.

Seeing us, Katie did a laughing, clapping jig of joy and raced over to give me a hug.

"Oh my God! I can't believe you're joining us, Mama! This is, like, the funnest night ever."

The more we slid down that chute, the more it filled with mud washing in from the saturated hillside. We were getting filthy. Sludge was finding its way into orifices it had no business invading. The rain continued to pound down, and I was chilled to the bone yet warmed by our shared exuberance. It was a glorious moment. An instantly treasured memory. An exploit I know the four of us will cherish and replay for years.

Occasionally, age does have its advantages. Returning to the room, mud-caked and exhausted, I told my kids I had first dibs on the shower. Since the back bathroom only had a tub, Katie was content to wait, busily texting blurry pictures of our nature-made waterslide adventure to Ori. With *Lord of the Rings* still playing on the TV, Charlie was in no rush to do much of anything.

When finally, we were all cleaned up and warmed up, we were still too revved up to sleep. Once again, it was my former-camp-counselor daughter who devised the perfect plan. After returning to her surprise-laden suitcase, she came toward Charlie, Clark, and me with something hidden behind her back.

"Guess what I brought." She grinned.

Charlie was ready. "Hopefully it's a foot-long meatball sub, 'cause I'm starving."

"Not even close."

She whipped her hands around in front of her to reveal original copies of the first two books in Clark's *Cow on the Lam* series. Seeing them, I had this rush of the too-numerous-to-count times we'd read those books to the kids when they were little.

"What're we supposed to do with those?" Charlie sneered.

"Read them! Like we used to. I think we should all get in the bed and have Mom read them to us." Then she looked to me. "But you have to do the funny voices like Dad always did."

"Sure, we can do that," Charlie grumbled. "But I'd still rather have a meatball sub."

Dashing over to my own suitcase, I dug into an unpacked compartment. "Well, your sister's not the only one with the Mary Poppins bag of tricks. Will you settle for popcorn?"

I whipped out the two packets of microwave popcorn I'd brought along and took great pride in seeing the love-filled gratitude radiating from my son's face.

Charlie claimed one bag of popcorn for himself, Katie and I shared the other. We snuggled together in the king-sized bed, with Katie and Charlie on either side of me; Clark was on Charlie's far side. I read *Cow on the Lam*, dutifully performing all the various character voices the way Clark had for the kids when they were young. Charlie took over to perform a hilarious recitation of the sequel, *Raising the Steaks*.

We talked about how much we loved those books. We talked about how cool it was that their father had written things that were so beloved by their entire generation. We laughed over some of the lines and memorable supporting characters. We couldn't help but reflect on the wonderful, blessed life Clark's creativity had provided for us.

I don't want to bust him or anything, but I'm pretty sure I saw my penguin husband swipe a flipper across his face to brush away a tear.

Although it seemed like it rained all night, the sun was up by the time we were.

Due to Charlie's teeth grinding and Clark's ragged penguin breathing, Katie and I had relegated the boys to the twin beds in the adjoining room while we happily shared the king in the main room. Following our busy day of carnival exploration, mud sliding, and bedtime stories, all of us had slept like proverbial babies.

(To be honest, that expression never made any sense to me. Most babies I've known sleep like shit, getting up to cry or be fed every few hours.)

Aware that checkout time was eleven, we decided to do some preliminary packing and organizing before we headed back to the Wander Inn for breakfast. Our clothes from the previous night were still soaking wet, so I was in the bathroom trying to wring as much water from them as I could when there was a knock on our hotel-room door. Katie, who was putting away the Uno cards and *Cow on the Lam* books, got there first. From the bathroom, I heard her giddy, lyrical "Good morning, you" and instantly knew it had to be Archer. I came out of the bathroom to see what was up.

Was he purposely trying to drive Katie and I mad? There he was, in tight running shorts and a sleeveless muscle tee, looking like he was heading to a photo shoot for the cover of *Men's Health*. His dark hair was floppy with sweat, one lock of it curling on his forehead with the rest of it plastered to the back of his neck, reaching down to his glistening shoulders.

"So ...," he started, "I've got good news and bad news."

Instantly I braced myself.

Was it totally impossible for our bliss to last one more day?

"As ya know, that was a pretty gnarly rainstorm last night and, well, I was just out for my morning run and got word that the bridge is out."

Out? What did he mean "out"? Like it left? Went for a walk? Went to visit its Mother Bridge in Brooklyn?

Charlie spoke up before I could. "So we're trapped?"

"Pretty much. Nobody'll be going anywhere for at least a day or two. First the stream flooded and washed over the bridge, then a couple of the central planks got swept away and, well, since that narrow little sucker is the only way in or out of Grover's Glen ... it's looking like you're stuck with us for a while longer."

"I don't mean to be rude," I said, "but what could possibly be the good news?"

"Since none of this is any fault of yours," Archer said with a smile, "I'm giving you another night in your room for free. And it's supposed to get pretty hot this afternoon, so please take full advantage of the pool if Clark needs some cooling down."

After our round of lavish thanks, Archer excused himself, off to alert the other patrons who had planned on checking out.

It was at that moment my phone rang. The caller ID showed the slightly cockeyed, grinning face of my sister-in-law, Lobotomized Wife. Gazing at it, I muttered to the kids, "This can't be good."

It wasn't.

How is it that some people make it past forty but still insist on behaving like children? LW didn't even bother to say hello before she blurted, "When are you coming home?"

"I have no idea. We're stuck in some tiny town with a washed-out bridge and no other way of escaping. What's going on?"

LW told me my mother and brother were in the kitchen, trying to plan the night's dinner menu; they were locked in a furious, protracted shouting match over the proper way to make a meat loaf.

In case I haven't told you this before, the two of them are the most stubborn, bossy, and opinionated people you'll ever meet. He's a Taurus—you know, the bull—and she's a Leo, the man-eating lion. Half of my childhood was spent listening to the two of them argue over the most inane topics, from the "right" way to open a bag of pretzels to whether Robert Mitchum or John Wayne was the better actor. (Are you kidding me? They both stunk.)

I asked LW to put Tits on the phone. With my gobsmacked kids standing by eavesdropping, I told him to knock it the fuck off and make the meat loaf the way Mom wanted to; I said she was going to be dead soon and then he'd be sorry he'd tormented her. When he tried to push back, I abruptly cut him off.

"No! This is not a debate. Be nice to your old mother. I have to go." I hung up to find Katie grinning at me.

"You're doing so good, Mama! Keep it up. You take care of everything for Nonnie every day. There's no reason in the world why he and his ass hugger of a wife shouldn't be able to deal with this for one pitiful week."

Amen, my daughter.

(I guess a brief word of explanation is in order here. My sister-in-law had the oddest way of hugging. She'd drape her arms loosely around your neck and then stick her disproportionately large ass out to keep her chest from pressing into you. Like some sort of strange, nonintimate intimacy. Hence we call her the ass hugger.)

I looked to both my children with a proud-of-myself grin.

"I have an idea: let's go get some bitchin' breakfast from Harold and Phyllis."

CHARLIE

Ya know, all the family-bonding crap was great and everything, but I really needed to be getting home. When I signed on for that trip, I thought we'd be gone two or three days. Between the popped tire and the washed-out bridge, I had started to wonder if we were *ever* gonna get back to L.A.

I was supposed to be moving to the East Coast in six weeks. My closest buddies would soon be scattering to schools all over the country. I wanted to be chilling, hanging out with them. That was the summer we were supposed to be having wacky adventures, getting caught up in crazy situations like Bill and Ted, or Rick and Morty. And where was I?

Trapped in Grover's Glen with my mother, my sister, and a father who'd turned into a penguin.

(Okay, I'll admit the penguin bit was a pretty wacky adventure but, shit, it was *my* summer to be the star of the story, not some supporting player in Dad's escapade.)

Anyway, I was smart enough to know not to bitch to my mom about any of that, so I managed to keep my mouth shut. Off I went with them to grab breakfast at Harold and Phyllis's café.

Since Dad was already somewhat of a local celebrity and nobody seemed to object to having him around, we figured there was no reason not to bring him along. Harold and Phyllis were delighted to see him and before we were even seated, Harold announced that he was headed into the kitchen to make Dad a "stellar" seaweed-and-anchovy omelet.

I had some sick chocolate-chip pancakes; Katie had a waffle with a side of hash browns. Mom said that after her "Fuck It Day," she wasn't eating anything but half a grapefruit and a scoop of cottage cheese. I will never understand why she's still so obsessed with her weight. At her age, who gives a shit? What, it's like she's afraid they might cancel her nude modeling contract?

Phyllis came over to let us know breakfast was on the house because she was so tickled by how much money Dad's one-hour stint in the carnival photo booth had raised for the local preschool. Man, between that and the complimentary night at the hotel, we were scoring big-time. Phyllis also asked if we wanted to order lunch to go because they would be closing early.

"It's our town's annual Summer Renovation Day at the high school and just about everybody shows up to pitch in. We paint the classrooms, wash the windows, polish the floors—"

"We'll be there!" Mom chirped.

Wait ... what? Who's this "we" you're speaking of? I don't do manual labor. I thought everybody knew that.

But ... I guess it was that old "when in Rome" thing because I stayed quiet and after breakfast, off we went.

All right, you know what? I'm gonna be the big man here and admit it: sometimes it actually can be fun to pitch in and help out when everybody's working for a common cause.

It seems like so much happened during our day at the school that I'm not even sure where to begin. Okay ... how about this? I think my dorky little sister finally developed her first real crush. At first, I wasn't sure how I felt about the whole thing, but I guess it was harmless enough.

Mom got assigned to repaint one of the classrooms with this couple named Marty and Wendy Knox. The Knoxes owned the local sports bar that had a regular Wednesday Karaoke Night; that was all Mom needed to hear. She was totally down to paint with them if it gave her the chance to grill them about every aspect of their lives. She's always had this fantasy of running a bar someday, but I'm sure the reality must be a total nightmare. Dealing with drunks and punks twenty-four seven? Pass-a-dena.

Katie and I were waiting to be told where we were needed. She had taken Dad over to a secluded patch of dirt where he could do his business when this kid about my age came wandering over to me, kind of sidling up, acting all coy. Nodding his chin toward the spot where Katie and the penguin were coming back into view, this guy goes, "So there with the little penguin, is that your sister?"

I nodded.

Then he said, "She's hot."

I'm not shitting you: for a minute I thought something had to be wrong with my hearing. My sister is loud, she's annoying, she's a drama queen ... but *hot*? You'll have to excuse me if I don't see it. (All right, I know; she's my sister so it's probably a good thing I *don't* see it but still ...)

This kid was tall, Jack Skellington–skinny, and had a full head of dark curly hair that looked like it belonged on one of those sheepdogs with the bangs that hang into their eyes. And speaking of eyes: his were like some shocking shade of bright-blue that almost didn't look real. He was like if *Saturday Night Fever*–era John Travolta had a baby with Timothée Chalamet.

Jesus, Village of the Hotties strikes again.

Katie saw me talking to him, and suddenly I was her best friend. She made a beeline right for us and stuck her hand straight out like some attorney meeting a new client.

"Hi. I'm Katie. Who are you?"

For a second, he just stared at her, maybe taken aback by how out there she was; he clearly had no idea who he was dealing with. My sister instantly jumped into his awkward void.

"Sorry," she said, "I didn't mean to start with the *tough* questions."

That snapped him back. He laughed and said, "I'm Tim." Then he spun around and pointed to a bucket, a hose, and a pile of sponges a few feet behind him.

"I'm supposed to start washing the first-floor windows over there. Wanna help?"

Man, I guess he really must have been into her because he was the first person we'd encountered in since, like, forever that didn't seem to care there was a penguin standing next to my sister checking him out.

I left Katie and Tim to do the window washing and wandered inside with Dad. We immediately ran into an old janitor dude operating one of those upright floor waxers, buffing up the long main hallway. Looking at him, then glancing back at Dad who was waddling along, checking out the huge trophy case by the front door, inspiration struck.

I asked the janitor, Willard, if he was expected to polish all the floors in the whole school.

He was.

I asked if he had another waxing machine. He didn't.

I queried him about whether he had any extralarge sponges, a bungee cord, a Velcro strap, and some rope.

He did.

A short time later, Willard wasn't the only one doing the waxing.

See, here's the deal with me and physical tasks like cleaning and building shit: unless I can make it fun, I don't really see the point. So this is where it helps to be a bit of a creative genius. (And a *Tom Sawyer* fan.)

I got Willard to pour a good amount of the liquid wax into a big metal washtub.

I used the strap to secure one of the big flat sponges to Penguin Dad's belly and then hooked the bungee cord to the top of the strap on his back. I threaded the rope through the cord, fashioning it into a long leash. Next, I told Dad to dip his sponge-covered tummy into the tub of wax to get it coated all around.

After that, I had him lay down on his stomach with his flippers splayed out to the side like he was flying; I started pulling him up and down the hall, with his gut pressing into the sponge so it would cover the floor with wax. He was like a living, breathing black-and-white Zamboni—ya know, those machines they use at hockey games to clean the ice?

When that step was done, I rinsed out the cleaning pad before pulling Sponge-Gut-No-Pants back in the opposite direction a few times to buff those tiles until they gleamed. I told you guys: I am the motherfucking Mother of Invention!

Of course, as you can imagine, a bunch of the little kids who were there with their parents immediately dropped their previous activities to watch me and my penguin doing our landlocked version of an Olympic-style ice dancing without the ice.

"Okay," I told them, "if you're watching, you're singing—and here's what we're gonna sing."

Using my improv song skills from drama class, I made up a brand-new version of "Mustang Sally" and taught those six-, seven-, and eight-year-olds to sing their tiny hearts out. That's the beauty of kids: when they're into something, damn, man, they learn fast. Soon parents were popping their heads out of all the classrooms where they were painting and cleaning so they could listen to our impromptu concert. The whole time, I kept dipping Dad back into the wax bath and then dragging him across one floor after another, making them shine.

The excited kids were reciting the lyrics just like I taught them, singing with limitless exuberance every time we came to the chorus of "glide, penguin, glide!" By the time we got to the final verse, they were practically screaming out the lyrics as they laughed and danced like little maniacs.

When at last I had finished, Dad hopped up on his webbed feet and raced to my side. The hall was packed with parents, kids, and teachers who were all applauding, cheering, and snapping pictures with their phones. I took Dad's outstretched flipper in my hand and together we gave a deep, tandem bow as the rousing hooting went on.

Hey, man, to hell with *Romeo and Juliet*. This was way better. Like a sold-out concert at Madison Square Garden–style status.

And those floors were looking almost as shiny as the glow in my cheeks.

With the day winding down, Archer came in search of Mom and invited us all to have dinner with him and Imani at their place. We found Katie out front, sitting under a tree, talking to Tim. She had this dumb-ass expression on her face like she thought everything this kid was saying was borderline amazing.

Wow. First love. Nothing like it, am I right?

When Mom said we were going to eat at Archer's house, Katie jumped up and asked if Tim could come too.

"Archer loves me," Tim said. "He'd be totally cool if I came along. He was my Little League coach for three years when I was in middle school."

Of course he was.

Mom went to clear it with Archer while Tim called his mom to get her okay. I'd clearly pooped out my Penguin Pop with all his crowd-pleasing waxing activity, so I took him back to the car to wait for the others; he immediately spread himself out in the rear compartment (do you still call it a trunk if it's an SUV?) and took a nap.

When we got to Archer and Imani's house a short time later, here's a question that popped into my head: How, in this modern world, are us guys supposed to be "woke" and aware and capable of treating ladies as genuine equals while still being allowed to acknowledge that some women just happen to be stunningly, awesomely beautiful?

I mean, are we supposed to go all Oedipus and poke our eyes out?

Yeah, you guessed it: I'm talking about Imani.

For sure Mom or Katie could do a much better job of describing what she was wearing when Archer brought us into their little house at the end of a cul de sac that backs up to a lush pine forest. It had been an unusually hot day for that part of the state, so Imani was in these white short shorts with a matching top that fell off her shoulders, like that sweatshirt Jennifer Beals wore in *Flashdance*. (This is how you know what a movie geek I am. There are probably only five straight guys my age in the whole country that would even know what the hell I'm talking about.)

Anyway, all Imani's long, skinny braids were coiled into a perfect knot on top of her head. Her killer legs were almost as long as Katie's whole body, and she had this, like, ring of light-blue makeup around her eyes making them pop out on her dark skin—and she just … she … okay, I'm guessing I should probably stop now.

But, see, doesn't this prove how evolved I am? I got through that entire description without saying a single word about her incredible tits.

This is where Dad got a total break being a penguin. He clearly realized he could go balls to the wall staring at her, and nobody would even notice.

Imani was in their dining room with knotty-pine walls, setting a table that looked like something out of a Williams Sonoma catalogue. Archer barreled in, pulled her against him for a hot kiss, and thanked her for being so chill about throwing a spontaneous dinner party. Mom, Katie, Tim, and I were heaping our thanks and praise on her too. Dad just stood there gawking. Imani turned to us with a dimpled grin.

"Don't think for a minute that you're guests here," she said. "If this dinner is going to happen, everybody works!"

Their two-bedroom bungalow was decorated with a mix of retro surfer-dude artifacts—that I assumed belonged to Archer—and African art and wood carvings. Imani's family was from Ghana, although she grew up in Palo Alto where her dad was a professor at Stanford.

They gave us a quick tour of the place and then, once we took turns hitting the bathroom to wash up after our day of hard labor at the school, each of us was assigned a task.

Archer was making his favorite linguine carbonara with a Caesar salad and garlic bread. He put Katie and Tim to work cutting the package of pancetta into small thin strips. Mom was chopping garlic and melting butter for the bread. Imani was cutting up the romaine for the salad while I shaved a block of fresh parmesan—some for the Caesar and some for the pasta. Archer was making his own salad dressing from scratch and also whisking together red wine, garlic, and black pepper for the pasta sauce. Once he had the fresh linguine in a pot of boiling water, he put a step stool beside the stove and gave Dad a wooden spoon to clamp in his beak. Dad's job, Archer said, was to keep the pasta stirred up and swirling to prevent it from clumping together.

Pretty weird that Archer assumed a rando penguin would be able to do something like that, right? But if we can take a brief time-out here, let me explain what I thought was going on. I've told you all along how Archer seemed like a magical being out of a Marvel movie, but Dad's job assignment was one more reason why I actually figured he might have some sort of sixth sense. (And not in the "I see dead people" kinda way.) As far as he knew, our penguin was just some runaway creature we'd adopted as a pet. He had no reason to think it was our dad transformed. He didn't know there was a human brain trapped inside that bird body, but everything about the way he accepted and interacted with my Penguin Pop made me suspect that he was somehow onto us. Yet he never felt the need to say a word.

Mythical entities don't have to spell it out. They just know.

Imani ducked into the living room and put on this amazing album by New Orleans's world-famous Preservation Hall Jazz Band. Of course, the music was piped directly into speakers mounted over the kitchen cabinets and soon, everybody was dancing while they sliced, diced, and chopped. I don't know if you've ever heard those guys, but it's damn near impossible to stand still when they start wailing. All those horns? *Shit!* Even Dad was swaying his penguin hips and wiggling his bird butt as he continued to stir the roiling pasta with that wooden spoon clamped in his maw.

When we moved to the table as dinner was served, Archer whipped out a huge piece of poached salmon to serve to Dad. Where that came from, I don't have a clue, but Dad couldn't have been happier. He eagerly bounced up onto his seat between Mom and me. Katie and Tim were seated across from us, locked in their own private conversation; they were talking quietly and laughing constantly, causing my smitten sister to blush from the sheer heat of her first true romantic spark. If I wasn't so bitter about women in general—and Amy in particular—I might have even thought they were cute.

Halfway through the meal, we heard Archer's phone knock, and he plucked it from the pocket of the denim shirt hanging on the back of his chair. As he read the text, he broke out into his famous dimpled grin.

"Good news, folks. Sheriff Hancock says the bridge is just about done and will be open by six tomorrow morning."

★★★

After dinner, Archer and Imani declared that they were "exhausted." (That's what they were saying, but it was so obvious they just wanted us gone so they could bone. Seriously. If you looked like the two of them, wouldn't you wanna be doing the mattress mambo every second you possibly could? I'm just sayin' ....)

Mom made some cute comment about wanting to take off before we wore out our welcome. (See? She also could tell they were jonesing to go at it.)

Katie was clearly doing everything she could to *not* have the evening end, so she lit right up when Tim asked if we wanted to join him to go miniature golfing. He invited all of us, but Mom said she needed to get back to the hotel to start packing so we could depart early the next morning. Archer and Imani declared that they were quite content to chill at home.

(Have sex.)

I was about to send my sister and her crush off on their own when I caught sight of Mom arching her eyebrows, vibing the crap out of me. She clearly wasn't cool with the idea of letting Katie go off with a boy she'd only met that afternoon.

Fine, I thought. *I'll take one for the team.* Plus, I was really looking forward to kicking their asses at minigolf.

We said our goodbyes to our hosts; carried on and on to Archer about what an amazing hotel owner, tour guide, and cook he was; and gave equally effusive thanks to Imani. Mom took Dad back to our room. Katie and I went off with Tim.

As soon as we were alone in his beat-to-shit 2012 Camry, Tim whipped out a vape pen and asked if we wanted to get high.

"My sister doesn't really do that stuff," I said.

"Says who?" Katie barked with a great deal of indignity. "Whitney, London, and I got high practically every weekend this year. With Whit's parents never home, it was the perfect place to get loaded and laugh 'til we peed our pants."

"Wow," I said, "talk about a good time."

Gesturing to Tim, wiggling her fingers in the direction of the vape pen, Katie swiftly took it from him and then turned her glare on me. "But you have to swear you won't tell Mom. She'd die."

In my head, I was chuckling my ass off. (Which, technically, I couldn't do since I'm pretty sure my head doesn't have an ass.)

Anyway, in a few short days, I had become the keeper of family secrets. Mom didn't want me to tell Katie she got high, Katie didn't want me to tell Mom *she* got high, and I got to get loaded with everybody. Lucky me.

Wanting to prove to me, the default chaperone, that he was a trustworthy fellow, Tim didn't catch a buzz until we were safely parked in the dark back corner of the Golf Land parking lot.

It was one of those janky complexes with an 18-hole miniature golf course attached to an arcade, a snack bar, and a batting cage, all on a much more compact scale than you'd find in L.A. On the golf course, the little windmills, corkscrew ramps, and tiny barn with the swinging doors were badly in need of a paint job, yet there was something old-school charming about the place—heightened, no doubt, by the rocking-strong Bali High in Tim's weed pen.

Despite my initial skepticism, I had to admit Tim was a decent-enough guy; he was fun to hang out with. He teased and flirted with Katie in a way that was genuine, not skeevy. Oh, and he was totally into *The Simpsons*, so how bad could he be? On the 8th or 9th hole, he made some comment about something that reminded him of the episode where Marge and Homer took the kids to Itchy & Scratchy Land; from there, he and I were off and running. We were quoting our favorite lines and talking about how Homer figured out that flashbulbs short-circuited the rogue robots. After that, we were laughing about a bunch of our other favorite episodes, chiming in with the best quotes and recalling some of the great bits that had showed up on the chalkboard in the opening credits.

Katie looked like she wanted to kill me.

We were closing in on the 17th hole. Tim was only two strokes ahead of me when I heard my phone and Katie's phone ping at the same time.

Shit.

I wanted to ignore the incoming text to focus on my crucial shot trying to get under a little waterfall to the green below, but Katie had to check.

"Oh no," she said.

"What's up?" Tim asked.

I looked at my own phone before Katie had the chance to respond. It was a message from Mom:

Something's very wrong with Dad. Please come back ASAP.

KATIE

It's Charles Dickens, right? *A Tale of Two Cities*? That's the one that starts with the "best of times/worst of times" business? That might have been fine for old CD, but why did it suddenly have to be *my* reality?

For the first time maybe ever, I was hanging out with a guy my age who was totally cute, supernice, and actually seemed to be as into me as I was into him. That, literally, had *never* happened to me before. Seriously.

Look, I wasn't a goober. I knew it couldn't go anywhere. He was living up there in East Bumfuck and we were leaving the next morning but ... I mean, couldn't it have lasted at least a *little* longer? Didn't I deserve my Cinderella run-off-at-the-stroke-of-midnight moment, acting all flustered and mysterious?

Apparently not.

Dad was in trouble again and Charlie and I had to get back to the hotel to help Mom. Fortunately, Tim didn't see Mom's text, so we just told him the penguin was sick and Mama needed our assistance.

As he was driving us back, out of nowhere, Tim suddenly piped up.

"Sorry if this is an insensitive question, but—where's your dad, anyway?"

We probably should have rehearsed our cover story, but I guess it had never occurred to me or Charlie. We biffed it Big-Time. At the exact same second, I said, "They're divorced," while Charlie said, "Away on business." Then I quickly added, "It's complicated." I started babbling about how much I loved the smell of the Grover's Glen pine trees and the wonderful fresh air up there; that seemed to get Tim off the subject. God bless stoners. They never can keep a train of thought going very long and, sometimes, that can be a good thing.

When we reached the hotel, Charlie was uncharacteristically cool. He made some stupid *Simpsons* reference that totally cracked Tim up but then said a quick goodbye. He dipped back into our room to let Tim and me have a minute alone.

I was superhot and nervous; I wanted him to kiss me, but I was terrified that I'd get freaked out and bash my teeth into his or make some other lame-ass move. He seemed like he knew everything I was thinking and just gently took both my hands in his. He said he'd had a great time all day, had a blast hanging out, and hoped we could stay in touch. I handed him my phone so he could put in his number. That's about the pinnacle of Gen-Z romance right there, know what I'm sayin'?

Then he took my hand again, smiled, and asked if it would be okay if he kissed me goodnight. Wait, what? He asked first? How sweet is that? I was *dying*.

I giggled. I blushed. I nodded.

He leaned down, tilted his head toward mine, and gave me the most gentle, lovely kiss. (Not that I had much to compare it to.) I kissed him one more time and then told him I had to get inside to see what was up with our bird. He smiled, waved, and almost looked like he was about to cry.

That was real, right? It wasn't just dust in his eyes? Are you kidding me? Dream man!

He even waited to watch the door close behind me.

I found Mom and Charlie in the bathroom, kneeling beside the tub where the penguin was immersed in cold water. More of his little feathers had turned gray and he seemed to be shedding faster than an Afghan hound in a hot tub; his eyes were glassy, sort of out of focus.

Mom said that almost immediately after they got back to the room, Dad had started doing that raspy, rattling breathing thing again. Scary.

She ran the tub with only cold water, added a few buckets of ice, and got Dad into it. That helped to calm his breathing, but for the last hour or so, he had been really listless and zonked. The tip of his tongue was poking out of the corner of his beak, and it looked like the little spikes on it were all shriveled.

"It *was* a really hot day today," I said. "Maybe he just needs to hang out in the tub, cool down, and get some rest."

The penguin nodded in lethargic agreement as his eyelids drooped and finally closed. Terrified, I had to press my hand to his chest to make sure he still had a heartbeat.

I asked Mom if she thought it might help to get Dad out of the tub and into the pool. Maybe being able to dive down deep and swim underwater for a while would be good for him. Mom said she was worried he didn't have the strength to do much swimming, but Charlie figured full immersion couldn't hurt.

It took all three of us to get the limp bird out of the tub, and then we sorta half carried, half steered him around to the back of the hotel so we could guide him into the pool. It was after eleven; technically the pool area was closed, but we knew Archer wouldn't mind. Plus, the goofy night-clerk kid was too busy playing *Fortnite* on his phone to notice us.

Dad did a little belly flop into the water and started floating. Mom, me, and Charlie were standing on the edge, watching him. He was face-down with his wings spread out looking like some wounded angel drifting in a pale-blue sky. When he stayed like that, just gliding in the water propelled by the breeze, I started freaking out.

"Oh my God, is he dead? Why isn't he picking his head up? Doesn't he need air? What if he's dead? He can't be dead. Is he dead?"

Charlie shot me one of his famous "shut-the-hell-up" looks, but I could tell by his eyes that he was really scared too.

"Should I go in? Should I make sure he's okay?" my brother asked. Fighting back tears, Mom and I nodded in sync.

Charlie hesitated for just another moment, then kicked off his sandals and jumped into the deep end where Dad was adrift with his bird face still pointed down. Charlie frantically dog-paddled closer and gently flipped the penguin onto his back. Dad exhaled a straight-into-the-air stream of water looking like some Vegas showgirl doing water ballet. He sputtered. He coughed.

He was alive.

I don't think anybody slept very well that night. We took turns hopping up to make sure Dadda, sleeping in a shallow bath in the master bathroom, was all right.

As soon as it was light out, a little after six a.m., Mom got me and Charlie up, announcing we needed to hit the road.

Dad was still looking pretty awful. We debated if we should try to find a vet for him, but I wasn't too optimistic that we'd find an experienced penguin doctor anywhere within a thousand miles.

I said, "I know there's no logic, and, obvi I can't fully explain it—but I just *know*, I feel it—we need to get him to Tahoe."

"Well," Mom responded thoughtfully, clearly doing everything possible to keep it together, "you *were* the first one to realize the bird was Dad, so I'm thinking we should trust your instincts."

Charlie agreed.

We packed up and took off while the sun was only beginning to make its morning debut. Mom said we could find some place with a drive-thru to grab breakfast in a while, but the immediate priority was to get some miles behind us.

Since this whole destination had been my idea, I was feeling a lot of pressure and responsibility, really hoping I'd turn out to be right. My head was spinning, my heart was pounding—and then I got a text from Tim:

[Smiling sun emoji] Good morning, you. Hope you had sweet dreams. [Line of Zs emoji] Also, hope your penguin is A-ok. [Red hearts and a rainbow emoji]

I had no idea what he was doing up so early but then, as we were texting back and forth, he said he was headed out for a morning run before he had to get to his job at the local CVS where he was a stock boy for the summer.

Okay … so he liked to stay fit and had a good work ethic? Whoa. Why in the world couldn't this boy be living in L.A.?

We'd been in the car for about a half hour when my lame-ass brother almost got us into a wreck. I think you know by now that Mom's a nervous driver, even in the best of times. Yeah, she's definitely a worse passenger but, still, she's always on high alert for doom and death around every blind curve.

Anyway, I was up front with her; Charlie was in the back seat with Dad who was sprawled out across the seat beside my brother. Out of nowhere, Charlie screamed out, "WHAT THE FUCK!" causing Mom to stomp on the brakes.

It was a total miracle the pickup truck behind us didn't fully smash into our rear end.

When Mom and I both whipped around to ask him what was wrong, he had tears in his eyes and looked like he couldn't even talk.

"Oh my God—Dad's dead?" I gasped.

Charlie gave me an incredibly annoyed glare and shouted like he wanted to take my head off. "Dad is *fine*. It's Amy."

"Is *she* dead?" I asked, trying to sound more horrified by the prospect than I actually was.

Charlie was getting angrier by the minute. "*Nobody's* dead, Katie! Stop it!"

By this time, Mom had started driving again and calmly wanted to know what the problem was.

"There's a picture of her on Insta kissing Jeremy, saying they're a couple now."

"Jeremy? You mean stupid Jeremy Lancaster?" I asked in genuine disbelief.

"YES! *That* Jeremy. The less intelligent, less attractive, less talented version of ME!"

Mom and I tried to talk my brother down, but he was incapable of listening to reason. We insisted that it was none of his business who Amy dated now that they were broken up. We tried to say that he was going to meet an amazing woman when he got to college so who cared what Amy did? She was the poor sucker who was going to be stuck in high school for another year while he was off having the adventure of a lifetime.

Charlie didn't want to hear any of it. He was in a totally illogical rage.

"Before I say another word," I began, "will you please promise me you're never going to get back with her?"

"Why?"

"Because you need to hear the truth once and for all: she's gross. And Jeremy's gross. They deserve each other. That girl is a total ho-bag. Don't you remember she was making out with one of your sworn enemies about ten minutes after you broke up the first time?"

Right then, my phone dinged again. It was Tim telling me I was an amazing woman. I could feel the lovestruck smile blooming on my face at the same instant that my bitter brother grumbled: "Fuck her. Fuck all women. Fuck romance. Love *sucks*. Fucking fuck-fuck-fuck."

I wanted to tell him I thought love was *won-der-ful*, but I figured in that moment, it was probably better to move on. "Trust me, brother bear," I said, "your whole world's gonna radically change the second you get to Hartford. I fully know those snowbound bitches will quickly be cravin' a heaping helping of California Charlie."

For the next hour or so, things were relatively calm. Charlie was sulking while I was texting with Tim. (I guess it must not have been too busy at CVS.) Dad still looked like holy hell, but seemed to be sleeping peacefully. His breathing was a little wheezy but not nearly as scary as it had been the night before when he was really struggling. Mom was fully focused on the road when the screen on the dashboard beeped with an incoming text alert from Tits-on-a-Bull.

"Oh shit," Mom said. "What now?"

She asked me to fish her phone from her purse at my feet, so I quickly dug it out.

"He says Nonnie has some weird white foam in the corners of her mouth, and wants to know if she's having a stroke."

Mom instantly went off. "Are you kidding me? What time is it?" She glanced at the clock on the dashboard and answered her own question. "Eight? How does he not know that she takes her antacid every morning and always has white shit in the corners of her mouth until somebody tells her to wipe it away? I swear to God, how far up his ass is that guy's head?"

She asked me to write my uncle back and tell him that the next time he had an idiotic question like that, he might want to simply ask Nonnie if she was feeling okay. I told Mom I didn't want to get in the middle of her family feud, but she said I wouldn't have to.

"Type it on my phone exactly like I'm telling you, and he'll assume it's from me. Overthinking anything, unless it's where to get his next drink, is not in your uncle's wheelhouse."

Not wanting to lose any more time than necessary, we buzzed into a McDonald's drive-thru right on the main road for Egg McMuffins with a giant coffee for Mom and those little bottles of orange juice for me and Charlie. Plus, Charlie also ordered one of those hashbrown bricks that are basically fried grease in a bag—*so* unhealthy. We tried to feed Dad a little bit of scrambled eggs, but he wasn't going for it. At least we got him to drink some water before he went right back to sleep.

When we passed a sign that said Lake Tahoe – 60 miles, I started to breathe a little easier. Maybe we *would* get Dad into the lake before it was too late. Maybe its cold water would be the thing that revived him. Maybe everything would be all right.

Oh God, I sure hoped so.

Of course, given how the rest of the trip had gone, I should not have been surprised when, only a few miles past that hopeful sign, all the cars ahead of us came to a sudden and complete stop. After five minutes of going nowhere, Mom exhaled. "Seriously?"

People were getting out of their cars and trucks to see what the problem was.

They were all gawking at something up ahead that they could see but we couldn't. Mom asked—or more like ordered—Charlie to go check it out.

When my brother returned a couple of minutes later, he was repeatedly shaking his head back and forth. Then, out of nowhere, he was standing next to Mom's open window, juggling three oranges.

(Yeah, it's one of the "special skills" on his acting resume: amateur juggler. You'd be surprised how often it comes in handy doing Shakespeare plays.)

"We're cursed," Charlie said, exhaling deeply. "We better hope Dad can hang on because, for the foreseeable future, we won't be going anywhere." After taking a dramatic pause for effect—another one of his actor tricks—he told us that there was an overturned truck up ahead that had been hauling a full load of freshly picked oranges; it was now lying on its side across both lanes. Of course, we had to be on one of those narrow mountain roads with a steep hill on one side and a sharp cliff on the other, so there was absolutely no way around the hazard up ahead. We were stuck. With a dying penguin and a ticking clock.

Charlie was on his phone, stalking Jeremy Lancaster's Facebook page just to torture himself; I was back to texting with Tim; Mom was sitting with her eyes closed, doing a deep-breathing meditation I knew was intended to keep her from flipping out.

Dad's intense wheezing had returned, in a quiet, shallow way; it was like that subliminal buzzing you sometimes hear from overhead power lines with their own brand of ominous subtext. His entire penguin body looked dried out and depleted. Every time I glanced back at him, I had to squint my ears to make sure I was still hearing him exhale. (Charlie says you can't squint your ears, but I disagree. It's like when you have to scrunch up your shoulders and really focus to be sure the sounds are sinking in.)

After about an hour, I was starting to go insane. Nobody ahead of us was moving. Nobody was offering updates. We could see the distant lights of emergency vehicles dealing with the situation, but we had no idea what was taking so long. The quiet all around us was making me want to jump out of the car and start running in little circles, screaming my head off.

"Can we please play a game or something? I'm seriously afraid of losing it."

Charlie wanted to do this movie game where one person says a film title, then the next person has to say an actor from that film, and then the third person says the title of another movie that actor was in. I told him I hated playing with him because he knows every movie ever made and every actor who appeared in them, and he purposely chooses the most obscure ones so he can stump Mom and me to guarantee himself a victory every time. So bogus.

Mom suggested we play "Geography"; that's where you have to say a city, state, country, ocean, lake, or anything like that and the next person has to come up with one that starts with the letter that matches the last letter of the previous choice. And you're not allowed to repeat anything another person has already said. That's a much more level playing field for the three of us, so we dove in.

It was pretty impressive that we kept the geographical train running for almost an hour. I finally won—SUCKERS!—after I followed Mom's "Utah" with "Halifax," and Charlie said there was no such thing as a location that started with *x*.

"Oh yeah, smarty-pants?" I retorted. "What about Xenia, Ohio?"

Of course, he tried to claim that was with a *z*, but when he looked it up, he saw that I was right so—*boo-yah, big brother*—I won!

Okay, ya know how I've told you my mom is kinda famous for her ability to see death and devastation in every imaginable situation? Well, sometimes that nuttiness works to our advantage. We'd been stuck going nowhere for almost three hours, and I was starting to get crazy hungry, bordering on hangry.

We each ate one of the oranges Charlie had pilfered from the spill, but that didn't do a whole lot to hold me. When I said I was pretty sure we might have to go full Donner party and resort to eating my brother, Mom replied, "Or we could get the emergency provisions I keep in the back for occasions exactly like this."

Wow. Big surprise. (So not.)

Returning from the rear compartment, Mom handed me and Charlie each a protein bar and a bottle of water.

Looking at my bar, I groaned. "Charlie, I hate this flavor. Trade with me!"

"Why do you have to be so disgruntled all the time?" my brother snapped.

"I'm perfectly gruntled, I just think the birthday-cake flavor tastes like soap."

"Oh, but it's fine for me?"

Mom turned in her seat and wagged the bar she'd chosen in my direction.

"Here. I'll trade with you. I have the chocolate-brownie one."

Charlie instantly got his back up. "No, Mom. You don't always have to be the martyr. Katie can eat the one she got."

"She's not being a martyr, Charlie. She's being a *mom*. And if she wants to trade with me, it's none of your stinkin' business—so shut up!"

With that, I swiftly swapped my birthday-cake bar for Mom's chocolate brownie and ripped off the wrapper to end the debate.

I think because he was trying to make me look bad, Charlie gently propped up Dad's listless head and cradled it as he urged him to drink some water. Without ever opening his eyes, Dad guzzled down the entire thing until he was sucking so hard, he made the plastic bottle collapse in on itself. Mom hopped out again to fetch Charlie another one.

"Hang onto that first bottle," my mom the frustrated Boy Scout said, "you know one of us is going to have to pee into it, probably sooner than later."

File that one under "ewww-but-true."

Settling back in behind the wheel, she glanced down at her watch. Discovering it was already early afternoon—we hadn't moved in over four hours—she had another realization. When we'd set out in the morning, our plan had been to get to Tahoe way before noon; we'd get Dad into the lake and then, depending on what happened, decide if we needed to stay over or could turn around to start the journey home. Now, even if the road cleared in the next ten minutes, we wouldn't reach our destination before five o'clock.

"We need to book a hotel room. No matter what happens with Dad, there's no way I'm going to be in any shape to start driving back down these mountain roads in the dark."

"Mom, you know I could always drive," Charlie said.

"No," my mother responded, instantly and with great finality. "Knowing what a terrible passenger I am in the best of times, after the week we've had, it's pretty much guaranteed that putting you behind the wheel would not be a wise idea for any of us."

Point taken.

So now we had a new challenge: finding a hotel room on a moment's notice in the height of the tourist season in a popular resort town. What could be difficult about that?

While Charlie started trolling the internet for an available place to stay, I got out to see if I could learn any more about when the road might be cleared. Walking about three hundred yards ahead to where a small crowd was gathered, I finally got a piece of good news: the overturned truck was now righted and had been hauled away. There was a bulldozer with a scoop shovel in the process of removing the gazillion pounds of oranges that were strewn and smashed across both sides of the road. A fire hydrant-shaped cop told me that we would be good to go in about forty-five more minutes.

Hallelujah!

By the time I got back to the car, Charlie had good news (from my perspective) and bad news (for Mom). The only place he could find with an available room was called The Landing Resort & Spa. One room with two queen beds was $530 a night! They claimed they were a pet-friendly establishment, but we figured it was still probably better to keep Dad on the down-low. Mom was freaking out about the money, except we didn't really have a choice. It looked totally luxurious to me, so I figured it was best to keep quiet.

"Fine," Mom groaned to Charlie. "Get my credit card out of my purse and book it. By the time we finally get there, I'm going to need a comfortable bed to crash in after I guzzle down a supersized Long Island iced tea. Or two."

I could already hear her ordering it: *No gin, lemon not a lime, tall glass.*

Exactly like the cop had promised, forty-five minutes later we were rolling once again.

As we dipped down a long, sloping road heading into Tahoe—the town's truly gorgeous lake filling the vista in front of us—another furious debate erupted. We were trying to decide if we should check into the hotel, get cleaned up a bit, and then take Dad down to the water, or just make a beeline straight for the lake. He had hardly moved in the last several hours, and nothing we did seemed to make him any more comfortable. Right before we approached our destination, Charlie accidentally bumped up against him while reaching for his book bag on the floor and reported that Dad seemed like he was burning up; his normally cool feathery flippers felt hot to the touch. Charlie gave him three more bottles of water, but Dadda clearly had a thirst that couldn't be quenched.

I didn't want to make things worse than they were, but I was terrified. He couldn't die. Even if he stayed a penguin forever, he was still my Dadda. He needed to be there to help me decide which colleges to apply to. He had to be around so we could go shopping for school supplies. We had to make fun of all the people at Disneyland as we sat on the bench outside the Haunted Mansion and I invented dialogue for the tourists going by looking totally over it.

I mean, c'mon, let's get to the real heart of it: one day he was going to have to be there to walk me down the aisle!

(And—bright side—if he was still a penguin, at least he'd already have the tux.)

After a bunch of back-and-forth between Mom and Charlie, I had to chime in. I said that we should park in the Landing's parking lot since the hotel was right on the water. They had little boats to rent, so we could load Dad into one, row out into the middle of the lake where it was probably the coldest, and toss him overboard.

"Then what?" Charlie asked.

"I don't know!" I said.

And then I burst out crying. So did Mom.

I swear to God, Charlie looked like he wanted to murder us both.

When the GPS led us into the parking lot of The Landing Resort & Spa, we did a slow loop around the property to get the lay of the land. We spotted a long wooden dock with the pontoon-boat rental shack beside it.

"There!" I shouted out. "Just park and let's go!"

We made the decision to crack all the windows a tiny bit so Dad would have air while we went to rent whatever they had available. Even though it was a cool seventy-two degrees out, Dadda was still burning up.

They rented us an inflatable dinghy thing that was little more than a blow-up life raft, but we were in no position to be fussy. Once the transaction was done, we went back to fetch Dad, rolled him into our trusty picnic blanket, and loaded him onto the raft when none of the workers were paying attention.

Charlie claimed he knew how to row from his two summers at the Lazy J ranch camp when he was twelve and thirteen but, let's be honest, if it wasn't for my mad skills, we'd probably still be going around in little circles two feet from shore.

We finally made our way out into the middle of the lake, far from any other people engaged in various water activities. I guess the fact that it was almost six o'clock in the evening was why it wasn't as crowded as I'd expected.

Thank God.

Mom and I slowly unrolled the blanket that enveloped Dad and found him looking worse than ever.

"I know the plan is to get him into the cold water," Mom said, "but is he even going to be able to swim? What if we drown him? What if we've all survived everything we've gone through, come all this way—and end up killing him?"

That stopped us cold.

We didn't know what we were doing.

We really had no idea what Penguin Dadda needed.

We still didn't know why he had become a penguin in the first place.

And we were 100 percent clueless about what it might take to bring him back.

After a protracted period of paralyzed quiet, Mom stared at me until my eyes locked on hers. Her voice was soft, trembling slightly, even though she was fighting to hide it.

"You have great instincts, Katie-Lady. You always have. I think the only option we have right now is to trust you."

Following a few more minutes of frantic strategizing, we had our plan in place. The three of us positioned ourselves to hoist Dad up and roll him over the side of the little raft into the lake.

He was hardly moving, barely responding.

"Jesus," Charlie said. "We're like Tom Ripley trying to get rid of Dickie Greenleaf's body after Ripley beat him to death with an oar."

While I stared blankly at my brother, Mom looked to me and nodded.

"*The Talented Mr. Ripley*," Mom clarified.

"Seriously, Charlie? You honestly think we need one of your stupid movie references *now*?"

Charlie shrugged. "Sorry."

I sighed deeply. On a 3-2-1 countdown, we roll dropped Dad into the water with an erupting splash.

He sank.

He didn't swim; he didn't come bursting back up through the surface to give us a penguin squawk of gratitude. He just slowly drifted down, going deeper and deeper, until he was entirely out of sight.

I was leaning so far over the side of the raft to try to see him, I almost made us capsize. Charlie swiftly scooted to the other side to balance things out.

Nobody was talking.

I'm not even sure we were breathing.

Dad was gone.

And there was absolutely no indication that he had the will or the strength to come back to us.

I looked over my shoulder to see tears sliding down Mom's cheeks. Her face was contorted in pain, but she wasn't making a single sound. Charlie looked deathly white. I felt like some gigantic monster was squeezing my breaking heart.

The thing I remember most was how quiet it was. I knew all of us wanted to be screaming our heads off, but the only thing I could hear was a chorus of crickets chirping far off on the distant shore.

CLARK

When I first hit that shockingly chilly water of Lake Tahoe, it felt like my penguin body was made of lead. No matter how hard I fought against it, I kept sinking, going deeper into the darkness below.

The cold water felt like an ice pick in my penguin temples. The enveloping darkness made me flash on tales of pilots getting disoriented in a storm, no longer knowing which way was up or down. Every time I tried to dispel the notion that was at the forefront of my brain, it kept recurring.

This is it. This is how, when, and where I'm going to die.

I wasn't sure if I was drifting, sinking, or tumbling. I'd lost all sense of my place in the universe. I started to think about the endless things I was going to miss. I wouldn't be around to see Charlie's Broadway debut or first major film role. Who was going to have the ultimate honor of accompanying Katie down the aisle? Julia and I would never get to take that long-discussed trip to Greece. I wouldn't write any more books or celebrate any more birthdays. No grandkids. No more sex. No more bean-and-cheese burritos from Taco Bell ...

Suddenly I heard my own voice in my head, giving the kind of speech I'd given to my kids a hundred times. Whatever it was, whatever their current crisis was about, my message had always been the same:

Life isn't about the obstacles that are thrown at us, it's about how we choose to respond to them.

If you want something, you fight for it. You fight like hell.

You. Fight. Like. Hell.

I was still sinking, I was still tumbling, but then, with no explanation at all, something changed. I felt this surge of electrical energy. I kicked my feet and felt a familiar sensation that made me glance downward, squinting into the darkness.

Why did it look like my feet were no longer webbed, no longer orange?

I kicked even harder, sending myself jetting upward. As I reached for the surface, I saw something startling in front of me. It was an arm. A human arm.

My arm.

I raised my head from under the water and forced my eyes to focus.

Then, from behind me, Katie shrieked like a little kid: "Oh my God—DADDA!"

Hearing my daughter's voice, I whirled around in the middle of that freezing lake. Feeling oddly weighted down as the water swirled around me, I glanced below the surface.

What I spied was a naked body.

My body.

Holy shit! I was back.

In their little dinghy a football-field's distance away, I spied my family screaming and waving in my direction. Katie and Julia were crying. Charlie was emitting these hooting-laughing cheers. With the furiousness of Michael Phelps, I dug in with both arms and practically flew through the water.

I reached the side of the raft and clamped my hands onto it. I was crying and laughing all at once.

The four of us were in some altered state of giddy hysteria. Julia leaned over the side, grabbed my face with both hands, and gave me a long, hungry kiss. When she pulled back to take a breath, I blurted, "Again, please."

Laughing through her tears, Julia took my face in her hands once more and gave me another delicious kiss. It was the first time I could remember that we were showing outward affection in front of the kids when they didn't act grossed out or tell us to "get a room."

Katie leaned in beside Julia to clutch my shoulder and kiss the top of my head. Charlie declared that he'd really like to get in on the lovefest, but somebody had to balance the weight to keep the little craft from flipping. For the first time, I could see that even my hard-ass son had tears sparkling in the corners of his eyes.

Catching my breath, I called out to him. "Hey, pal, are you wearing boxers under those shorts?"

"What the hell, Dad? You've been a penguin for months and this is the first thing you have to say to me?"

Realizing how absurd that had to sound, I gave out a hearty laugh and went on to explain. "I'm naked here. I need to get out of the water, but I'd rather do it without traumatizing your sister for life. It would be swell if you could give me your shorts."

Catching on, Charlie complied. He tugged off his cargo shorts, emptied his pockets, and tossed the shorts over the side to me. Clinging to the craft with one hand, I used the other to hang on to Charlie's pants as I guided my legs into them.

"Okay, now you guys all shift over to Charlie's side so I can climb aboard."

With more grace than I would have expected, I was able to tug myself up and pretty effortlessly flip over into the dinghy without causing a mini-tsunami. (I guess my daily swim really did have its benefits.)

Scrambling into a seated position on the raft's floor, I was grinning from ear to ear to see my family, clustered together across from me, staring in my direction with such overwhelming affection. I hoped I was looking back at them with as much adoration as they were projecting onto me.

After an elongated moment of us all taking each other in, savoring the joy of it without needing to speak, it was Katie who broke the silence.

"So ... what the hell, Dad? Would you mind telling us what this whole penguin thing was about?"

I took a moment to gather my thoughts. I exhaled as I came to an inescapable realization. "Man, I wish I could explain it to you, baby doll, but I don't have a clue. It's just ... sometimes shit happens. And we don't always get to know why." I paused for a breath and went on. "But there is one thing I *do* know: I am really, *really* happy to be back."

The instant we had returned the boat and Julia had put her security-deposit driver's license back into her purse, real life came barreling toward us at warp speed.

Julia had both arms wrapped around my right arm, pressed into me, reluctant to break physical contact; it was as if she was afraid I might slip away again. Even as we were melded into a single human form, she was the one who launched off first.

"Okay, I really should call my brother to tell him we can be back by tomorrow afternoon. You know he's been freaking out that something's going to go horribly wrong with Nonnie under his watch, so the least I can do is let him know the end is in sight."

"We also have to figure out when we're gonna make the Bed Bath & Beyond run to do my school shopping," Charlie said. "We're seriously starting to run out of time."

Katie piped up. "Do you think maybe I can come back up to Grover's Glen over Labor Day to see Tim? I'm sure I could stay with Archer and Imani."

"But wait, wait. The very first thing we need to do is hurry up and check into the hotel," my wife announced. "For the price we're paying, we can at least try to enjoy it a little bit."

They were all talking at once, making plans, worrying about logistics, fretting about things that wouldn't be happening for months.

"Stop!" I said, raising my voice to be heard over their three-part cacophony.

I paused for a moment, reveling in the joy of realizing I had a voice again. They'd heard me! They stopped and looked at me.

Wow.

"C'mon, guys. May we please take a little moment here?" I turned around to face the lake. "Look where we are!"

Julia, Katie, and Charlie pivoted in unison.

Directly in front of us was a long wooden dock that stretched out into the water. On the far side of the lake, the mountains rose behind the opposite bank, guarded by a platoon of ancient pine trees. The sun was beginning to sink in the pink-and-blue sky. The interwoven streaks of color could best be described as majestic.

"I get that real life is calling," I said. "But ya know what? It's always going to be calling—and that's okay. I love our life. Seriously."

It was impossible not to notice the three "Are you sure there, buddy?" looks being trained on me.

"Okay, okay. I know I wasn't always the best at recognizing that— but I really, truly know it now."

I paused for a moment as I could feel myself starting to choke up. I took a deep breath and went on.

"I'm wondering if maybe we can't just go out to the end of the dock and *sit* for a minute. Ya know, take this all in. We've been through a lot. Wouldn't it be nice to have a second to celebrate the fact that we're here, we made it, we survived this crazy ordeal?"

"And," Katie chimed in, "not one of us is a fucking penguin!"

"Always with the mouth." Julia laughed.

Chuckling over the familiar rhythm of it all, I said, "So may we do that? How about we take a moment to just ... *be*?"

And that was precisely what we did.

Watching the neon-orange sun glide elegantly into the sparkling lake, there we sat. Feet dangling over the end of the dock. Side by side.

Together.

ACKNOWLEDGMENTS

I want to thank Lee Constantine of Publishizer for putting me on the path that led to Warren Publishing and PipeVine Press.

Huge thanks also to Geradeen Santiago whose generosity led to the second step on that yellow brick road to PipeVine.

Thanks to my incredible colleagues in the UC Riverside Department of Theatre, Film, & Digital Production for sharing their artistry, their wisdom, and their generous hearts daily for the past sixteen years.

Deep gratitude to my editor, Amy Ashby, who provided the most positive and productive collaboration I've experienced in my forty years as a writer.

To Mindy Kuhn and the entire PipeVine team: thank you. From the first time we communicated, it was abundantly clear that you understood what I was attempting to do with *Raft* and only wanted to assist me in making it as good as it could possibly be. Bless you.

To my social media team, Amanda Biggs, Ava Fojtik, and Rosie Hicks: thank you for gently guiding me into this terrifying new world to help spread the word on *Raft*. And to Paul Ingoldsby and Clark Barclay who were always there to generously pitch in as needed.

To anyone who has gotten to this page, thank you for still caring about the printed word. Stories are how we connect and acknowledge our shared humanity. At the end of the day, the Beatles got it right those many years ago: "All you need is love."